Praise for
The Past Leads a Life of Its Own

"Wayne Fields's stories stand out with a rare and calm splendor on the current literary horizon. They are both simple and subtle, cunning and earnest. They create a self-contained world of post-war rural childhood and retrieve an America that is so neglected and overlooked as to seem exotic. . . . Fields is a poet of the natural world. . . ."
—Lynne Sharon Schwartz

"A rich and complexly flavored work of fiction, a book to be savored. . . . Wayne Fields presents sixteen episodes from the life of a boy who grew up poor but loved, as the author did, in a series of small towns and hamlets in northern Missouri, Iowa and Illinois. . . . Fields writes as well about nature . . . as anyone alive."
—Harper Barnes, *St. Louis Post-Dispatch*

"Beautifully subtle. . . . These narratives are like stones skipping on water, capturing the struggles of a family leaving one way of life behind for another. Fields remembers the feeling of a time and a place gone forever."
—*Library Journal*

Praise for
What the River Knows

"*What the River Knows* is nothing less than a compelling confrontation with nature that is also an excursion down the river of the soul. It merits a place among the great books of its kind, those by Thoreau and Annie Dillard."
—Richard Selzer

"His god never reveals himself to the author with a thunderclap. His god is in the details of this beautiful, beautiful book."
—Christopher Lehmann-Haupt, *New York Times*

"A masterly achievement. . . . One of those rare literary achievements that, like a great painter's work, changes reality."
—Roger Starr, *Washington Times*

"He seeks the grace of a perfect cast, the grace of a well-wrought line, the grace to forgive himself a lifetime's accumulation of small failures. . . . What the river knows, and what Wayne Fields learned in his 42nd summer, is that the task of middle age is to live with the knowledge of death rather than drown in it."
—Le Anne Schreiber, *New York Times Book Review*

THE PAST

LEADS A LIFE

OF ITS OWN

wayne fields

THE PAST

LEADS A LIFE

OF ITS OWN

THE UNIVERSITY OF CHICAGO PRESS

CHICAGO & LONDON

The University of Chicago Press, Chicago 60637
The University of Chicago Press, Ltd., London

Copyright © 1992 by Wayne Fields

All rights reserved. Originally published 1992
University of Chicago Press Edition 1997
Printed in the United States of America
03 02 01 00 99 98 97   6 5 4 3 2 1

Library of Congress Cataloging-in-Publication Data

Fields, Wayne.
    The past leads a life of its own / Wayne Fields.
        p.   cm. — (Phoenix fiction)
    ISBN 0-226-24858-5 (paper : alk. paper)
    1. Middle West—Social life and customs—Fiction.   2. Family—Middle
West—Fiction.   3. Boys—Middle West—Fiction.   I. Title.
    II. Series.
[PS3556.I4212P37   1997]
813'.54—dc21   97-11754
                                                              CIP

For Karen Johnson Fields and Sarah, Elizabeth,
and Aaron Fields;
For Bill and Esther Fields and Jack, Jerry, Marilyn,
and Eric Fields;
And, too, for Ruth and Loyd St. Clair, Guy and Ruby
Fields, and Ivan Cull

CONTENTS

Introduction

Remembering, we aspire after a single story, a narrative, edifying and admirable, that runs from our unquestionable beginning toward some satisfying close, the conclusion that yet remains beyond us. Like David Copperfield in his story, memory longs to discover in time that it is the hero of its own account. And heroism means above all else to become one thing, to be whole.

Things work out for Copperfield because he is a fiction, his an imagined memory and not the thing itself, which, at its best, finds stories but never the novel in a life. Real memory leads not to the one but to the many, and though inevitably related these are just as inevitably broken from one another, resistant to any ultimate synthesis, to any bottom line.

I have, in this volume, tried to remember, not simply to recall but literally to "re-member" those bits and pieces, to join that which I am able to cobble together to some larger body. Though we like to pretend, especially those of us who take pride in our recollecting powers, that we can "re-call," conjure back the past reliably, memory does not work that way. It is fictional from the start. The past returns piecemeal, and we make of it what we can; it is we who give the meaning to the meaningful glance, who find a conversation to contain the poignant phrase, who draw a setting for the surviving detail too beautiful to abandon.

So my confession, an honest word in this celebration of dishonest memory. Some of what I remember I know did not originally belong to me, was rather incorporated from someone else's story, the anecdote of parent or grandparent that so long endured in me I have forgotten it was ever the property of another. Some of what I remember even comes in another's voice, a story told by someone else but taken in so wholly that only the disparity of syntax from that more typically my own betrays its secret.

Sometimes, in memory, I am a character outside my remembering self, watching like a stranger, while at other times I am inside that remembered body, seeing with its eyes and hearing through its ears. Strangest of all, sometimes I remember the opposite of what I know in fact occurred, recall with terrible clarity the danger actually escaped, the tragedy I was spared, as if the avoided possibility has become the reality. It is as though the past contains not only the things that happened but those that merely could have, and sometimes the latter more fully and powerfully than the first.

This re-membering is a bewildering business, full of imaginings by which we strive to find the truth about our past, full of fictions by which we struggle to define the self we truly have become. When it all begins, for me, with a haunting image (two women beside a fire, a fossil on a creek bank) or a phrase ("built a big-as-hell house," "never had much luck with rivers"), I have, long before I ever thought of writing them down, tried to place these shards in some credible history made of other recollections, other fragments, like a house built of spare parts rescued from the ruins of a dozen different structures.

Here is the way I re-member it, out of the storehouse of my own past and, like all memory, always incomplete, rarely consistent, one piece to the next, but somehow, I trust, reliable in its own presumptuous fashion. The past is nothing if not persistent, refusing to go away, denying us the last word; everything reworked as each new experience adds to the treasury and changes the value of what was already there. We remember out of who we are as much as out of who we were, and so it is all constantly rewritten, the present unceasingly transforming the past, striving toward the end we will never witness.

The inferno of the living is not something that will be; if there is one, it is what is already here, the inferno where we live every day, that we form by being together. There are two ways to escape suffering it. The first is easy for many: accept the inferno and become such a part of it that you can no longer see it. The second is risky and demands constant vigilance and apprehension: seek and learn to recognize who and what, in the midst of the inferno, are not inferno, then make them endure, give them space.

Italo Calvino, *Invisible Cities*

Prologue

The air is cold, a damp, end-of-March cold that cuts through my wool coat. I am on the creek bottom with my father and my mother's father and my uncle. I am eight. My grandfather has notched a locust tree and now watches as my father cuts through from the opposite side. My father, legs apart, balanced like a fighter, strains against the chain saw, holding the whirling teeth away from his body. He is young and small and wiry and is smiling as small, wiry men smile—cocky, defensive, contemptuous all at once. We are cutting fence posts. A short distance away my uncle, still in his teens, hacks branches from an already fallen tree. I smell the rich, singed smell of new sawdust.

Last year's weeds, brown and broken by winter's weight, still shelter occasional pockets of snow, and slivers of scum ice cling to the edges of the creek. This is the place I love best: the creek with the woods high on the opposite bank and, where we work, the flood plain dotted with willows and locusts. Behind us a grove of leafless hickories casts a web of branches across the distant farm.

All morning the sky has been gray, a snow sky, but now the clouds are broken and intermittent openings let through the yellowed slants of dull sunshine. I watch stripes of light and shade slip across water and trees as the saw screams.

The saw stops. Instinctively I turn, afraid for my father, but he stands unharmed, looking to the south. Then I, too, see them, low on the horizon, in great V's shaping and reshaping behind the leaders, and at last their muted honking drifts down to us. We stand there on the narrow ground between seasons. My father holds the chain saw, its stilled tongue touching the earth. My grandfather, thin and straight, has tilted his head back and to the side. Beyond the older men my uncle leans against his ax.

The geese come like swimmers crossing the sheets of gold, gleaming for a moment before they darken in the gray sky, then gleaming and darkening again and again, scores of them, necks stretched straight and slender and their black wings pumping, keeping the heavy rhythm unbroken. Then they disappear, all the wobbling V's lost in the grayness to the north.

Later, between my grandfather and father in the front seat of the truck, I ask where the geese were going.

"About as far north as you can go," my father answers.

"Where did they come from?"

"About that far south, I reckon," he says.

"I wish I could go to those places," I say, surprised at the words, unsure of what they mean since I get homesick whenever I leave the farm even with my family.

The pickup bounces over the track that leads away from the creek, bounces so hard that only the weight of my father's arm keeps me from flying off the seat. After a while my grandfather says, "If wishes were horses . . ."

My father smiles, not the smile of short, wiry men, but another smile, as the truck slides and bucks away from the creek and the woods.

Grant me, Lord, a little light,
Be it no more than a glowworm gives,
Which goes about by night,
To guide me through this life,
This dream which lasts but a day,
Wherein are many things on which to
stumble,
And many things at which to laugh,
And others like unto a stony path,
Along which one goes leaping.

PRAYER OF AN AZTEC CHIEFTAIN
UPON HIS ELECTION (AFTER
BERNARDINO DE SAHAGÚN)

From *Many Mexicos,* by Lesley Byrd Simpson

ONE GOES LEAPING

The dog saw it first and dropped belly down to the matted leaves. Instinctively, the boy knelt alongside, trusting his companion, then he saw it as well and with an almost imperceptible movement pulled tight against the dog. Below on a limestone shelf lay the snake, its thick body black against the bleached rock. The stream, just a few feet beyond and glutted by thaw, rushed by, but on the ledge the snake was still, its flat, triangular head elevated, tilted skyward where the serpent had coiled upon itself, seemingly all observant yet responding to nothing. On the bank the boy and dog hugged together against the chill and waited. Gradually the sun warmed their backs and stirred around them the odor of decaying vegetation, but the snake lay unmoved. So long and intently did the child watch that eventually he could see only the snake clearly; the creek below, even the limestone, faded from view. He did not blink to readjust his eyes, but grew oblivious of all but the snake's coiled body and the sound of sucking, pulling water. After a long while the dog stirred beside him, nudged at him with its nose, and the boy—who was called Lonnie—chilled and damp, slipped silently away from the limestone ledge.

When they were safely removed from the creek bank both dog and boy rose and hurried up the hill. As they crossed the ditch below the road, a covey of quail broke from the high weeds, a sudden, startling thrash of wings and birds taking flight in low, flat lines then swinging free in looping crescents before scattering to a distant windrow. Lonnie waited for a moment, the dog still calm beside him, and when his heart had quieted, slithered under the strands of barbed wire and ran until he reached the house.

For as long as he could remember Lonnie had come with the dog to play in the gullies surrounding the creek. Sometimes he would jump on the brush piles his grandfather had thrown up against erosion, flushing rabbits into alarmed flight, then watch as the dog harried them into other cover. Lonnie was not allowed to go alone to the heavy timber along the river bottom or, in the other direction, beyond the pastures above the house. So he spent his free days in the grazing lands to the north and in the fields below the road, diverting himself among the weeds and along the creek, watching for the first cottontails to emerge and for the Queen Anne's lace to fan into blossom.

There is much on a farm for a child to do. Lonnie searched out quail nests in the thick grass, moving carefully so as not to disturb them, and waited for the chicks to break through their shells. And then, as the spring progressed, he went to the fields with his grandfather, sometimes to ride on the tractor's draw-bar, sometimes to wander along the grassy margins where vegetation grew wild along the restraining fences. Often he went to a half-buried boulder, a strange granite intrusion in this limestone country, its top deeply indented in a wide bowl, darker and smoother than any other part of the rock—the result, he had been told, of Indians grinding their cornmeal. And always beside him like a second shadow, black with white patches at the throat and ankles, was the dog.

But this year they came most often to watch the snake. Even when there was no longer hoarfrost in the mornings and the days grew warm into June, the snake remained, coiled upon itself, head uplifted, triangular eyes unblinking. Each morning the boy and dog rushed from the house, slowing only at the road, then, as they approached the stream, bending low until they reached the point where they had first huddled together above the creek. Each morning the boy grew oddly anxious that the snake might be gone, but each day when he looked down to the ledge the serpent was still there.

Lying flat against the now green earth, Lonnie suspected he was hearing and smelling and seeing with a new intensity and that things previously hidden were being revealed to him. The creek, long past the spring runoff, still ran swift and loud, but he could hear above its racket the whirr of the grasshoppers in the field at his back, the call of the red-winged blackbirds in the river bottom, the comfortable sounds of cattle in the pastures above the road. And every breeze brought new complexities of scent: the deepening smell of honeysuckle from the bush at the corner of the field, the fullness of new-plowed ground, or the rich cloying sweetness of cut hay. But when the wind blew across the stream, beneath a fragrance of water grass and mud, beneath even the damp cellar smell of the limestone, was the pungent odor of decay. It burned in his nostrils even after the winter's effluence of dead leaves had disappeared under the summer's green.

His field of vision remained more narrowly confined, and he saw with clarity only the snake etched against the limestone. But this he saw vividly, profoundly, saw the blacker pattern on the black body, a series of intersecting lines triangulating, subtle diamonds that sometimes seemed, even on the unmoving snake, to flex and glide as they wove around the thick body.

He took pride in the ritual of his daily return, came to think that he drew from the snake some power beyond his ten years, and perhaps for that reason he was vaguely troubled by the thought that one morning the ledge would be deserted. Yet he knew a deeper fear, the fear that somehow, sometime he would be pulled down toward the cottonmouth, that its attraction would grow irresistible, and he would discover himself embracing it rather than the dog that held him safely to the higher ground. At times his anxiety was so great the bank itself seemed to be slowly sliding into the creek and so, above the ledge, he clung to the dog and, for good measure, clutched with his free hand at the long grass on which they lay.

Snakes, as a general rule, did not frighten Lonnie. Often when he picked blackberries in the thickets behind the house, blue racers would dart unexpectedly from the bushes, and an old bull snake sometimes came with a geriatric deliberation to sun itself beside the Indian rock. Though Lonnie would start at the sudden lash of a blue racer through the weeds, he just as quickly recovered. And the bull snake lacked all ambition for surprise, pulled itself into the warm light slowly, heavily, neither fearful nor threatening, made no effort to conceal its approach. Lonnie knew that cottonmouths differ from bull snakes and blue racers, not only in being poisonous but also in their fierce aggression; he'd heard the terrifying stories of their sudden, venomous attacks, accounts of swimmers lost to swarms of vipers and of waders pursued by a single determined snake.

Lonnie had seen cottonmouths before, had a perspective other than folklore. Sometimes, when a spring flood carried snakes up from the river bottom, his grandfather would discover a cottonmouth in the willows by the lower pasture and kill it to protect the cattle. Then he would carry it to the house, and with everyone gathered around, pull apart its jaws to expose the cottony white.

The snake on the ledge did not open its mouth, did not move at all in Lonnie's presence, but there were daily changes, slight variations in the tilt of the head or the arrangement of its body. The boy never tested it with rocks or sticks, never tried to coax the dog into any act of harassment, but let the cottonmouth be as it chose and watched respectfully through a summer's progress, waiting for some sign, some explanation, memorizing the pattern of the coils and the subtle design burned deep in the black skin.

The last week in July, Emmett Moncrief died. Moncrief was an old man, old as Lonnie's grandfather, who lived alone on the neighboring farm. Once he'd had a family, was married to the sister of Lonnie's great-uncle, Tull. There had been two sons, but they died within a year of one another, just as each of them approached his fifth birthday. The children had at first seemed healthy, but then began to waste away and be racked with convulsions. The first was newly buried when the second showed the symptoms. Moncrief was crazy for a while, and Lonnie's grandfather, a young man then, would hear at night the engorged cows bawling in the barn lot. While his neighbor did the milking, Moncrief tried to help but would soon give it up and curse and beat his fists against the barn wall. Later, after several months, he quieted down, and did his own chores again.

Moncrief's wife never left the farm after their second trip to the cemetery, and six months after that she too was dead. Moncrief found her in the barn when he came back from planting. Afterward he closed off all the house but the kitchen, where he put down a cot and lived the rest of his life.

These things happened even before Lonnie's mother was born, but he knew the story because the farms were so close and because Moncrief had been a friend to the boy's grandfather, and because Tull, who was also his grandfather's brother-in-law, was friend to them both. Tull sometimes preached in the little churches that dotted the countryside, but he also kept a farm, a farm he ran in his own way, continuing to work with horses even after all his neighbors had switched to tractors. He was a quiet man with large hands that held attention, not like other preachers' with their movement, but with their stillness, as they hung at his sides or lay on the pulpit while he spoke. He was also gentle and, besides his father and grandfather, the only other man with whom Lonnie felt wholly at ease. The boy liked horses because Tull raised horses; he believed in God without hesitation or even thought because Tull spoke of God as matter-of-factly as he spoke of horses and with the same respect and unstrained formality.

So when Tull rose at Emmett Moncrief's funeral to speak about death, Lonnie listened, listened because death was new to him and because Tull was a man worthy of attention. That day the broad, callused hands held no Bible. And the furrows and ridges around Tull's eyes and mouth did not relax into the familiar contours of the preacher's face, but rather held deep and fixed as Tull looked over the open casket toward the congregation. Funeral-home fans, emblazoned with pastel-tinted pictures of Jesus blessing the children, swept methodically back and forth or brushed at flies that came through open windows. But Lonnie watched only his great-uncle's face, the hazel eyes, the burnished skin and thick black hair, all familiar but different, and he listened to understand the difference.

When Tull spoke he ignored the people seated in the oak pews and looked somewhere above them, through the clear windows at the back of the church, out across the old cemetery with its crumbling limestone slabs and its newer granite markers, and toward the dark cedars that lined the distant river. His voice, as was often the case when he preached, seemed almost two voices, or one voice and its echo, each utterance sounding rich and full and yet, an instant later, deep and hollow. There was nothing disconcerting in this, rather something profoundly affecting, as though Tull were speaking from the mouth of a deep cave.

"I have stood in pulpits for as long as some old men have lived," Tull began. "And I have tried always to tell the truth whether I preached here among my neighbors or somewhere else to strangers. Always, no matter the text, the question has been the same: 'Who are we?' or as the Bible says it, 'What is man, that Thou art mindful of him?' " Tull spoke more slowly than usual, and quieter. He fell silent for a moment, then shook himself slightly, a kind of shudder.

"When a baby becomes a child, strong enough to place the earth beneath its feet, and to walk by itself, when it becomes a man or a woman and parent to another baby, that person grows into a joy worth dying for. Then, when life seems unspeakably good, when nothing seems better than to be what we are, that's when we ask, 'What is man?' and it's not so much a question as a statement of praise and wonder. 'What, then, is man!' A work of God, a God-like work, that's what man is. Praise God. Praise man." Tull's voice came hard, the word "praise" dull and lifeless and "man" spoken with a twisting both of mouth and sound.

A mud dauber circled above the pulpit, its drone underlining Tull's voice, its jerky, darting flight a nervous counterpoint to his still presence.

"In times when we are full of life and affirmation, we celebrate ourselves and a God who was wise enough to make us." He paused. "But then there is Moncrief. Where is the celebration for him? What comes of our self-congratulation when we remember Moncrief?" The words carried little of inflection, their cadence regular, their volume low.

Drifting down from the ceiling, the mud dauber settled on Tull's wrist just below the large right hand that clasped the pulpit's edge. Lonnie's gaze had shifted to follow the spiraling flight, and he slid back into the pew, watching as the insect crawled slowly across the preacher's hand. The words kept coming, quiet and even, and the boy heard them, but all the while he watched the erratic movements of the wasp as it explored Tull's tanned flesh.

"I do not regret Moncrief's death. I welcome it as he did. I regret his life, and I despise the waste." A stir of uneasiness rustled through Tull's audience, but he seemed not to notice. "What is man if his life is such a trivial matter to his creator? If his child is given merely to be taken away, his wife found only to be lost? If his living is only grief?"

Tull stopped speaking and in the silence the wasp lifted with a clumsy delicacy from the pulpit and drifted up among the exposed rafters. When Lonnie looked back to the preacher's face, Tull had lifted his eyes above the congregation and was gazing once more toward the river. Then slowly he lowered his attention to the people before him and with a softer tone began again.

"When creation was finished, God told Adam to name the other things of this earth, and Adam did what he was told. And doing that he became higher than that which he named." Tull's voice had begun to rise and fall, as though he were trying, through careful wording and subtle emphasis, to explain a thing to very young listeners.

"Something was gained. But something was lost as well, since Adam, to move closer to heaven, had distanced himself from earth. And then he fell, fell likely because, despite his efforts to the contrary, he loved the world too much and that made Heaven jealous. Which is why Adam poured out his wrath on the serpent, why he ground beneath his heel the first snake to come his way. He attacked the earth he loved too much and the creature which was so near the earth as virtually to be one with it. Mad as Adam was, he knew his choice, and knew it came with a price, but, in spite of death, he declared himself for our life and our dying. That was the bargain: death is what we pay for the world, for this life."

Lonnie hunched forward, a little ball on the edge of the pew, vaguely aware of the uneasiness that was building around him.

"Moncrief is dead. He has paid the price, lived up to his part of the bargain. But Moncrief paid more than the serpent could rightly demand, paid more than the world—or Heaven—has any right to charge, paid more than God Himself. I don't know why. His sacrifice saved none of us. The dying of his sons spared no one else's child, the rope around his wife's neck pulled no other woman to safety." Tull stopped, surveyed the troubled congregation. He shook his head, a small side-to-side movement.

"We are Moncrief's witnesses, and we must tell the truth or all our truth will turn to lies." He hesitated as though pondering something and then continued. "The truth is this: Moncrief was a good man who suffered terribly and unjustly. He did not suffer mildly, praising God despite his pain. Moncrief cursed God, cursed Him with silence, rejected the words which are, as John tells it, the very stuff of God. As he got older the silence and the outrage only deepened, until, at the end, few of us remember ever hearing his voice." A few people nodded, and Aunt Minnie Shumate, the oldest member of the church, whispered in a deaf woman's whisper, "I remember. I do. A sweet voice, too, a sweet voice then."

"If it's right to ask who we are, not just in times of joy and self-delight but also in the presence of terrible suffering and doubt, and if the acceptable answer remains 'We are God's children,' then it is also right to ask that other question." Tull paused. No one stirred, but above the open window facing the cemetery the mud dauber had begun battering its strange body audibly against the glass. " 'What then is God that we should be mindful of Him?' " Again he waited, then, his countenance both stern and sorrowful, continued. "Wrong is wrong no matter the offender. Sometimes the only true, the only responsible worship must be full of indignation and complaint." He looked toward the window where the wasp struck the glass again and again. "Justify yourself," he whispered in a voice as low as Aunt Minnie's whisper.

Tull stopped, but for a moment Lonnie was not aware that he had finished. The old man's chest rose and fell as though he were still preaching and his breath came out through parted lips though not as words. Tull abruptly turned away from the congregation and, without a glance toward the coffin, left, walked down the center aisle and out the front door. Lonnie's grandfather watched his brother-in-law depart, then said quietly, "Amen." The rest of the people sat confused until finally, with a solemnity that pinched up his face, the undertaker, a short man, and remarkably fat, hurriedly ushered the first row past the open casket. Bessie Craig sat at the still untouched piano and as people began to file by, started playing "Just as I Am," though in her confusion she quickened the tempo. The line speeded up until people were trotting with hurried, choppy steps to the casket, stopping to peer in and then running to close the gap in front of them.

The undertaker, Girst, moved his bulk around the coffin, waving his arms like a man shooing invisible flies from the corpse and rubbing the sides of the casket as though trying to smooth wrinkles from the shiny metal, darting like the mud dauber as it beat against the window. When Girst moved, his pants cuffs pulled up high over tiny pointed shoes, revealing blue socks limp around his ankles. Lonnie followed his grandfather and mother as they left the line early and started for the door, but the undertaker, thinking him neglected, ran over, grabbed at the boy, and turned him toward the casket and the corpse. Lonnie's grandfather, when he saw what was happening, pushed through the line and seized the child from the fat little man's eager grasp.

That night Lonnie found it difficult to sleep. He turned but could not get comfortable. When he lay still he felt a vague discomfort, a kind of crawly sensation under his fingernails and in his toes, an itchy feeling deep under his skin, and he alternately stiffened and relaxed his joints as he sought relief. There was no continuity to his thoughts in those fitful minutes, only images, and when at last he slept, he dreamed. In his dream he was looking down at Moncrief while Tull walked into a distant darkness. The casket's metal shell was black, but as he peered deeply into its surface bursts of pinks, yellows, reds, and silvers seemed to radiate from somewhere deep in the blackness. They did not erase the blackness, they were the blackness, and the intensity of that contradiction made his eyes ache. Lonnie felt himself drawn toward the center from which these colors erupted but, at the last minute, pulled himself free.

Inside lay Moncrief; his face, where it was not rouged, was colorless—not white, but colorless. There was no movement, no bursts, not even in the reddened cheeks, and his flesh was like the papier-mâché vases that hold drooping flowers at funerals. The lining of the casket was silky white crepe. But again, as the boy looked to the very heart of the color, bursts of pinks and yellows became visible, and they were the whiteness. Gradually Lonnie saw within the folds, no longer cloth, two delicate porcelain fangs curving to points too fine to see. Translucent, they held the pinks and yellows in a creamy ice, and they, in turn, nestled in the billowing folds that, while lacking the brittle stiffness of the crepe, retained its dancing colors.

Lonnie slowly drew back and saw the rest of the snake, black and vibrant, with deeper, shifting hieroglyphics. He felt no fear until he found the eyes—flat black diamonds against a dull

yellow background. No bursts of color, no reflection, no movement; they stared lidless at him, through him, and as he cried
out he awoke.

A few days later he rushed past blooming thistles and blackberry bushes bowed with their late summer burden. When he
reached the ledge, the dog trailed behind, reluctant, and then
slipped away. The following morning the animal was badly
sick, unable to walk, and Lonnie stayed beside him. With his
grandfather's help he carried the dog to a corner of the porch
and covered it with gunnysacks to ward off the chill that racked
its body. In the afternoon the veterinarian, on his way back to
town from working on Les Gibson's cow, stopped, examined
the eyes, felt the slack belly muscles, and then, after stroking the
ears for a long time, stood up and said it looked like poison.

"Somebody must have been baiting foxes," he said. "That's
it. He's dying. No use making him suffer unnecessarily when I
can stop the hurting now."

The grandfather nodded his head in agreement, but Lonnie
cried, "No!" and the men accepted it.

The day had started mildly, cool as May after a week of
ninety-degree temperatures and high humidity. Now clouds
had begun to move in, not the dark, menacing thunderheads
of August, but the lighter bearers of gentler rains. Already, as
Lonnie entered the windrow, a shower moved in a gray curtain
across the wheat field to the north, not so thickly as to block the
view but more like a thin veil floating above the grain. But the
grass beneath the boy's feet was still dry, and grasshoppers
whirred up around him, brushing against his face and clothes.

Before he crossed the road the dog had died, but Lonnie did
not know and had he known it would have made no difference.
He was terrified, and almost hoped the snake—though it was
his only hope—would have vanished. Yet he went on, and this
time did not drop to all fours but rushed upright to his post
above the ledge.

The snake was there, untroubled by the approaching rain.
Lonnie stood, looking down on the black coils, the triangular

head, stood so long and so intently that his leg muscles began
to twitch in little spasms, and then at last he ran down through
the Queen Anne's lace, the milkweed, and breaking free of the
vines and thistles, he jumped the treacherous mud on the bank,
landed on the limestone, and in one brief sprint crossed to the
snake. He leaped, feet forward, body twisted to one side, and
at the same time reached down, dragging his hand across moist
stone until it reached the dry, muscular body. Then he
screamed and continued to scream even as he fell heavily on
the far side of the ledge.

It was night, and the corridors were dark. A black man in a
white pullover stood bent in a pool of light as he mopped the
floor in front of the nurses' station. The mop sloshed over the
tiles, the sound slowly retreating as the janitor worked his way
down the hall. His clothing grew luminous and floated in the
dark.

Waylon sat in a straight-backed chair beside a gray metal
desk. Somewhere a child wept in short panting bursts, and
under the lights, perched on a high stool, a nurse wrote short
messages as she leafed through a stack of papers. No one else
was in sight, and the man sat quietly, staring at a panel of
blinking lights on the opposite wall, his fear inseparable from
the acrid smell of disinfectant.

All around him evidence of children testified to other presences; circus posters were interspersed on the wall with brightly
colored finger paintings and through the open door of a play-
room the silhouettes of rocking horses and swings loomed,
dimly outlined by the glow of distant streetlamps. But neither
animals nor clowns could conceal the terrible tension, neither
horses nor swings deliver Waylon from his dread.

He was disoriented, set down in a place whose rules he did
not know. He tried to find some pattern in the blinking lights,
tried to understand the occasional calls that came over the
intercom, but his frustrated efforts only increased the bewilder-

ment and fear. He wanted to run, to rush through the halls, down the stairs, and onto the sidewalk. Across the street there was a park with big sycamores. Under their branches he could think, would know what to do. But he did not leave, only sat where he was, watching the lights, listening to the weeping of someone else's child, muscles tensed against an unknown oppressor.

The intern who came to talk with him was young, but he had "Doctor" written on his nameplate. "We are examining your daughter," he said. "And we need some information." He took out a pen and held it expectantly over the first sheet on his clipboard. "How old is the child?"

"Two and a half." Waylon's voice was raspy, and he cleared his throat with a harsh, choking effort. He needed a drink but none was offered, and he did not ask.

"Has she been sick before?"

He thought carefully; it had become difficult to remember things. "No, nothing serious. Ear infections sometimes, and she had chicken pox. But never anything serious."

"Has she been examined regularly by a doctor?"

He stiffened defensively at the implied neglect. "Yes."

"Regular checkups?"

"Yes."

The intern sensed the defensiveness, was confused by it, but softened his manner. "Have you had any major illness?"

Again an accusation. The old guilt began to rise, the idea that somehow he had caused this suffering, that he was to blame. "No."

"Diabetes?"

He hadn't been believed. "No."

"Heart disease?"

"No."

"Venereal disease?"

"No."

"What about the child's mother?"

Waylon did not understand the question. "What?"

"Has she had any major illness?"

"I don't know. No, I don't think so. No."

"Perhaps I should ask her. Will she be at the hospital tomorrow?"

"No."

"When could I talk to her, then?"

Waylon cleared his throat again and tried to make sense of the question, understand what in fact was being asked of him. "She is gone."

"I beg your pardon."

"She's gone."

"Is she dead?"

"No." He tried to find the right words. "She left. Things got too hard and she needed to get away."

The intern glanced from side to side as though looking for assistance. "Ah . . . well, there are other questions. Are any of the grandparents surviving?"

"No."

The interrogation went on for several minutes, just as when Waylon and his daughter had arrived at the hospital several hours earlier. The woman at the admitting desk, without turning from her typewriter, had asked the questions then, asked them and pecked out the answers with only the faintest sign of interest in any of the proceedings. She had typed "Waylon" as he spelled it out, slowly, enunciating each letter, but she put it in the space for the last name and had to redo it on another form and in its proper space, insisting that once again he spell it out for her. She had looked directly at him only when, after he'd said he was a carpenter, she had asked for the name of his employer and he replied, a little too quickly, "I'm unemployed." At the word "unemployed" her eyes came up involuntarily, and then, as if recognizing a mistake, she forced them back to the typewriter.

The intern finished the interview. "Your daughter is very sick." He said the words slowly, more loudly than necessary. "We are doing everything possible for her."

Then he pointed out a parents' waiting room down the hall, stood up, and walked into the darkened corridor. The lights continued to blink, and names, now growing familiar with repetition, were called by the voice high up on the wall. At last, unable to stay away, Waylon rose from the chair, his body stiff and unsteady, and went to the room where they were examining his daughter. He was turned back at the door.

In the parents' room people slept in grotesque positions. They looked like the bodies in old battlefield photographs. Some had pulled cushions down and lay on the floor; others were curled like great fetuses in vinyl armchairs. Waylon stood outside the door and lit a cigarette, but it burned at his tongue and tasted bitter.

Driven by a growing restlessness, he walked round and round through tiled corridors, past doors and numbers, desks and names, until, finally, a doctor came and said they had to operate as soon as possible—the next morning—and gave him papers to sign. He signed, unsure of what he signed, unsure if he should sign, but signed furiously, cutting through the top copy, and then he ran to the room where she lay, feverish and tossing. He sat there clinging to her hand through the rest of the night. He tried to pray but could never finish a sentence before the effort at piety was interrupted by curses of fear and anger; and so at last he crooned an unintelligible sound and knelt down to be as close as possible to his daughter.

When sunlight first touched the sycamores across the street, whitening their naked trunks, the orderlies took her to surgery. When they wheeled her away from him, she roused up and called out, "Daddy." Waylon ran, but before he could reach her she had disappeared behind the elevator door.

Four hours later the surgeon came, his face unmoved but his voice oddly off key, and said that she was dead. The tension of the past hours moved from Waylon's shoulders and chest down into his body, collecting like enormous weights in his stomach, his hands, and his feet. And he stood there, sagging like an old tree whose roots have broken but which still stands, held by habit and inertia. He did not think or weep or cry out. He just stood there, humped and sagging, as the surgeon, torn by his own impersonal grief, watched.

Mechanically, Waylon signed more papers, refused some pills, and went back to the apartment. He lay down and was almost at once swept away by sleep.

When he woke it was evening. He walked to the hospital and went to her room but another child was there. At the desk he asked where she was, and the nurse looked into his face without comprehending and called for the intern. The intern told him she was dead, and he said he knew but where was she? The intern gazed back at him, confused, but then understood and told him that the mortuary had taken her body.

"You agreed last night." He spoke the words softly. "You signed all the papers then."

Waylon had not been thinking of mortuaries. He could not remember what had been said the night before, could not remember signing for his daughter to be sent anywhere.

"Can I see her? See her there?"

"Of course. They will need to work out the arrangements with you." The intern shook his head. "They should have called you or sent someone by."

"We," Waylon began, then caught himself. "I don't have a phone, and I've been sleeping."

"Of course," the doctor said, "It's all right. You can work things out in the morning, during their business hours." He spoke as if to a child. "There's no need to worry about it tonight. They will see to things. They're dependable people."

For the next two hours Waylon sat in the apartment, sat slumped in upon himself, sat without outward movement but all the while sliding deeper inside. Forty-eight hours earlier his daughter had played beside this table, thin and pale but with no outward sign that she was less than a whole child. Now whatever had been lurking unnoticed had taken her from him, taken her forever.

He felt as though he had made a terrible mistake, committed

an irredeemable error. Grinding accusations into his deep
wound, he became aware of an unbearable possibility, one
whose very irony made it seem likely. How could he be sure
that she was so desperately ill? He knew only that she was
running a fever and kept falling asleep. Perhaps it had merely
been the flu. Without question, he had given her up. He had
required no proof. He did not think she was dying when he
took her to the hospital. Why should he have come so quickly
to believe it? She had called to him in that last moment,
perhaps aware of some trick. She had given him one last
chance to save her, and he had refused, stopping at the elevator
door.

She was his trust, and he had given her up to strangers. He
had given her first to doctors and now, mechanically, without
any clear decision, to morticians. He became outraged at his
own weakness and knew he had to reclaim her, take her from
the indifferent hands that held her and make the last duties his
own.

From under the bed he dragged a tool kit, his movements
painstakingly deliberate as he unfolded a nail apron, filled it
with wood screws, and tied it around his waist. He regretted
having to use screws, preferring to lock the wood together with
mortise and tenons, but there was no time. The oak dining
table had been built fifty years earlier by his grandfather. After
setting his marks with the square, Waylon snapped chalk lines
and, cutting first the leaves and then, with the legs removed,
two identical lengths from the top, took the pieces he needed.
The broad grain stood dark in the light wood, and he turned
each board gently in his hands, as though afraid he might
bruise it, checking to see that it was true.

The sides and ends were single pieces, but for the breadth of
the top and bottom Waylon beveled two boards·until they fitted
together with an almost imperceptible seam. The oak cut, he
took an old router, its walnut surfaces polished by hours spent

in the hands of other carpenters, and routed a groove where the pieces would join. After he had set the screws below the wood's surface, he cut the dowels that had joined the leaves to the table, then carefully tapped them in to cover the screw heads. When he had varnished all the new surfaces, it was one o'clock.

He went into her room and took the patchwork quilt from her bed and put it in the coffin. Then he took her piggy bank from the dresser and broke it. He poured money into a little cloth coin purse she had left beside the lamp and pushed it into his pocket. He put on his work shoes and a heavy wool shirt, and after he had stood for a moment looking at what he had done and thinking of what remained, he lifted the coffin to his shoulder and, closing the apartment door behind him, de-scended the stairs.

The alley was unlighted, and he had to push his way past garbage cans and boxes, but he did not set his burden down until he reached the car. The coffin would not slide into the back because there were only two doors, and the frustration and anger which had dissipated as he worked at his carpentry returned, and he tore at the seat on the passenger side, trying wildly to break it free. Gradually he calmed and with a crescent wrench removed the bolts, then dragged out the seat back into the alley. Careful not to mar the wood, he slid the coffin into the car, one end resting on the back seat, the other on what remained of the front passenger's side.

The car was old, and as Waylon started down the street it shuddered while the engine warmed. He had driven little in recent days but still the gas gauge showed empty. He pulled into an all-night service station where the attendant, young and uncertain, peered through plate glass into the dark, reluctant to leave his sanctuary, but at last came, jerking the hose away from the pump and thrusting it toward the car.

The money from the piggy bank, except for three folded dollar bills, was all in coins, and while the attendant watched, Waylon turned and counted out three more dollars in change. A breeze sent paper cups and a twisted cigarette pack rattling across the concrete. He faced back to the attendant, who anxiously flexed his fingers on the nozzle trigger.

"Stop at six dollars," he said.

"That won't fill it, mister."

"It will do," he said. "Stop at six dollars."

The attendant watched the pump until he had carefully balanced the last zero in its box and then, money in hand, he rushed back to the lighted island of the station.

The mortuary seemed unattended, but Waylon found an unlocked door at the rear of the building and entered. Inside he climbed three stairs and stepped through another door into a room filled with open caskets, some enormous on their stands, others quite small. He did not know where to look and so moved carefully through the darkened display room, threading his way between the caskets until he reached a hall. In the back of the building he found a large room dimly lit by a night light. Something in the room brought the sting of tears to his eyes, a sharp burning that lingered in the air, an acrid presence that cut through disinfectant and deodorizers. He saw around him metal tables and unfamiliar machines with hoses and switches dark against their shiny finish. On a counter lay a length of hollow steel, sharpened at one end like a weapon and connected to a hose on the other. Beside it was some kind of a pump and another appliance that looked like a vacuum. Stainless steel sinks gave the room the appearance of a high school science laboratory. The rest of the building had been carpeted, and the sound of his footsteps on the tile floor startled him, but he crossed behind the tables and there, in a deep drawer, he found her.

She was freshly bathed and even in the dark he could tell that her hair was newly washed. But he did not dare look closely, did not kiss her or even touch her face. Rather he lifted her and carried her tenderly, as he used to do when she fell asleep on the sofa, back through the unlocked door and to the car. She was draped in a plain piece of cotton like the kind she had worn in the hospital, and so, after covering her with the quilt, he drove back to the apartment for her nightgown.

· · ·

He was still driving southeast when the first dull light of dawn appeared, and when at last the sun broke free of the horizon in a great crimson bubble, he was there. Clouds filled much of the sky, yet the low sun shone beneath them, casting a pink light over fields and trees. Wheat, at once water and fire, rippled before a west wind, but the trees, already in leaf this far south, did not move and stood a dark host on the distant hills. The farm was no longer his grandfather's, for his grandfather was dead. Waylon did not know who owned it, and he parked the car off the road at some distance from the house. As he walked toward the buildings a dog barked and ran growling in his direction, but then quieted as he approached, content to smell at his hands and ankles. Scrawny and blotched with mange, it followed him in silence. He crossed the open lot and entered the barn through a side door. No animals were housed there, and what hay was visible in the loft seemed years old, but leaning in the northeast corner were a shovel and mattock, dust-covered and webbed to the barn by generations of spiders. The wood bore the burned "S" with which his grandfather had marked all of his tools.

Waylon carried the shovel and mattock up the road, then across to a knoll overlooking the creek. He was far from the house, and the field across the stream was empty. Leaving the tools, he walked back to the car and lifted the coffin to his shoulder. On his return he carefully set the oak chest where a patch of violets were just beginning to bloom. Again he returned to the car, this time to start it and drive further down the road, off onto a rutted track lined on either side by tall blackberry bushes.

Waylon chopped and dug for three hours until he reached limestone. Once, in the distance, he had heard a machine start, but on a farm down the road from what had once been his grandfather's place, and no one came into sight. But the dog came, crept to the top of the ridge behind him, and crouched in last year's weeds as Waylon worked.

When he finished, the sun had clouded over; the farm remained strangely silent, as though it had been abandoned. For
the first time that day Waylon looked around him and saw the
dead elms shedding old bark and the cottonwoods awakening
from their long winter with young yellow-green leaves. A squirrel chattered in the branches high above him and a red-tailed
hawk rode in wide circles to the north. There had been
changes—a swath of broken trees marked where a tornado had
in recent years crossed from the southwest—but in the bottoms
the river still moved in its own thick timber, and he thought of
the great thrust of limbs reaching out from either bank, extend-
ing far over the dark water as they curved upward toward the
light.

Waylon lifted the lid from the coffin and set it carefully on
the grass. When he had taken her from the mortuary, he had
refused to see how awfully changed she was, did not look even
as he slipped her into the nightgown, but now he saw as he
smoothed the quilt around her body. From his pocket he took
a thick carpenter's pencil, and, when he had found an old
envelope in his billfold, he drew an X across the addressed side
and printed her name on the back and, below that, his own and
placed the paper at her feet. He hesitated, then retrieved the
envelope and added the name of his grandfather.

Waylon fastened the lid to the oak box, tightened the screws,
and pounded down the dowel plugs before stepping into the
hole and cleansing the rock with his creek-dampened handkerchief. When the chalky surface glistened, he placed the coffin
upon it and then, scooping dirt with his hands, slowly filled in
around the box. From the surface he broke the largest clods
and sprinkled the earth carefully until the oak disappeared.
After that he worked with the shovel, sliding dirt down the sides
of the grave until, at last, the hole was gone. Then he smoothed
the sod which, in the beginning, he had carefully cut and
stacked to one side. The violets had not yet withered, and he
gently patted them back into the restored earth.

The sky was gray, a winter sky in spite of the April warmth,
and in the distance a bobwhite called. This place where he had

lain for so many hours beside his dog was, despite his landless-
ness, his, claimed through a special act of possession, the only
place he could think to bring her. Below, the limestone ledge
was empty, covered with dust and humus, and for the first time
since the dog died he looked at the outcropping and thought of
the snake.

He stood, exhausted, his hands so blistered and chapped that
he no longer felt the slivers of wood deep in the quick. He
stared down at the ledge and remembered, absurdly, the snake.
After all these years and after burying a child, the old obsession
returned. He tried to explain the phenomenon, the serpent that
remained—so openly—always in the same spot, the cottonmouth that had not struck at a crazed boy who dared to touch
it. He wondered if there had ever been such a creature, if he
had not imagined it all. Perhaps he'd needed such a thing, a
personal totem fleshed out from shadows or a fallen limb.
Suddenly it seemed important, given all that he did not know,
to find the truth about this one event, to test the reality of his
own past. With the logic of his boyhood he became convinced
that the snake must have died here, rotted and left a skeleton,
left a sign, and he sat on the ground and slid down the loose dirt
to the ledge. There on hands and knees under the gray light of
an April sky, he scratched for flecks of ivory in the twenty years'
debris.

After my grandmother's funeral, her six oldest grandsons carried her coffin from the church and across the road to the cemetery. The undertaker insisted on leading the way in his four-wheel-drive truck, making a real processional of it, and we followed just behind, lurching from side to side because of our uneven heights, moving across gravel and then grass, six cousins who hardly knew one another. We carried her through a high wooden gate where black letters, undaunted against a chipped and faded field of white, proclaimed LIBERTY, carried her down the hillside to the place where her parents and grandparents already lay.

STONE FLOWERS

During breakfast his stomach had ached, not badly, just a vague, unsettling turbulence, but by the time he left for school the hurt had gone.

Lonnie started off across the high pastures behind the house, moving quickly till the farm fell out of sight behind the first ridge. As he walked the sun burned the haze from the damp ground and warmed his neck and ears. He was small for his age, and his lunchbox snagged the tall plants until, not far into the meadow, a bouquet of broken weeds had collected around its handle. Surrounded by open pasture, he slowed, watching for animal signs, burrows or nests, and when he came to a deep gully, he carefully slipped his lunchbox down the bank and then half slid, half fell to the bottom. He had read on the back of a cereal box that Indians walked silently by stepping first on the ball of the foot and then lowering the heel, and as he crept down the ravine he took high exaggerated steps, concentrating on every footfall in his effort at stealth. He halted before an old fox den that he checked every morning and that every morning was empty. As he peered in, head bent to shoulder and body rounded to one side, he imagined the fox curled against the nighttime cold in that small place.

Lunchbox banging against his leg, Lonnie tried to climb the embankment in one full charge, but near the top he faltered and was forced to claw at the ground with his free hand to avoid slipping back downward. The short dash changed the tempo of his walk, and so, free from the gully he ran, leaped hummocks of weeds and bounded over puddles and rivulets. Along his way he stirred the smell of damp earth, sweeping it with him through the yellow vegetation. Meadowlarks rose before him, and in his wake winter's waste divided, exposing the first green shoots. The cattle that usually grazed this pasture had been moved, but Lonnie still watched for the white-faced bull that harassed him, not through pursuit, but by standing between the child and the fence at the far end of the meadow, moving in lazy interference until at last Lonnie sprinted for the wire. It was a contest both seemed to welcome on dull winter mornings, a challenge of a boy's wit and speed against the bulk of that inscrutable beast.

This day Lonnie did not slow until the fence was crossed and he reached the road. Then, as he walked along the shoulder, scuffing the gravel with his boot, his stomach renewed its complaint. At first it did not actually hurt; it was just there, a slight dis-ease with every step. After he passed the Caldwell place, the disturbance grew into an ache. He thought of turning back, of asking to use the Caldwells' bathroom, but he kept walking, uncertain, until the house was too far behind. Gradually the aching changed to cramps that followed one after another in quick succession. He kept walking, bending at the waist to lessen the hurt, until he knew that he could neither wait until he reached school nor go back to the Caldwells'.

Frustrated and ashamed, he looked for a spot beside the road, rejecting, despite his urgency, trees and the shallow ditches as too exposed. Then as stomach and bowels clenched, he rushed ahead to the one refuge he could see, a creek bridge at the foot of the hill. Scrambling down beside the small stream and tripping over limbs and rocks, he undid his overalls and then, hidden below the planking, pulled down his underpants and relieved himself.

Gradually the cramps ceased, the aching lessened. He cleaned himself as best he could with the dead leaves that lay in drifts beneath the bridge, and only when he had finished did he see that his underwear was stained. Crouched over, his pants and underpants around his ankles, he scrubbed at the cloth with more leaves, but a slight discoloration remained. He told himself it did not matter, that no odor would penetrate his clothes and reveal his secret, but still he could not bring himself to pull the soiled underwear next to his skin. Finally he sat clumsily down, worked his overalls over his high-topped shoes, and removed the offending underpants. When he pulled his overalls back on, the rough seam of the crotch felt strange and uncomfortable, but he fastened the suspenders, satisfied that he was clean, then took the underwear to the stream and dipped the stain into the cold water. After he had washed the garment and wrung it out, he opened his lunchbox, removed the waxed paper from around his peanut butter sandwich, and wrapped up the underpants before pushing them deep into his coat pocket.

That done, he felt better, but he did not consider going on to school—not without underwear—nor could he bring himself to return directly home. He did not know what to tell his mother, and most of all he did not want to be sent back late, with necessary explanations, to the schoolhouse. He sat beside the stream for a long time, hesitant and confused, but gradually his uncertainty lessened and the sense of expectancy with which he began the morning returned.

Lonnie stood up, brushed himself off, and instead of climbing back onto the bridge, followed the creek as it flowed easterly away from the road, picking his way cautiously along the bank. He did not give thought to where he was going or how he would, in time, explain the diversion; he simply took his direction from the water, thinking at first he'd go only a short way, but as he rounded a bend and lost sight of the bridge, he kept on, intrigued by this departure from his usual way.

The life of the stream differed from that of the meadows. In quiet oxbow pools Lonnie discovered tadpoles wriggling small and black, still legless and slow moving, but when he tried to catch them in his hands, they slipped through his fingers as easily as the water. Occasionally, along the edges of the stream, the bulbous eyes of leopard frogs would jut above the surface, silently inspecting him until he came too close and then dropping, audibly, out of sight. Once with a long rainbowing leap, a frog that had sat bunched and fat on the bank stretched in midair to a surprising thinness, escaping from a strand of water grass to the safety of the creek.

Less than a half mile from the road, the stream made its way through cultivated land, but except in the flattest stretches its banks were everywhere covered with brush and trees, sometimes reaching up in steep-wooded hillsides that continued wild for two or three hundred feet, a self-contained world, radiating from the noisy stream and held together by the joyous clamor of tumbling water. Squirrels chattered in the surrounding oaks, echoing the call of the creek, and cardinals cried redundant declarations from the highest limbs.

Lonnie found himself following the small precise tracks of a raccoon that had spent the night feasting on tadpoles and crawdads. Inspired, the boy stripped off shoes and socks to leave his own prints, giantlike, alongside the raccoon's. He kept their trails parallel until he came to a place where the sand was saturated with water, cold as ice, and even then he remained barefooted, just moved to drier sand higher on the bank.

As the sun climbed, its light danced, aslant, among the trees, sparkled on spray as the stream hurdled rocks and branches. An elm felled by a winter storm, roots uplifted on the far side of the creek and, on Lonnie's side, limbs miraculously in bud, provided a bridge to the other shore and so—after putting his socks and shoes back on—carefully, one foot in front of the other, arms outstretched, he crossed. The roots, still clutching clumps of soil, fanned out in a bristling wall. Quietly he edged up against their mossy dampness and on tiptoe peered through toward the land. On this side the water cut without margin or floodplain into a high tangled ridge that rose before him like a richly worked tapestry. Lonnie studied this thicket, sorting out details, ordering and identifying what he saw. Violets bloomed in little hollows, and though much of the hillside was covered with vines and brush, part of the bank stood bare, newly exposed by a sudden slide of earth loosened by moisture and the tree's falling. Here, where the clay showed red in the morning light, he could see the first work of gophers and groundhogs. As he watched he realized, startled to have been looking at something without seeing it, that a bobwhite sat immediately in front of him, her thick brown body frozen against the dark background. With the slightest movement, another quail appeared behind her. Then, magically, he saw higher up on the bank a third and a fourth. He expected them to erupt into flight, braced himself for it, but instead they simply vanished. One moment he could see all four and the next all were gone, lost in a wilderness of weeds. Frustrated, Lonnie searched for them with quiet urgency, but the quail did not reappear.

He crossed back to the other side of the water and continued downstream until, sun nearly overhead, he stopped to eat at a spot where the sand gave way to limestone. He took the sandwich from his lunchpail and sat, legs crossed, body hunched forward, and as he chewed, he ran his left hand aimlessly over the rough stone surface. Gradually he became aware of patterns he was tracing in the rock and, bending closer, he could see delicate circles, whiter than the limestone, hollowed out as though they were beads to be strung in a necklace. Some were detached circles with smaller circles inside, but others were embedded one on top of the other, like vertebrae, in short, jointed chains. Where the ledge had dissolved around them, they jutted nearly free, so thinly anchored by the surrounding stone it surprised Lonnie they did not loosen at his touch. On hands and knees he examined the rock shelf, discovering an elaborate intricacy of fossils scattered over the entire surface, so thick in places there was no other stone. Where dirt obscured the broadest part of the ledge, concealing the pattern etched upon it, he carried water in his lunchbox, and, taking his soiled underpants from his pocket, scrubbed until the stone was nearly clean, its grayness flecked with small flat crystals glistening from the damp. Here among fans of shell, snaillike coils, and bits of bone as delicate as lace, the white circles had been joined into long, curving stems, branching, dancing across the face of the rock until suddenly flowering into fragile, inward-curling blossoms that seemed aflutter before some stony breeze. The fossils, somewhat lighter in color and more tightly textured than the limestone, rose and fell in the rock like an elaborate mosaic, sometimes arching far out and other times nearly disappearing in the matrix from which they were emerging. It was as if Lonnie were looking through water at deeply sub-merged flowers, distorted and unreal but more beautiful than anything he had ever seen, their presence here as unaccounta-ble as their gentle curved response to that never-changing wind.

After a while Lonnie began to think of getting back. He had never been on this part of the creek before and did not know his precise location, only that eventually the stream must de-scend to the heavy timber and the river below his grandfather's farm and, in between, cross the gravel road that led home. He knew he had left behind the steepest decline of the creek, had passed into the flatter land of the river valley, that the water had widened and slowed, and its song, so high-pitched when he began, had lowered. Even the floodplain had broadened, and though the stream remained narrow, the exposed sand through which it flowed came in increasingly broad expanses. As he made his way once more, Lonnie became fearful of quicksand and climbed high on the bank, but with the elevation came more interference and his progress slowed as he bypassed bushes and climbed over fallen branches. Thorns and burs tugged at his clothing. Once more he was in shadow, more of limbs than leaves since the scrub oaks and elms were still bare, carrying only the unruly nests of squirrels, sometimes four or five to the tree, like badly made hats stuck on their branches.

As he thrashed through the underbrush, Lonnie began to breathe more rapidly. He stumbled frequently and the vegeta-tion struck out at him, stinging his face and blurring his eyes. He fretted now, not about getting lost, because he knew the stream would lead him to familiar ground, but about the missed school and the shame of his soiled underpants and what he would tell his mother.

He came to a fallen limb barricading his path and carefully climbed onto it. As he shifted his weight to step down on the other side, the dead wood snapped and Lonnie fell backward, crashing heavily into the brush. As he fell, face up, looking into a high oak that had been maimed by lightning and wind, his body still sinking into the leaves, he saw a dark shape, wider than his own outstretched length, drop from above, its thick body falling toward him as though burdened by some awful weight. But its fall slowed, then just as slowly the shape spread enormous wings and moved ponderously into flight. Talons caught the sun, and the hoarse, hooting sound of night filtered down as the owl beat its way through the forest. The boy rose and ran, telling himself even as he ran that the bird was as badly frightened as he, but he rushed up the bank, forcing his way through the trees until even the noise of the creek was lost.

He stopped only when he glimpsed a clearing in the distance. Leaning against a tree, he waited for his breathing and the pounding in his chest to slow, trying as he waited to locate himself once more. The creek had been his guide, but it had disappeared in the tangle of brush behind him. While he was unwilling to retrace his steps, without the stream he was unsure of the way home. The sun might indicate general directions, but it was high enough in the spring sky that he could not discern the line of its path.

At last he decided to enter the open land and plot his course. When he came to the last tree before the clearing, he stopped again and gazed out onto a field somehow familiar, yet never before encountered from this vantage point. Eventually recognition came. Lonnie remembered that during the previous year's harvest he had ridden here, high on the back of the combine, but now the field was newly broken and the smell of freshly plowed and harrowed soil rose with the breeze. In the center of the clearing a hundred yards away, unaware that he was being watched, Lonnie's grandfather walked toward him. The old man wore striped overalls and a light blue shirt, and as he moved his work shoes sank heavily into the earth. He was hatless, and his gray hair blew lightly around his head. Slowly he came across the field, swaying, sweeping his right arm in long, rhythmic arcs. He carried something on his back and bent slightly before its weight, yet he seemed to be moving to some restrained but joyous dance, his right arm swinging back and forth in tune to a subdued melody. The boy watched and, then, in what for a lifetime would be a miraculous memory, saw the old man suddenly haloed by bursts of light. In rhythm with his gait, as though the music were being made visible, light blossomed above and on either side of him and then fell glittering to the ground.

Clutching his lunchbox, Lonnie crouched low in the growth beneath the tree, waiting, watching as his grandfather came to the end of the field and turned to repeat the pattern again and again. At last, tired and content, the boy moved along the clearing's edge until he reached the pickup. Quietly he opened the door and crawled inside. There in the warmth of the truck he nestled against a bag of seed and watched his grandfather cross and recross the field, watched the gray head surrounded by the gold light of spring until he drifted into sleep.

three

Every night a toad sits on the cement blocks by the door to our cabin. When I go out to drown the last embers of the campfire or wash in the lake before bed, he is always there, positioned so that as I exit and enter, the screen door nearly touches his mottled head. He never tries to cross the threshold himself but sits, facing the cabin and watching with unblinking eye until I nudge him from the steps and out of the doorway's light.

THE ASCENSION

OF

REVEREND WATKINS

Whenever someone at Mt. Canna School wanted to call someone else stupid, thoroughly, irreparably stupid, they would say, "You must be Russell Shockley's lost twin brother." There was no way to misinterpret the accusation because Russell, with his round face and perpetual ripe-melon grin, was everyone's model of ignorance, and if he knew enough to understand his reputation, he accepted it with the good nature of a hound that keeps coming back to the master who abuses it. Big, physically a man, he had red spots, more like moles than freckles, all over his face and hands, and thick and unruly hair the color of barn paint. But what set him apart was that huge slack-jawed grin and a laugh, virtually his only public utterance, which came in a series of long hiccups that jumped without any intermediate steps from a low scale to a high one as though he were about to yodel.

For the most part Russell was ignored. He sat quietly beside the stove at the back of the room where his constant grin would distract no one but the teacher. During recess, when we chose up sides for games, he was never picked because, despite his size, he always managed to lose. In baseball he never tagged

anyone out; when we played Red Rover he was always cap-
tured by the smallest kid. He didn't understand the nature of
games, and so at recess he wandered off by himself, poking
around the storm cellar and coal shed or drifting down to the
road.

Mt. Canna's one room housed eight grades and, the years I
went there, twelve students. Russell was fifteen and had completed four grades—after a record-setting three years before his
promotion from fourth to fifth—but if he was dumb, he was
also persistent. Every fall, returning from a setback that would
undo lesser beings, he would reappear at the desk by the stove
grinning away as though there wasn't any place he'd rather be.
He had a special incentive, as his father told anyone who would
listen, because he would inherit the Shockley farm only if he
graduated from the eighth grade. The old man had considerable faith in education even though he had no schooling himself.
Russell's brother, Chester, had left home at thirteen, and the
boy's father attributed the desertion to a lack of learning, vow-
ing not to see the mistake repeated with his youngest son. So
Russell lived with his father in a tarpapered farmhouse that
could be seen from school and came every day after morning
chores to sit silently through another droning day of classes.

Actually Mt. Canna was not a bad place to spend your days.
The school, a square frame building, was perched on an oddly
rounded hill that sloped sharply in every direction except on
the north, and even on that side the land fell steadily if less
dramatically. The hill was situated on a section corner, and two
dirt roads, tracing the plat lines, formed a right angle to the
southeast. This lofty location offered a great advantage: perfect
for sledding in winter and in the spring placed to catch every
breeze, and since windows ran the length of the building on
either side, students could be indoors, at their desks, and still
know all that was happening outside. Behind the school were
three frame outbuildings, the boy's toilet, the girl's toilet, and
a coal shed, while in front, half buried, was an igloo-shaped
storm cellar that had for years been collapsing in on itself.

The teacher for two generations had been a motherly woman everyone called Aunt Nora, and it was largely her benevolent spirit that recognized sufficient knowledge in Russell to get him through four grades in nine years. But she was gone now. She had fallen during the summer and broken her hip, and all through August the school board had searched for someone willing to shepherd twelve children for the pittance Aunt Nora was paid.

Their prayers were answered by the Fox Creek Baptist Church. Fox Creek was to conventional churches what Mt. Canna was to conventional schools. Its membership dwindled as roads improved and more of the nearby farmers bought automobiles. Finally, all that kept the church alive was the cemetery. It was less that the living weren't willing to leave the dead and more that they had an investment to protect, their families being regular depositors in the past. So they stayed on and the ruling body of the church stopped being the deacons and became the cemetery committee. But this they decided was the critical year. If the church was to endure, new life was required. In August there was a revival led by a preacher imported from Indiana, and by week's end seven new members—four reforming Methodists, two backsliding Baptists, and one middle-aged man of uncertain origin—sent the optimism of the cemetery committee soaring. They decided this was a go-ahead sign and that, after ten years of part-time preaching, they were being given divine instruction to call a regular, every-Sunday minister. They began their search.

Late in August they found Reverend Watkins. They declared the old Ewer house, after five vacant years, a parsonage, and when Reverend Watkins argued that his family couldn't live on the salary the church offered, the cemetery committee convinced the Mt. Canna school board, of which three of them were members, that Reverend Watkins could teach school as readily as he could preach.

On the Sunday morning before Labor Day, Reverend Watkins, accompanied by his wife and their three children (a four-

year-old whose nose ran constantly, one nearly two with a
purplish rash tattooing its body, and a new baby) who were
duly installed in the front pew, claimed the pulpit of the Fox
Creek Baptist Church. His text concerned a woman who lost
a coin and then found it after much crying and worrying.
Reverend Watkins was convinced that she then gave that coin
to God and concluded that people should give their money,
even when it hadn't been misplaced, to the church. He asked
everyone who tithed to hold up their hands. The chairman of
the cemetery committee held up his hand, but his wife pulled
it back down. One of the new members held his hand high,
waving it in fluttering little movements. Most of the other
people stared at the floor as though distracted by something of
profound interest in the planking, then on the first chord of the
closing hymn, looked up, all together, with a surprised expression, as though their minds had been wandering and they just
that moment realized where they were. After services most of
the congregation, pleased by the novelty of their very own
preacher, declared themselves satisfied and fussed over the
Watkins children. I never heard him preach again, because the
next Sunday we joined Liberty Baptist Church.

But I saw Reverend Watkins at Mt. Canna the first day of
school and every day thereafter for the rest of the year. He was
a man of average height but extraordinarily thin, and when he
stood behind his desk he leaned toward the class as if a hard
wind were blowing against his back. His schooling had ended
after a year of Bible college, yet he held strong opinions about
what a classroom should be like and how it should be run. He
had us bring old bricks from the collapsed wall of the storm
cellar and build a brick platform for his desk and chair. Instead
of the old arrangement where we sat together by grades, he
made us sit in alphabetical order. It deeply troubled him that
there was no dunce stool in the front corner but eventually he
was content to send students he declared ignorant to sit by
Russell Shockley. He always called us "children"—even Lyle
Webster, who was six feet tall and in the eighth grade—and he
made us call him "Reverend Watkins, sir."

The thing I remember most about Reverend Watkins, besides the strap he kept on his desk, was his smile. It was always
the same, as if he had just stopped sucking something of unbearable sweetness. His narrow face clenched around that
pouting smile regardless of what was taking place in the class;
he smiled it most energetically while fawning over Ernest and
Patsy Goring (the only girl at Mt. Canna), whose father was
chairman of the Fox Creek cemetery committee; and the same
expression consumed his features when he caught Lyle Webster
leaving through one of the windows at lunchtime. It was a
strange feeling, especially when the weather got cold and the
windows were steamed over, to sit there trapped between Russell Shockley's gaping grin and that pinched-up smile of Reverend Watkins'. Some days the interval between all that happi-
ness seemed pitifully small for the rest of us.

School started every morning with a drawn-out prayer in
which God was thanked for families like the Gorings and asked
to be merciful to unnamed others who bore a striking resemblance to my own. Next Reverend Watkins would make one of
us read from the Bible, at least one chapter, preferably one with
a lot of unpronounceable names begetting other unpronounceable names. Then we all sang a hymn which we were supposed
to know by heart, something lively like "There Is a Fountain
Filled with Blood" or "Beulah Land." Except for the first verse
no one but Patsy and Ernest ever knew the words, so we mostly
mouthed nonsense syllables. Next we said the Lord's Prayer.
And finally one of us had to give a thought for the day, a catchy
phrase such as "You are not fully dressed till you put on a
smile." Then class would begin. By this time we had already
been in school for an hour with only another forty-five minutes
until recess.

Our studies were not so carefully organized as the opening
exercises. Reverend Watkins never knew who was in what
grade and so he handed out the textbooks with complete arbi-
trariness. No one was in second grade, but Reverend Watkins
was fond of the second grade reading book and made everyone
under five feet in height read from that primer. It was not

altogether a waste because he did most of the reading himself—
did it in an affected way, trilling adverbs which he added to the
text and thundering the more impressive nouns—even though
the book was familiar to all of us except Robert Lee Moore,
who was supposed to be in first grade. Reverend Watkins
seemed genuinely moved by the stories and talked as affec-
tionately about that little boy and girl and their dog and cat as
a mother about her own children. One day he insisted that
everybody, even the oldest kids, listen, and he read about how
Puff, the cat, got lost, and then, just as his voice started to
quaver with affected emotion, how the boy and girl found Puff
in a neighbor's tool shed. Reverend Watkins said that was a
good story, that it could have come right out of Jesus' mouth
because it was just like the story of the lost sheep—which he
told at great length—and showed how much God loved the
lost. Lyle Webster asked if after they found the sheep did they
butcher it or just shear it. He had to go back and sit next to
Russell.

Afternoons Reverend Watkins always gave out arithmetic
texts and we had to trade books until we got ones we understood. Then after we did some problems he would have us pass
our papers to the person in front of us, and that person was to
turn to the back of the book where the answers were. But since
the person in front almost always had a different book from the
person sitting behind, it was rare that an answer was not
checked wrong.

But autumn passed quickly. Since Reverend Watkins didn't
know which grades should be doing what, those of us in third
grade—there were four altogether—could use the triangles and
protractors normally reserved for the older students, but which
we found amusing. Much of the time, however, Reverend
Watkins was so involved with preparing next Sunday's sermon
that he didn't pay us much attention, and we stared a lot
through dirty windows at the infinitely interesting world
around Mt. Canna's hill.

All this time, Reverend Watkins was also busy separating the sheep from the goats, deciding which of the bigger boys it was safe to punish and which of the younger kids lacked influence with either the school board or the cemetery committee. Those of us in the latter category were made to carry coal each night for the next day's fire, to clean the blackboards, and, as the year progressed, to suffer when things went badly. We were the ones who had to stand in the corner for dropping a pencil or were ordered to stay after school for missing all the questions on the math assignment. But Reverend Watkins did not stop smiling even as the school days grew increasingly dreary and punishment more frequent. The puckered mouth merely drew his face up all the more.

Traditionally winter was the best time of year at Mt. Canna. Several kids brought sleds since the hill was covered first with snow and then, inevitably, with a sheet of ice. Those without store-bought transportation improvised with pieces of cardboard or even the scoop shovel from the coal shed. When conditions were perfect we could go more than seventy-five yards in one long slide by crossing the ditch and turning up the icebound road. So at recess, at lunchtime, before and after school there was a steady flow of people sledding down and then trekking back up the hill. This year it was different. Not that Reverend Watkins kept us from playing in the snow; far worse, he joined us. With a glee that was terrifying to behold, he would "borrow" a sled from one of the smaller boys and then launch himself down the hill. At the bottom he abandoned the sled for its owner to retrieve and then hustled back up the slope to take out another loan. He was much impressed with the largeness of heart that led him to share our recess, but he broke two sleds—mine included—and generally destroyed the tempo of our play.

Of the several sled runs that radiated out from Mt. Canna, Reverend Watkins always took the same one: a discreet path down the gentlest part of the slope that topped a low ridge halfway down, then went beneath the limbs of a large maple before leveling out where the roads cornered. One night Lyle

Webster and Calvin Jennings drove over on the Websters' tractor and, with a rake point attached to a log, gouged a trench where Reverend Watkins' sled run crossed the ridge. Then they filled the trench with soft snow. The next day word spread and at recess everyone bounced around restlessly, trying to appear normal, as we waited for Reverend Watkins to commandeer a sled. For most of a recess that seemed as long as Christmas Eve night, he stood beside the building all bundled up with only that pinched-up face sticking out between his ear flaps. At last, as I was working my way up the hill, he moved, walking at just the right speed to intercept me as I pulled my sled up the last few yards of the incline. He patted me twice on the head in benediction and took the tow rope from my hand. I was torn. As much as I wanted to help him toward that trench, I was convinced the shock would ruin my newly repaired sled. But the longing for catastrophe and revenge won out.

All other movement ceased as Reverend Watkins walked with the small mincing steps by which he avoided the indignity of a fall. Everyone froze, afraid somehow they might miss the grandeur of the thing. No one dared even blink. No one, that is, except Ernest Goring, who, with his sister, had not been trusted with the secret and so tagged along dutifully at the schoolmaster's heels. Reverend Watkins stood at the top of the hill, holding my sled high above his head so as to slam it to the ground all the harder, when, for some inexplicable reason that might provide argument for a special providence, he turned, patted little Ernest on the back, and sent him down the hill on my sled. At the trench, Ernest took to the air, floating angel-like until he hit the maple tree. It was the better part of five minutes before he regained consciousness, and even then he acted peculiar for the remainder of the day. My Flexible Flyer never did recover.

As the winter dragged on Reverend Watkins seemed to tire of playing school. He never stopped smiling but by the end of January it required such an effort that the muscles in his neck appeared ready to break through the skin. Whether or not he was simply bored no one knew, but he no longer read *Dick and Jane*, nor did he give out the arithmetic assignments that had kept the entire class in confusion throughout the fall. His role changed from teacher to tester and periodically he would, with furious zeal, give quizzes. Standing in front of the class, he shouted out questions and then pointed to whoever of us was to answer. There was no rhyme nor reason to these tests, at least none we could discern, but he would get as excited as if it were the last session of a slow revival.

"What is the capital of Arkansas?" he would shout and then bend forward and thrust his bony finger toward someone. If the answer came quickly and was the one he thought correct, Reverend Watkins would immediately straighten up and cry out, "Who was King David's grandfather?" and without leaving time for even the best student to sort through the begats, would lunge toward someone else. The questions covered a wonderful range of subjects, from "What do Catholics call the anti-Christ?" to "What time of night should you plant cucumbers?" And it was rare that we gave two satisfactory answers in a row. When one of us gave the wrong response or admitted ignorance, Reverend Watkins would close his eyes ever so slowly, like a river shrinking during a drought. He'd stay like that, leaning forward with his eyes shut and his lips pinched up in that immortal smile. The class would sit paralyzed. Then in a voice that was low, almost soft, he would whisper—all the time his face, impossibly, drawing tighter—"I must do the work of him that sent me while it is yet day, for the night cometh when no man shall work."

One day, just after lunch, Reverend Watkins rose from his desk very quietly and then, as though the question had just occurred to him, hollered out so loudly that we all jumped, "Who called the bears down on mocking children?" I tried to remember if it was Elijah or Elisha, but when he jabbed out his finger both names immediately flew from my mind. For some reason this time he pointed over everyone's head to the back of the room. It was not clear whom he meant to identify, but Russell Shockley, the only person we all knew couldn't possibly be the one called on, was convinced that the question had been addressed to him. The red began to run down from his hair, drowning all the freckles in its path, until it covered the whole expanse of that round face. The hiccuping gurgle started up as if it were coming from his toes. It may have been embarrassment but that seemed unlikely. More probably it was simply the surprise of being called on after all those years and more than likely he had no idea what was being asked of him. At the first hiccup everyone turned to stare, an act which unleashed a long series of key-changing "un-huhs" from Russell's throat. Only Lyle Webster, who had been sent to the back earlier for blowing his nose on a curtain, seemed to grasp the state of things. He leaned his head slightly toward Russell and said something. Russell hiccuped again. Reverend Watkins turned white and, for the first time in our experience, repeated the question, his voice dropping to its lower register: "Who called (pause) the bears (pause) down on (pause) mocking (pause) children?" Lyle edged closer to Russell, and in mid-hiccup Russell burped out, "Goldilocks."

From that moment Reverend Watkins set out after Russell like he was the Pope. He called him the son of darkness and a Philistine and various other piously slanderous names. All the while Russell sat by the stove, slightly dazed but with his broad grin undiminished. For nine years he had been left peacefully in a backwater at the edge of class; but from the moment of his Goldilocks answer on, there were days when the entire scholastic enterprise seemed centered on him. Reverend Watkins would call him to the board to do arithmetic problems (a recovered enthusiasm), and when Russell just stood there slack-jawed, holding the chalk as if it were a long-legged spider, the preacher would look as smug as though he had just caught a glimpse of the new Jerusalem and call the youngest person in class to supply the answer.

In late February, Reverend Watkins started bringing his

four-year-old to school. She was a scraggly-looking child, always clothed in dresses made from feed sacks and tucked inside
blue coveralls. Her face, around her mouth, was like a well-
used strip of fly paper with a coat of honey or sorghum in which
crumbs had been trapped and, no matter how they struggled,
had been held fast and died. Even without this decoration she
would not have been a handsome child; she too greatly favored
her parents for that. In fact, only the breakfast rubbish identi-
fied her as a child at all. Like a ferret's young, she was just a
smaller version of Reverend Watkins, her ancestry complete
but miniaturized. Mornings, we were now given vague assignments while Reverend Watkins, who again lost nearly all interest in the finer points of teaching, settled into the role of doting
father. He let his daughter crawl over his desk and rifle the
drawers, and he didn't reprimand her when with savage skill
she pinched one of us to whom she had taken a dislike.

By now one of Reverend Watkins' favorite pastimes was to
ask us to recite the Bible verses he had chosen as the text for
next Sunday's sermon, and whenever he called on Russell, he
turned from that red silence to the wizened creature scurrying
around the class and asked her to repeat the passage to this
backsliding young man. Instantly she would stop, blink a time
or two, and in a voice like a nail on slate recite the passage
perfectly. Reverend Watkins would glow, become a regular
northern light, and beaming out at Russell would, in tones of
insufferable patience, say, "A little child shall lead them." At
this cue the daughter would promptly bite the first available
student appendage.

One day she bumped the stove and burned her elbow, not
badly, but enough to redden the skin. Reverend Watkins
grabbed her up as the screams riveted the rest of us to our seats.
He called her "angel" and "love" and "heavenly light," but she
kept up her hellish cries, though no tears ever appeared on her
cheeks. Then Reverend Watkins told Russell to give her the
apple Russell always brought in his lunch bucket. She became
like a corked bottle, all the noise completely sealed off by the

fruit. Russell, however, from that day on was expected to keep her away from the stove and to bribe her into obedience with his own lunch.

Every spring the Mt. Canna attic had to be cleaned. It was never explained to any of us just what made this ritual necessary, though it was darkly hinted that a state law required the annual cleaning of public school attics, even that a state inspector could, unannounced, suddenly appear in the classroom and demand to see our attic. Since the whole of Mt. Canna School only took up a space about fifteen feet by thirty-two, the job was not particularly imposing, but it was one usually done quickly and without advance warning. Some parents worried that the old books and papers harbored scarlet fever because, during the war, and for three years running, several cases had broken out within a week of attic cleaning.

One day late in March, Reverend Watkins had Lyle and Calvin move his desk—which sat directly below the trapdoor to the attic—and bring in the stepladder from the coal shed. Then all the boys, except Ernest Goring, who was troubled by heights, were sent up to clean. A layer of coal soot made the chore a dirty one, but it was fun to explore the old stuff that had been stored away. There were books that contained the names of uncles or aunts, and those of us who could find something our parents had left behind got a peculiar sensation knowing we held an object our mothers and fathers had used when they were our ages. Each year during cleaning time we had a contest, and the winner was the one who found the most unusual relic. This year it looked as though Calvin had the prize when he found a picture of Teddy Roosevelt in perfect condition except that the teeth had been clipped neatly out, leaving the smiling lips unblemished. Then, while sweeping up an elaborately constructed mouse nest, I found the teeth, a little crumpled, but otherwise in good shape. Still that didn't take the prize. Late in the day Charles was shaking the grime off a copy of *In His Steps* when out fell a love note with his father's name at the bottom. And the name at the top did not belong to his mother.

We finished by patching up holes a squirrel had made in the back wall. With that the job was over and Reverend Watkins pushed the ladder to the precise center of the opening, climbed halfway to the top, and stuck his head through for inspection. Little of the late afternoon light reached the attic, and Reverend Watkins' eyes weren't used to the darkness. He screwed his head all around, making an elaborate show of checking our work, but when he turned to peer into the remotest corner, he lost his balance and, tottering, grabbed the trapdoor to steady himself. It kept him from falling but his weight tore one of the hinges away from the wood, leaving a corner of the door so damaged that it required major repairs, which Lyle's father—a good carpenter as farmers go—agreed to fix when he found time. That's why the entry to the attic was open and the ladder still in place during show-and-tell days.

Show-and-tell represented the longest sustained assignment Reverend Watkins ever thought up. Each of us had to bring in something that indicated the approach of spring and to talk about that something for at least fifteen minutes. As the teacher, Reverend Watkins said he would go first, and of course he brought in the March edition of *The Word and Way*, which contained Easter poems and devotionals. He read for an entire hour and then explained how the Easter edition was a surefire sign since it only came out in the spring. Lyle Webster said he thought that was cheating and the next day brought in the calendar from his folks' kitchen and said that when you get to March on the calendar and it's got written at the bottom of the twenty-first box "First Day of Spring," you know exactly where things stand.

The rest of us weren't so daring and, besides, it was fun to think up new things to do. All in all, this was Reverend Watkins' most successful venture in education. Patsy brought the new garden seeds that had just come in the mail and told how her mother had said she could plant her own flower beds and maybe she would plant hollyhocks but she didn't really like fuzzy flowers so it would probably be petunias and snapdragons. Reverend Watkins said how nice that would be and how he would be sure to come by and see her garden all in bloom.

Things picked up, though, after Patsy's report. Her brother had brought in a baby chicken, and to keep the surprise till just the right moment, he left it in a box in the back of the room, buried beneath some coats to muffle any chirping. Sometime during his sister's long presentation, the chick suffocated. When Ernest opened the box and found the dead bird huddled in one corner, he started to rant and yell, out of anger, not sadness. First he blamed the chicken, as though it had died in order to disappoint him, but then he found a more vulnerable target and claimed that since Russell was the one closest to the tragedy, somehow he was responsible. Reverend Watkins didn't acknowledge the absurdity of the charge but instead declared that a special funeral service would be held at recess and sent Russell straightway to dig a hole for the burial.

Russell dug the grave in front of the coal shed, but when the rest of us marched out for services, Reverend Watkins said that was not a proper place since whoever carried the coal bucket was sure to step directly on the deceased. Russell dug another hole behind the girls' outhouse, a spot safe from desecration, and we proceeded with the sad affair. First Reverend Watkins prayed, reminding God that he knew even when a sparrow fell and so must be equally aware whenever a chicken died. He pointed out some other pertinent information that might have slipped the omniscient mind, and then said "Amen" and Patsy and Ernest said "Amen" right after him. The praying over, at least for the moment, Reverend Watkins began a sermon that promised to go on for some time, but when he looked over and saw his daughter doing peculiar things with the departed, he hurried the dead chick into the ground. Finally he led us in one stanza of "When the Roll Is Called Up Yonder." By this time the recess period had been more than used up, so we all filed past Ernest and Patsy, shook their hands, and went back into the school.

After that, show-and-tell proceeded without any remarkable interruptions. Henry brought in a jar full of tadpoles, and though some died, none required burying; I brought a new sweet potato plant and someone else found some quail eggs. Calvin hauled a dead groundhog to class—which Ernest claimed he had killed specially for the occasion. At last, on the third day, only Russell remained, and this time he had come prepared. By now he was so eager to redeem himself in Reverend Watkins' eyes that he had spent long hours searching out just the right sign of spring, and that morning he carried a gunnysack, tied at the top with binder twine, and left it inside the storm cellar doorway. After lunch he brought it with him into the classroom, walking straighter than he had in weeks, clearly convinced that he had done his job well.

It was nearly two by the time Reverend Watkins called Russell Shockley's name. Perhaps he had not seen the burlap bag sagging under its heavy limp load, not noticed the erect gait of Russell as he entered the room, because he called out the name with both a weariness and disdain that declared his expectation of being disappointed yet again. But not this time. Russell jumped from his desk before Reverend Watkins had finished the first syllable and in the same bounding effort snatched up the gunnysack from behind his desk. "It's another damned groundhog," Lyle muttered from the back of the room, but the shape—or rather the lack of shape—didn't seem right for a groundhog.

When Russell at last stood beside Reverend Watkins' desk and was facing the class, the enormity of his undertaking finally caught up with him; the burping-laughing noise began and his oversized hands, all blotched with red, went to his head and began twisting his hair into straggly little horns. Reverend Watkins, with the tone of infinite patience infinitely tested, said, "Well, Russell, just what little thing have you brought to show the class?" Everyone expected Russell to wither up and rush to his desk, but this was a day for miracles, and Russell pushed the hiccups back down his throat so that they rumbled and shook but with less than their usual violence. He grabbed the bag with his right hand, his left working all the while at his hair, and seemed, incredibly, to be preparing himself for a speech. The class sat quietly. Not only might Russell actually speak, but there was also the awesome spectacle of those two smiles, side by side. We'd never seen that before. There was Russell's great face glowing around his huge grin. On the other hand, Reverend Watkins had his tightest possum look, teeth clenched, mouth tight up at the corners but working in jerky little movements as though he were chewing a green persimmon.

Russell just stood there as if he had lost his place, his hair twisted into a dozen sprouting braids.

"Well, Mr. Shockley?" Reverend Watkins said and Russell turned to see if his father had entered the room. "Is that all? If you have something to show us, put it here where we can see it. If not, please stop wasting our time."

Russell seemed to remember where he was. "I brought this," he said. He sounded almost confident, intoxicated by his own few words, and Reverend Watkins looked more angry than surprised.

"Yes, boy, we know that. I've put up with dead chickens and slimy tadpoles. What is it this time?" Russell ended his curiosity. While Reverend Watkins had his eyes lifted to Heaven as though expecting an answer from that region, Russell untied the gunnysack, heaved it upside down, and shook a half-awake bull snake onto the floor at Reverend Watkins' feet. The snake was large, and sluggish from hibernation, but the heat of the room had roused it, and it began to stretch in front of where Reverend Watkins stood. Or rather, in front of where he had stood. No sooner had the snake dropped heavily to the floor than Reverend Watkins' eyes fell from higher regions to behold this answer to his prayers, and at the sight, in a single gravity-defying bound, jumped to the middle step on the ladder, scurried up two more, then grabbed the opening to the attic and vaulted out of sight. It was an amazing maneuver, impressive as any gymnast's routine; one moment there he was and the next he was gone as though snatched, like Enoch, right out of our midst. But while his body had vanished, his voice, a little

shaky at first, echoed down from the attic in a great hollow
roar. No preacher has ever been more impressive, not in over-
all performance.

"Russell Shockley," he cried out. "You are an ass, a slobber-
ing moonfaced ass. Damn you! Damn you! You heathen! You
son of Baal! You child of perdition!"

He was wound up now and had gotten the tremor out of his
voice, having put a full story between himself and the bull
snake.

"You have been the devil's instrument. But you have
mocked me for the final time. You will not undo my work any
longer. I judge you now. Look out that window at your father's
farm. Look, you gaping idiot. Look."

Russell had that dazed look people have after they've gone
to sleep and run the corn cultivator through the fence or have
hit the accelerator instead of the brake and driven through the
back of their garage. But the smile, or the better part of it,
remained as he slowly turned to look out the window toward
his father's house.

"Look at it now," the voice repeated. "I tell you this place
isn't Cana but Pisgah, and you can look on that promised place
but it will never be yours. You fool."

And we could see that finally, after all these years, Russell
understood that he would never make it through the eighth
grade, would never inherit his father's land. It had all been
some farce played at his expense, everything building to this
moment. The smile drained off, a little at a time, and without
it he became a different person. At first he looked bewildered,
and he crossed to the window as though to better view what
he'd lost. When he turned again, he no longer seemed confused. Nor did he seem angry. The corners of his mouth began
to pull up again, maybe out of habit, but not into his old grin,
just pulled up a little into a small smile, and he walked back to
where the snake, thoroughly warmed and curious, leisurely
rubbed its belly on the floor. With one swift move he grabbed
it behind the head. The snake livened up considerably, lashed

out with its heavy body, and flattened its head. Then Russell underhanded it so that it went looping through the air and into the dark of the attic opening, landing with a heavy thud above our heads at the very moment that Russell kicked over the stepladder.

"I mightn't ever be a farmer," Russell said, "but then I guess I won't be no damned preacher neither." As Reverend Watkins hollered and stomped his way around the attic, Russell walked away from Mt. Canna School for the last time.

f o u r

The lake lacks depth but the German was a man of great determination. For nearly a year he had lived alone in the Morrissey shack carpentering and cutting pulpwood for Morrissey. The spring day he decided to commit suicide, he put on all the clothing he owned, loaded a straight-backed chair—to which he had tied all the cabin's window weights—into Morrissey's boat, and rowed to the middle of the lake. The water was so shallow that when he climbed out of the boat, his head and shoulders must have remained well above the surface. But he took the chair and sat down, hands tightly clasping the rungs, and, with his pockets full of rocks, the lake covered him as effectively as could any greater body of water.

FROM
SHIRE'S END

They made the journey the same time this year as last, the same as the year before that, but whether the date was determined by the calendar or the weather, Lonnie never knew. Most probably it was the weather, the first sure evidence of winter's end. What his grandfather called mud time. In a country with few paved roads and with fast-rising creeks that annually overflowed their banks and the low bridges that in drier months spanned them, early March was not the best time for traveling, but that was precisely when Lonnie's family made their yearly pilgrimage to the city. The errand required only his father, and yet they all went—Lonnie, his mother, and this year a baby brother—all of them climbing, on the appointed day, into the old Ford coupe, which during January and February his father, when not working on the farm machinery, had taken apart and painstakingly reconditioned.

The same tensions arose every year. Not just worry about roads made treacherous by thaw and flood, but a greater, though unspoken, worry for the news the day would bring. But great as well was the excitement of going to town, of leaving winter and the farm, and driving through the awakening countryside with the warmth of a spring sun spreading through the car.

For Lonnie an air of mystery surrounded the trip, but it was enough to know this journey concerned the future and the new life his family was always about to begin. He liked living on the farm, his mother's parents' farm, but it was not his home. It was where his mother had grown up and where he had been born, but it was not a place where his father belonged and therefore it was no longer the place for any of them. On cold winter mornings when Lonnie awoke in the attic room he shared with his uncle, he would lie in the gray light, look through the gable window across the stubbled fields toward the woods and the frozen river, and think of all the bedrooms in which he had slept and of the one that eventually would be his own. On one wall he had tacked pictures of a glacier tumbling into the sea and of a log cabin surrounded by an arctic meadow, pictures cut from an old *National Geographic*. The previous year his father had talked about homesteading in Alaska and had even written for a government booklet explaining official procedures for claiming land. But eventually talk of Alaska stopped, and Lonnie kept the pictures only for decoration. Still his family would soon move someplace else, and while he would miss the farm, he was eager to get on, to see what lay ahead beyond the winter and the gray light.

In the days before the trip, his father always became subdued, distracted. Lonnie, in response, more regularly accompanied him in the barn, where the man readied his father-in-law's machinery for another season of farming. Normally, as he worked, the father explained what he was doing or told stories about the machine, or the machines that had preceded it, or at the very least whistled. Now, however, little was said, and Lonnie came after his school day only to watch and be near.

Every year, the last job before they went to the city was tuning up the big John Deere diesel tractor. All winter, its bulk dwarfing the smaller tractor used for cold-weather chores, it remained in the barn. When at last the points and plugs had been changed, gaskets replaced, and the power takeoff serviced, his father—ducking his head—would drive the machine through the double doors of the barn, and the roar of its engine declared, irrevocably, the arrival of another spring. Then Lonnie would scramble up onto on his father's lap, and while his grandfather watched they would thunder down the road. When they returned, his father would pull up in front of the barn, kill the engine, and say to his wife's father, "That's done." And Lonnie's grandfather would say, "Well," and the three of them would walk through the dusk to supper.

On the appointed day Lonnie awakened to the cries of cardinals in the walnut tree outside his window. Patchy fog covered the lower pasture and as he watched, cattle appeared and disappeared in drifts of gray, while to the east the sun had climbed above the clouds and sparkled on the morning dampness. He had slept later than usual and could hear from the porch the whirring of the cream separator as his uncle divided the morning's milk. By the time Lonnie had dressed and come downstairs to the dining room, his mother and grandmother had already packed lunch in a shiny lard bucket and were setting the table for breakfast.

He found his father in the barn lot filling the Ford from the red gasoline tank that leaned drunkenly, on skinny angle-iron legs, against the garage.

"Is it time to go?" Lonnie asked, more to confirm the day than the hour.

"Not till after breakfast." His father replaced the gas cap and hung the nozzle back on its hook. "Plenty of time. No reason to rush things." He picked the boy up, lifting him to a man's height, and Lonnie pounded on the red tank. The drumming sounded low and heavy with only a short-lived reverberation. "Still plenty left," the man said and lowered his son to the ground.

Then, slapping him lightly on the shoulder, "Race you to the house."

Inside they took turns washing their hands in the green crockery basin and smoothing their hair before the wall mirror. When everyone was seated at the dining room table, the grandfather, with Lonnie's father and uncle on either side, asked the blessing—not a ready-made prayer but one for the particular concerns of this day, one that asked for safe travel and good news about the future, and ended, as always, "Thy will be done."

The family ate in silence, passing sausage and fried potatoes and biscuits whenever a plate had emptied. The baby lay quietly on a blanket on the floor, deeply enthralled by the fingers of his left hand. To Lonnie everyone seemed unnaturally subdued, overly deliberate in gestures and words, polite as with guests. He itched to get on with things, and even the slow movement of the sorghum with which he normally coated his biscuit became intolerable; he put down the pitcher after the first heavy drip stretched to his plate, rather than piling up his usual reserve. He squirmed in his chair, frustrated and yet unwilling to break the near silence that prevailed around the table.

When the meal was finished, everyone stood at once as though rising for a hymn at church. Everyone, that is, except Lonnie. He had been eager to jump up throughout breakfast, and yet when the others at last rose from their chairs, he remained seated, momentarily frozen. In that instant, looking up, he saw the adults hesitate beside the table, and he noticed the way they lingered, glancing briefly one at another before breaking the circle and moving on toward the day ahead. Then the spell was broken and he leaped from his chair.

The car fueled and lunch already packed, little other preparation remained. Lonnie's face was inspected, a lingering stain was thumb-rubbed away, and his shirttail was tucked in. His mother changed the infant, and his father got the dynamite box, which served as a baby bed, the white pine softened with a small, brightly colored quilt. At last they all proceeded, single file, to the car. His father, in the lead, carried the baby. Then came Lonnie, followed by his mother and grandmother, his uncle carrying the dynamite box on one shoulder, and his grandfather with a thermos jug and the lard bucket of food.

For the first half mile his father carefully kept the tires astraddle deep tractor ruts, and from the crest of each hill Lonnie looked through the rear window to the farm and his grandparents, shrinking in the distance beside an already invisible gate. When they had driven as far as the mailbox, his father turned the car onto the gravel of the county road. Westward the way ran past the farms of relatives and friends, past the one-room schoolhouse and between the church Lonnie's family attended and the cemetery in which their dead were buried. In that direction lay the town where they bought their groceries and other supplies, a town two blocks in length that faced itself across its only street and whose biggest business establishment was Girst's Mortuary and Furniture, an imposing structure with two enormous plate glass windows that displayed caskets and bedroom sets side by side.

Today, however, they turned east and the road led away, past the hill country with woods and creeks in every hollow toward the broad floodplain of the Mississippi, there to cross a long bridge suspended high above the great river, into Illinois and the city: a city with enough streets that they required numbers to keep track of them all, with Sears, Roebuck and Montgomery Ward and J. C. Penney and Western Auto, with motion picture shows and cafés. Like a mail order catalogue come to life, it was a place of uncountable things, not pictures but the things themselves, things so shiny that wherever Lonnie looked, in nearly everything he examined, his own face, distorted and transformed, reflected back at him. The city always amazed Lonnie, excited and troubled him, and left him exhausted.

This year the morning drive proved uneventful. Occasional clouds cast wide shadows over barren fields and darkened the patches of frost that still survived in sheltered places. But most of the time they drove in sunlight through a damp and shiny landscape. Sometimes Lonnie pointed out lambs and calves to his brother, and the baby responded with appreciative gurgles and smiles. Sometimes one of the parents spoke, either to check on the infant or to have Lonnie notice something they were passing; sometimes, but not often.

By the time they approached the Mississippi bridge, the

clouds had clumped more thickly together and the streaks of sunlight moved farther and farther apart. The drawspan had opened for a barge and they had to wait beside the toll booth. Lonnie strained to see what was happening below, but the railing blocked his view, and he could make out only the top of the locks as they pushed outward to admit the waiting vessel. Farther ahead and in clearer view, water fell from the open gates of the dam, and an eagle soared in easy circles above the torrent. The baby fell asleep.

When the bridge slowly lowered in front of them, grinding back once more into a road, drops of rain splattered heavily on the windshield, but as they passed over the river and then descended into the city, the sun broke through once more.

As they entered the city, Lonnie thought his father and mother sat straighter and more rigidly. They spoke more frequently now without turning to one another, instead keeping their faces toward the windshield.

"How much shopping do you have?" asked his father.

"Not much," his mother answered, her voice, like her husband's, monotone and low. "A few groceries and some yard goods."

"Then I'll stop first to see what I can learn."

They drove past the stores to a side street. Traffic lights gave way to stop signs, and Lonnie tensed each time his father braked and steadied the baby's bed whenever the car accelerated more quickly than usual. His mother looked straight ahead, and as he waited for lights to change, his father tapped his fingers on the steering wheel. At last they parked next to a vacant lot across from a shiny yellow and black building that looked as if it were made of metal. On the big windows, in yellow letters, was written "Lindeman-Mitchell Coal and Construction." Next to the building the boy saw a yellow pickup and a battered dump truck, both with the same words painted on their doors.

The father looked at the woman and then back at the children and forced a grin. "Don't leave without me," he said. Then he climbed from the car and crossed the road to the yellow and black building, his wife and son watching until he disappeared inside.

Lonnie's mother continued to stare at the building, saying nothing, sitting stiffly, her head tilted slightly back, chin thrusting forward. For the first time her son recognized his grandmother in his mother, less in appearance than in the way she looked at things around her, looked at them as though she were looking beyond them at something else.

Outside the sun shone. Two starlings waded stiffly in a mud puddle, and a collie ran in circles around a vacant lot. When the baby stirred, Lonnie patted him and he quieted into sleep once more.

In a few minutes the father returned, entering the car stiffly—hips first, then the main part of his body, and finally his head—as though the door had become too small for him.

"Lindeman's on a job," he said, "so it'll be Mitchell. One-thirty," he added.

He started the car and made a U-turn in front of the building.

"Seems like it's always Mitchell," the mother said. Then both sat silently. In the dynamite box the baby began to fuss, and Lonnie reached to comfort him.

"It's all right," his mother said. "Time he woke up."

They drove past white houses with long porches and ginger-bread trim. Lonnie saw, behind picket fences, grape arbors and sandboxes, and high upon a clapboard house, a boy his own age standing on a widow's walk looking out over the surrounding buildings, and he wondered if the river was visible from that height.

They turned beside a Western Auto store that had a row of bicycles standing out front, then passed a gas station where a man on a ladder was painting a red horse. Lonnie's father stretched his right arm around his wife. "Well, it's Mitchell and time our luck changed." He slapped the back of the seat and began to whistle "Little Brown Jug," slapping out the rhythm on the back of her seat. The woman said nothing.

They stopped at an A & P and, while his father stayed

behind with the baby, Lonnie went in beside his mother. He pushed the shopping cart while she picked out canning rings and boxes of Sure Jell. "That's all," she told him, and he pushed the groceries toward the cashier, "unless," she added, as though an afterthought, "you wouldn't mind going back for bananas." He started to run toward the produce section. "Don't run," his mother called to him, and he slowed to a fast walk.

Next they drove to Ward's and this time they all went inside, Lonnie's mother in the lead, moving quickly down the aisles, followed by her son and then her husband, who carried the baby on his shoulder, bouncing him lightly whenever he started to cry. As they passed through the shoe department, Lonnie slowed in front of a pair of boy's black engineer boots, smaller versions of those his father wore, then caught himself and sped up again. Beside him his father whispered with a confiding tone, "Maybe this summer. Let's see what Mitchell has to say."

They went upstairs to fabrics. Towering bolts of material rose up on either side, a forest of gingham and chintz. Lonnie walked among gauzy cheesecloths, chambrays with stripes and flowers, flannels figured with dogs and horses, and puckered seersuckers in unnatural colors. They came, in the back of the store, to the remnant bin, and his mother held up pieces of light cotton until she found one with pale blue stripes. She ran it through her hands, measuring. "There's enough for two pairs of pajamas," she said.

"What about you?" the father asked as she started for the cash register. "You were going to make a skirt."

She hesitated. "I don't see anything I like. Let's wait until we know where we're going."

"Wherever we go you'll need a skirt," the man said. She shook her head and started for the cashier.

"Can I get the buttons, Mom?" asked the boy.

"I don't need buttons for pajamas," she said, "but you can look through the cards while I pay."

Outside the sky was grayer and the air, which had earlier felt so warm, had grown chilly. The baby fussed, refusing to be distracted even by the father's bouncing and tickling.

"Well," said the father, "we better go to the park and eat before it rains."

At the park Lonnie rushed for the swings. While his mother, seated at a picnic table, nursed his brother and his father unpacked lunch, Lonnie launched himself skyward, leaning far back, legs outstretched and body flattened, then, on his return, pulling upright with the chains and pumping forward again. He worked the swing higher and higher until his body paralleled the ground and he faced the clouds. Then he relaxed and let his momentum drain away.

After they had eaten the sandwiches and potato salad and drunk the milk from the thermos, Lonnie waited for the bananas, but his mother cleared the table without mentioning them. He walked to the far side of the park beside his father, who moved at an even pace, carrying the baby upright, the infant's head resting against the man's chest. On the way back Lonnie ran, waving his arms and yelling, toward two crows feeding beside an overturned trash barrel, stirring the birds into dark, reluctant flight.

Heavy drops of rain, falling singly and at long intervals, blotched the picnic tables. "We should head on over," Lonnie's father said.

The rain splattered on the windshield as they drove away from the park. "A lot of building going on." The man spoke lightly, trying to sound casual and only partly succeeding. "Shouldn't be any problem this year." The woman remained silent, looking far ahead between the blurs of raindrops.

"Maybe afterwards we'll have time to look for a place," Lonnie's father said. "Lots of For Rent signs around."

They parked across from the yellow and black building and the man switched off the engine. He did not move for a while but sat as though he were still driving. The rain continued slow and deliberate, thumping the roof with a hollow sound. Still looking out over the hood, he reached across to touch the

woman's shoulder. She did not turn or speak but raised her
own hand to cover his. Then he was out of the car, striding
toward the dark opening in the metal building.

Lonnie's father was gone a long time. The baby slept in his
box; the mother, sitting stiffly, stared straight ahead through
the windshield and down the street; Lonnie waited. Only the
erratic splashes of rain broke the silence. The starlings and
collie had disappeared. There was nothing to watch except the
yellow and black building beside a broken road bordered by
dead weeds and covered by a darkening sky.

When the baby awoke with low complaining noises, Lonnie
patted him but with no effect, and the cries grew louder. Still
their mother did not turn, and Lonnie, not knowing what he
should do, sensed only that it was important for the baby not
to start crying in earnest.

"Could he have something?" Lonnie asked. "A banana
maybe?" The words were rusty in his mouth, and his mother
did not hear. The rain fell more heavily now, blurring glass
which had already begun to steam over.

"Could he have a banana?" Lonnie tried again.

His mother turned, looking surprised, and at first her eyes
seemed unable to adjust for something so close at hand. Then
she blinked in understanding.

"Not a banana. Not for a baby, not just yet." She opened her
purse and took out a piece of muslin twisted around a lump of
brown sugar and tied with heavy thread. The boy put it in the
baby's mouth and the baby sucked with soft contented noises.
Then the woman took the brown sack containing the bananas
out from under the seat.

"Here," she said, handing a banana to Lonnie. "You have
one." She brushed his hair. "I forgot," she explained.

Lonnie sat watching the building, nibbling at the fruit, making it last.

When his father opened the door of the building it made a
black hole in the yellow wall. He came in long strides while the
hole filled in behind him, came head up without ducking his

face out of the rain, and entered the car quickly, sliding under the wheel and starting the engine in the same unbroken movement. Then he pulled out his handkerchief and wiped a clear circle on the fogged windshield.

No one spoke. The man and woman looked straight ahead, expressionless. The baby sucked at the sugar. Lonnie stared at the backs of his parents' heads and continued to wait. After a while he felt the car lurch up the bridge, and only then did he look out the rain-streaked window.

When they had crossed the bridge the man spoke. "There's work," he said. "All summer's worth." He hesitated. "Maybe something here in the fall." The woman looked ahead. The rain slowed and the windshield wipers screeched against the glass.

"Where?" she asked, her voice steady, as unbending as her gaze. The man watched her out of the corner of his eye as he drove.

"Pretty far away this time. A state highway up north, up above Amity." He paused but the woman did not respond. "I go in the morning."

The woman turned quickly toward him, then caught herself. He shut off the whining windshield wipers.

"Lindeman will be driving up in a couple of weeks, maybe a month. If the baby's ready, you can all come then." He pulled around a truck, accelerating quickly so that the car lurched forward.

"They're staying in cabins. Some sort of trailer court, Lindeman says."

Lonnie, tired from the day and warmed by the car heater, sank down in the back seat. He steadied the baby's box, first with a hand and then with his body as he leaned over and pressed against the wood. He turned his head until he faced the top of the car. The gray-brown upholstery seemed to be made of lint. The dome light was broken, one jagged edge roughly overlapping the other. He wondered how the pieces could ever have fit in a seamless surface. He tried but could not remember a time when the crack had not been there. Next to the light, fabric had torn away from the roof and bulged downward as though the rain had leaked through. He half expected the cloth to break and, wet and clingy, to engulf him, his mother and his father and his brother. But the gray bulge had been there a long time; the ceiling would hold and they would return to the farm at dusk, unchanged. He closed his eyes.

His mother finally spoke, soft now, consoling. "Remember three years ago," she said. "We got to Fairmont and the creek was out. Water all over the road. I thought we'd be caught there forever."

His father laughed. "We nearly made it. Would have, too, if it hadn't been for that chuckhole."

"That chuckhole was all that was left of the road," she said. "According to you, water wouldn't cover the hubcaps. And then when it came in over the floorboard and we had to keep our feet on the seat, you decided we were in a chuckhole."

They both laughed.

"Where'd we go that year?" she asked.

"Fort Lyons," he answered, "but on to Midland. Midland, I think, when you got there."

They were quiet for a while. Then the man spoke. "Better that time than the spring I came back on furlough—before they shipped me out. The year the levee broke at Wayland. I could see you standing on the other side of the water, you and the baby. You and Lonnie. You wore that flowered dress, and I could see you beside the car. You were waving but I couldn't get across. Couldn't hear you or call to you or anything."

It was getting dark. Lonnie, eyes closed, still lay against the box, its edge hard and sharp against his shoulder. He did not move, but neither did he sleep.

In the front seat his father said, "I never had much luck with rivers." He sighed. "Someday we'll get a place where I don't have to cross water to get to anything."

five

Because there had been no rain in June, the July berry crop was nearly nonexistent. The few blueberries that came to maturity were hard and dry, more shriveled little nuts than berries. The moisture had been driven out of the ground so that no grubs or angleworms were to be found under rocks or rotting logs. Everything looked burned; the ferns were yellowed and brittle, as though taken from between the pages of a book, and the high meadow grasses gave off the dry acrid smell of ash. By the end of the month birches had begun to lose their leaves and the younger spruce had turned brown and died. Only beside the lake did any green persist and even there it was dull, grainy with dust.

One night in the driest week a raccoon, desperate with hunger, attacked the storage shed behind our cabin, came at it from the top, ripping off cedar shingles, then clawing at the inch-thick boards that underlay the shingles. It did not get through, did not gain access to the half-bag of dog food stashed inside, succeeded only in removing nearly a square of roofing and littering our yard with the urgency of its desire.

A CHILD'S
HISTORY
OF WORK

As a child Lonnie conceived of work less as a thing man was condemned to do than a thing man was condemned to seek. Work was what Lonnie's father and his father's friends "looked for," couldn't "find," got "a lead on," a term that came with a prospector's vocabulary, suggesting a commodity that was rare, even if only modestly valuable. Those who lacked it followed rumors of its presence from one place to another, time and again pursuing a promising vein only to discover upon arrival either that the claim had already been staked or that the ore was low-grade. The labor, hard and soul-breaking, of finding work he learned from observation was among the most difficult of all jobs, and the fact that more secure people—in the absence of such experience—failed to recognize it as work at all only intensified the anguish.

His father, when Lonnie was older, settled in one place, and while he didn't work for a single employer more than a few months at a time, employment was more regular and always in the same geographical area. But earlier, when Lonnie was still a little boy and his father a young man fresh out of the army, the family's life was built around the search for work. Sometimes the father went job hunting without the rest of the family, hitchhiked or joined with others in the same dilemma, pursuing a place where construction was about to boom, heading to Texas where a new plant was supposed to go up, to Utah where a hydroelectric dam had been funded, to Kansas where men were needed to lay a pipeline. Dams, pipelines, large industrial complexes, these Lonnie knew to be the mother lodes for construction laborers, big projects that promised employment for years rather than weeks, where there would be overtime and promotion. But always his father returned in frustration: the project had been delayed or was much smaller than rumor had advertised; there was a surplus of men already in the area; employers wanted skilled workers and wouldn't give him a chance.

What was more often available to his father was road work. In the years following World War II Midwestern states began to rebuild and extend their highway systems, an effort that required large numbers of men willing to work long hours for low pay and few other benefits. Lonnie's parents and their friends, in those pre-lottery days, never aspired to an Eden of not working; rather their ambition was never to be out of work, never to be dislocated by its absence. Highway construction is neither reliable nor locating. It is seasonal, interrupted by bad weather and, in most places, halted every year by winter. In contrast to what Lonnie's parents called "steady work," the whole point of a highway project is to get finished and as quickly as possible eliminate the jobs of those whom it employs. And, of course, highways do not stay in one place, thereby displacing those who labor on them that others might more easily find their way home. As the road moves, so do the road builders and their families, uprooting every few weeks to go to another town farther down the way.

It was this reality that most divided Lonnie's parents and the other husbands and wives in the road business. Even a boy could tell that the men liked at least the idea of movement, of going places, even if those places lacked any real significance for them personally. Many of them, like Lonnie's father, were sons of farmers and many had been soldiers, and sometime during the war, as Lonnie had heard more than one of them say on more than one occasion, they had promised, "If I'm alive when all of this is over, I'll be damned before I go back to the farm." But in fact working the land was what they knew best apart from marching and cleaning rifles, and as laborers that's what they'd gone back to, only this time they'd broken free of the fenced-in fields and careened across country, plowing, leveling, remaking a narrow strip of the earth's surface.

But for the women road work meant continual packing and unpacking, a never-ending chain of new neighbors, none of whom got to be real neighbors; it meant living in other people's houses and being regarded with suspicion and contempt in small towns where other people had spent a lifetime in houses their parents had built; it meant never having a family doctor and carrying their children's lives around in a box for delivery, upon demand, to new schools or public health officials. What their husbands experienced as liberating meant for them imprisonment among strangers. For them the remedy for unemployment was nearly as deadly as the disease itself. Lonnie, of course, saw more of his mother's life during these days than of his father's and was himself always aware of the strangeness brought by constant moving. And yet he too was impressed by the work his father did and came to associate his own location less in terms of the steady stream of unfamiliar towns and people and more with what was familiar about the road itself.

Job sites were always the same, the same machinery clawing at the same raw earth, the same spectacle of men and equipment. While Lonnie cared little for the actual blacktopping with its attendant heat and the stink of asphalt, he liked to go with his father evenings or on rainy days to wander through the mingled smells of freshly broken ground and diesel fumes, in part because all this reassured him that although they had been moving, they remained on the same path. Occasionally his father would take him to the job during working hours, and he could watch the graders and big tractors as they reshaped the landscape. He liked to sit far up on the bank or in the cab of a truck parked to the side and just watch, all the while filled with an excitement and a sense of well-being that he took to be the point of work, the sensations his father so conscientiously pursued during the periods of his joblessness. This feeling was what made it all seem worth the trouble. Such was the vocation he expected one day himself to pursue—drive a dump truck, or run a big grader. This seemed natural enough, a construction site is a child's fantasy, an extravagant sandbox bordered with huge heaps of earth, the stuff of the last leveled hill held in reserve for exalting the next valley. Everywhere is something to look at: beribboned grading stakes, tripods topped with survey-ing instruments, stacks of shiny culvert pipe, huge belly-drag-ging earth movers, and fat rollers, and in every direction men imitating boys, playing with trucks, pushing dirt around, mak-ing loud noises. From Lonnie's privileged position as a child watching at the margin, already an expert on the anguish of adults, the masculine pleasure offered by such a vocation, no matter how intermittent, was all that justified growing into manhood.

When they returned—he and his father, in the evening, after the new paving had cooled—the road wound like a clean black ribbon through the green countryside. Steam drifted up from its surface and dew dulled the smell of asphalt to a gentler pungency, nature and construction in apparent harmony, labor and amusement perfectly combined.

The envy Lonnie felt for the workers, however, disappeared whenever the work ended. The Herculean figures of summer labor became desperate in midwinter idleness, their power over the earth mocked by unemployment and sometimes poverty. On those occasions when his family did not return to his grand-parents' farm, there to outwait this embarrassment, he wit-nessed the desperation as his father looked for other work, looked without precondition or lofty requirements. One winter no local jobs could be found, and Lonnie's father went west, left his wife and Lonnie and Lonnie's little brother while he tried to find something to do, left with the promise that he would somewhere find work and return for the rest of them and buying just before his departure enormous bags of soup beans and cornmeal to ensure their survival in his absence. It was a hard time, one that, among other things, gave Lonnie a lifelong distaste for soup beans and cornbread. When at last the father came back he seemed much older than Lonnie remembered, seemed nearly as old, for a while, as the boy's grandfather.

At such times Lonnie's father did anything that offered compensation, no matter how small the reward, sold magazines, shoveled snow, took day jobs of every description. In the same spirit Lonnie's mother sewed clothing from remnants, feed sacks, whatever material came to hand, and made meals of anything she could get cheaply or, in summer months, for the picking. So the boy was instructed in two expressions of labor: first in the make-do employment of getting by, the temporary work of attending to other people's homes and chores, of finding necessities in their cast-off possessions and their surplus food; and, second, the rare and mysterious work that went with "having a job." The first was a matter of salvage and survival, the second one of security and self-respect. The central text of Lonnie's literary education was the Bible, and the Genesis account of our human contract declares work the consequence of sin, but the boy discovered early on that people in the towns through which his family migrated regarded the lack of an official job to be the ultimate sin, and Lonnie suspected nearly as soon that the pain so evident in his parents was as much the result of guilt as of poverty. Thus he learned the meaning of work as only the children of the unemployed working class understand it, that it is not just the consequence of the Fall but that its absence means to keep right on falling. Unemployment pulled at his young parents like some redoubled gravity, and, contrarily, finding a job produced a buoyancy that changed the way they looked and moved and spoke.

Inevitably Lonnie "worked" as well, did all the things kids do to make money. In some of the towns through which they drifted he found yard work, already at seven able to push a lawnmower, though never quite at the right angle and always, of course, with someone else's mower. Despite a deeply ingrained shyness, he became proficient at going door to door in strange neighborhoods, asking if there was anything he could do, and often there was—attic cleaning, gardening, and general maintenance.

His father, when he scrambled between jobs, often found something to sell. Lonnie's favorite product was a kitchen tool called a Salad Master, a cutting machine with several cone blades that, when turned with a crank, sliced and diced and performed other acts of violence on tomatoes and onions and potatoes. As a result the family often had french fries, a previously rare delicacy for the child, made from potatoes cut during sales demonstrations. Not surprisingly, then, Lonnie, also tried selling as he got older, despite finding it embarrassing and being unable to represent forcefully the virtues of any product. He sold the kinds of stuff pushed on budding young entrepreneurs from the last pages of boys' magazines, ads found next to the Charles Atlas sand-in-your-face strips: Cloverine salve, *Grit*, Christmas cards. He had the most luck, when he was about nine, with Christmas cards, largely because he merely carried the sample boxes to women with whom his mother had already spoken, women already resigned to the purchase, who would flip through his wares while he, eyes downward, gripped the order sheets and mumbled appropriate prices.

Lonnie did not like anything about sales, not the speaking with people and certainly not the asking for money. Every aspect of the transaction made him uncomfortable, but it was employment—even if it was never clearly, to his mind, work—and he did not complain; only unemployment, he knew, justified complaint. Still the jobs he preferred involved physical labor, carrying, shoveling, raking, anything where he actually got tired in body; only when he felt the labor in his arms and legs was he confident his activity was truly, undeniably work. While selling also made him feel exhausted, he could never locate or explain the tiredness and could never, as a consequence, quite believe it justified his pay. He suspected the purchaser was merely being charitable and that Lonnie's portion of the proceeds was unearned.

The general principle of compensation was, in fact, a thing he never understood. When he overheard other boys talk of becoming firemen he was bewildered, since he thought that life especially difficult. He had lived in towns with firehouses, and whenever he passed by, the firemen seemed unoccupied. Lonnie knew they lived in the firehouse but thought it was because they were paid only for the time it actually took to put out a fire, and since fires were relatively uncommon, he supposed their earnings to be quite meager. He assumed firemen lived at the fire station, their accommodations charitably provided, because they could not earn enough, in the usual absence of conflagration, to afford homes of their own. While he found the idea of living in a sort of hayloft over a big garage otherwise appealing, he was saddened by the shame of unemployment so publicly and constantly displayed.

Eventually Lonnie's father found his way into the building trades, first as a laborer, then as a carpenter, and finally as a millwright. This was how the family came to settle in one town, and though this work too was seasonal, they waited out each stretch of bad weather, each economic recession, each contract dispute, rather than go prospecting in a different territory. There were times during exceptionally long layoffs when Lonnie's parents would talk once more of moving, but as their children got further into school they became increasingly reluctant to uproot them for the always uncertain prospects in another state. Lonnie sensed an element of despair in his father's remaining in one place, a surrender of belief in hard work eventually rewarded, the reluctant substitution of a more stable life for personal dreams and freedom. Lonnie missed the circus atmosphere of road construction, missed the swaggering men and their big machines. And he missed the something his father had given up for his children's sake.

The place where Lonnie's family eventually settled, a small

city in western Illinois, had a double flood plain because it was located at the junction of two rivers. The land there was rich, and Lonnie eventually found work on truck farms, topping onions, picking beans, pruning tomatoes. His parents thought he did this for the money, but mostly he wanted to work, really work, and this employment, though not as satisfying as grading and blacktopping, fit his narrow definition. The pay came only to twenty or twenty-five cents an hour and the work was hard. At eleven and small for his age, he strained against the weight of heavy cabbage crates, carrying them alongside older boys the hundred and more yards from the patch to the farmer's waiting truck. When he pruned tomatoes he nearly always broke out in great itchy splotches that he concealed from his mother so she would not become alarmed and make him quit.

It was at this time, when he first embarked on an agricultural career, a thing happened that, over Lonnie's lifetime, told him more about the nature of work than did even the biblical account of man's Fall. Over the years he thought of this event so often, recounted it to himself in such a way that it became less a personal experience and more a kind of storybook story, the sort that gets moralized in the end. But it did happen to him, happened when he was eleven, working on a truck farm.

He was hired to pick green beans, not at the height of the crop, but later, after the regular harvest, when all that remained were the end-of-season leftovers. The farmer who hired him, along with two older boys, paid by the basket, ten cents a peck. "Good money," he repeatedly told them, "good money for kids," as though they were taking advantage of his generosity. "But," he qualified, "I won't allow any damage to the plants." The bean fields were already in disarray from the earlier pickers and looked like a garden after a hailstorm, plants falling in every direction and the paths between them blocked or twisted by the wreckage. It was hard for Lonnie to imagine a way to damage them more.

The farmer was a man somewhere between the ages of Lonnie's father and grandfather. He dressed like the other farmers Lonnie had known, and yet something struck the boy as odd about his clothing. The blue demin coveralls, the work shoes, the chambray shirt were standard enough, but Lonnie realized by midmorning that they all looked as though they had been purchased the same day, and they all showed exactly the same amount of wear, whereas Lonnie's grandfather and father would have on one item that looked old, maybe even patched, and another relatively new, and something else somewhere in between. He placed no significance on this aspect of the farmer's appearance, only noticed it and puzzled over what he had noticed until finally he had pinned it down.

While the boys worked, the farmer sat at a desk in a small building at the end of the bean field. Bent over his letters and ledger books, forehead wrinkled, eyes squinted, he copied numbers into columns and jotted notes on sheets of paper, pausing every little while to shake his head angrily.

Lonnie picked all that day, but the plants had been so thoroughly culled it took a long time to fill a basket and earn a dime. Still, after nine hours of work, he had collected nine of the little brass markers the farmer gave out whenever he was presented with a full container. One of the older boys quit during the morning, and the one who remained, a tall kid who sometimes sneaked a smoke and who called Lonnie "Squirt" and punched him in the arm whenever he passed by, had harvested no more of the metal tokens than Lonnie. With nine tokens in his pocket and the day nearly gone, Lonnie hurried to fill his tenth basket and earn an even dollar. When at last he finished, tired and proud, he started toward the farm. Two rows over, the tall boy trudged along in the same direction.

The farmer had ridden out on his tractor to meet them, had parked at the end of the field and had raised himself up from the seat, as though to better inspect his property. With his back to the west, he was, as Lonnie approached, only a dark shape against the sun. When the boys came to the machine and lifted their baskets to him, Lonnie sensed the anger he had noticed in the shed, but no longer directed at books and papers. The

man wore a green and yellow John Deere cap pulled low over
his forehead, and his eyes glinted pale and blue from the
shadow that darkened the rest of his face. His mouth was a
short straight line. Whenever the farmer took the beans from
the boys, his hand shot out abruptly as though he were snatch-
ing at a bird. Earlier he had quickly emptied the baskets into
a small wagon parked to one side, but here, on the tractor, he
clutched them, one atop the other, on his lap. Then without
speaking he started the tractor and drove back to the shed.

After he dumped these beans in with the others, he turned
to the boys who waited, their brass tokens in hand. He shook
his head: "You made a mess of things. There's nothing to pay.
You ruined the plants."

"Not us," Lonnie said, "the first pickers." The farmer looked
angrier and shook his head again. "I only pay for honest work,"
he declared. "You destroyed my beans. You ought to be the
ones paying."

The older boy looked at Lonnie, and in a voice both whining
and angry declared, "He made the mess, not me. He's just a
little kid, and he tore up the plants."

The farmer looked at the boys and then reached into his
pocket and withdrew a half-dollar. "Here," he said to the older
one, "take this and be glad I don't call the police."

"What about me?" Lonnie asked, already resigned.
"Where's my pay?"

"You heard him," the man snarled. "You ruined my bean
rows. Now get out."

Lonnie walked home bewildered and ashamed, unsure of
what to tell his parents. He tried to tell them nothing, to avoid
all discussion of work. They, however, asked questions, asked
if he hadn't put in too many hours, if the work hadn't been too
hard, asked, finally, if he had been fairly treated. The last was
always his father's question. Not "How much were you paid?"
but "Were you fairly treated?" It was, Lonnie knew, an important matter, too important to lie about, and so he told the truth,
told how he had been cheated, that he had worked hard, had

been careful of the plants, and then had been falsely accused
and denied his pay.

His father listened quietly then said, "Let's go." They walked
in silence, the man straight, his pace steady, but not so hurried
that the boy couldn't easily keep up. They walked past the last
house on the street, past the last intersection, past the "Dead
End" sign to where the road, less well maintained now, divided
the vegetable fields. Lonnie's father still had on his work
clothes, and his high-top shoes, cracked and stained with cement, made a crunching sound on the blacktop. As they approached the farm he began to whistle a slow version of "Little
Brown Jug" and seemed to his son remarkably relaxed. As they
turned up the gravel drive the farmer was just closing the door
on a large machine shed and did not see them until they
reached the front steps of the house at virtually the same moment as he. The farmer looked at Lonnie's father and, finding
nothing familiar in his face, turned to the boy. Lonnie too
seemed unrecognizable to him.

"The boy worked for you today," his father said.

"Ah," the farmer responded, placing Lonnie at last, "the kid
that broke down my beans." He gestured toward the field they
had just passed.

Lonnie's father turned to inspect the damage, then faced
the farmer once more. "That whole field is in bad shape. Did
the boy pick every row? That would be an admirable day's
work, even for a grown man." The word "admirable" rolled
on his tongue like a musical phrase. There was nothing in his
tone to suggest sarcasm or anger, just easy talk between two
men at the end of a workday, and yet the farmer, someplace
in the middle of "admirable," stiffened ever so slightly, became defensive.

"His part's beat up the worst," he declared, his words both
belligerent and hesitant. "The rest will come back, but he
ruined his rows."

Lonnie's father did not speak, only shook his head slowly, a
bemused look on his face. "But it's not worth arguing over,"

the farmer said, digging into his pocket. "The season's almost over. How many baskets was it?" he asked the boy.

"Ten," Lonnie answered. The farmer unrolled a packet of bills and peeled off one from the top.

"There," he said, "now you've no cause for complaint."

"No," his father said, "not about the pay, but I believe you owe the boy an apology."

The farmer's eyes widened in disbelief, then quickly narrowed. "Who the hell do you think you are, coming to my door and demanding an apology for some snot-nose I just paid for destroying my beans? Get the hell off my land or I'll call the cops."

"Maybe that would be best," Lonnie's father answered as though that would, indeed, be a reasonable course to follow, and he sat down on the porch steps. "Maybe they can tell which of those rows are more broken down than the rest. We'll just wait here while you place that call."

The farmer was furious. He grabbed at the John Deere cap with one hand and squeezed the crown, then stomped onto the porch. "Dammit," he cried, "that kid did more damage than work."

"Why did you keep him all day, then?" Lonnie's father asked, still sounding calm and curious.

"Goddammit, I'll not apologize," the farmer insisted, repeating himself three times, but in the end, the other man still positioned on the porch steps, he muttered, "Maybe the other kid did it. Maybe it wasn't your kid's fault."

"Close enough," Lonnie's father said. And they left.

On the walk home the father took his son by the hand, and since it was too dark for anyone to see, Lonnie did not resist. "The pay's important," the man said, "even when it's not much, but the work deserves its own due, a kind of respect, whether there is pay or not." The two walked on a little way before he added, "It's all right to work even when the pay is bad or when there's no pay at all. But never without respect. You always owe the work that much, that it be respected."

That, of course, is what Lonnie remembered, and what made it all, later, seem a storybook story, but he never doubted the truth of his father's words.

Lonnie did many things after that, but his image of work, the kind of work he always associated with his father, remained through childhood and youth that of the men on the road-construction sites, carving away with their graders, wreathed in diesel smoke, and sitting high above the highway they were pushing forward, proud to the point of arrogance in their short season of employment, throwing their labor back in the face of a god who had intended it to be a curse.

The cub had carried the garbage bag ten feet from the cabin and was buried up to his shoulders in corncobs and fish bones. When the flashlight's beam caught him, he scrambled backward clumsily, then stopped, blinking against the light. Golden strands of corn silk stuck to his nose. Somewhere in the night, his mother made hard guttural grunts, but he did not respond. Transfixed by the light, he remained facing the cabin, an overgrown toy, head cocked, ears erect.

Suddenly the darkness reared up, blocking the light's path. The female, standing on two legs, slashed out with one enormous paw. She swung at the light, claws glistening as she thrust down through the beam. She swung again and again as the cub rushed into the woods behind her.

EASTER

Tull came at ten o'clock Good Friday morning. Lonnie met him by the gate.

"Where's your grandpa?" Tull asked.

"Castrating hogs," Lonnie answered.

As they walked toward the barn, Tull a step behind the boy, they could hear the squealing and thumping. Inside the barn, Lonnie's grandfather and uncle were releasing a pig from a narrow chute into an outside pen. The grandfather crossed to Tull. The uncle sat on the edge of the chute.

"Can I borrow your tractor for an hour or so?" Tull asked.

The grandfather brushed at dirt caked on the bib of his overalls. "Got a horse stuck?" he asked.

"Got a pond to check," Tull said, "over at Gibson's."

"Too bad the river's so low," the grandfather said. "His pond can't be much cleaner than anything else Gibson owns."

"Probably not," Tull agreed, "but it's the only one around that hasn't had cattle or hogs in it all spring."

"A pond's a poor substitute at best," the grandfather said.

"But it can't be avoided," Tull finished the sentence.

"Tractor's by the well," said the grandfather.

"Teaching it to drink?" Tull asked. "If it's all right, I'll take the boy, too. You don't need him for this work."

As Tull drove, Lonnie stood between the driver and the wheel, one hand holding to the tractor seat and the other braced against the fender. Gibson's farm lay a mile to the east of his grandfather's, but the two men had little to do with one another. As Tull pulled into Gibson's barn lot, he had to weave carefully around dilapidated machinery. An old border collie with a matted coat sniffed at the tires but did not bother to bark. Skinny chickens scurried frantically in and out of buildings and under the scattered farm equipment.

Gibson came from around the barn in an unhurried walk. He took a long time opening the gate because the hinges had been replaced with loops of wire, and it had to be lifted and carried open. When he reached the tractor, Tull shut off the engine.

"I'd like to take a look at the pond," Tull said.

Gibson leaned to the side and spat tobacco juice at the dog. The stream faltered, fell short of the mangy animal. Some of it caught in the stubble of graying whiskers on Gibson's chin.

"Well," he said, after he had straightened up and wiped at his face with a dirty hand, "reckon it's still where we put it. Don't move much." He smiled a brown smile.

"You can never be too careful," Tull said. "Things get misplaced."

"Well," Gibson said, "I'll just come along and keep you company."

He called out, apparently to one of his two sons, who were the only other inhabitants of the farm, but neither of whom was in sight, "Going to the pond. Gotta keep the preacher out of the deep water," and then climbed up onto the drawbar.

Tull turned the tractor and drove down the road a half mile to another tumbledown gate. Gibson got down, opened the gate, then said, "You can drive right through here. Ain't got to this field yet." He swung his arm out over the unbroken ground. "Hoped to have it harrowed by now but nothing went right. Ain't even been in here with a plow."

Gibson climbed back onto the drawbar, and they bounced across the field until they reached a fenced-in corner, banked higher than the surrounding land. The pond, while larger than those on surrounding farms, was still only a depression gouged out by a bulldozer, the displaced earth pushed into a levee to hold the water. Tull pulled apart two slack lines of barbed wire, held them while Gibson and the boy crawled through, then ducked between the strands himself.

"S'pose your people can manage that fence?" Gibson asked. "I'd hate to cut it."

"They'll manage," Tull said.

At the far end, cattails filled the pond and fat bullfrogs jumped heavily into the water, grunting loudly with their effort. Eventually their eyes popped above the surface at the edge of the weeds, surveying the activity at the opposite end of the pond.

Tull sat down and loosened the suspenders of his overalls. Then he untied his work shoes, took them off, removed his gray socks, and tucked them into the shoes. Next he pulled off his overalls. When he stood, he wore only white boxer shorts and his white shirt. As he waded into the pond, Gibson sat down beside Tull's shoes and added to the chaw of tobacco already bulging his cheek.

"Checking the depth?" he asked as Tull worked his way beyond the weeds growing in the shallow water, out to where the pond came to his waist.

"No," Tull answered. He watched the water as though reading something beneath the surface.

Gibson sat silent for a while, then spat, laughed, and said, "Snakes. It's snakes, ain't it? Never knew a preacher that weren't hell on snakes."

Tull still didn't look up but began making his way parallel to the bank, still watching the water. "No," he said, "not snakes."

Gibson ignored him. "When Tompkins had that church, he baptized here all the time, even when the river was full, 'cause he hated snakes. Even the little water snakes like you get in these ponds. But at least here, he said, there weren't no cotton-mouths. He got real worked up about cottonmouths." Gibson spat at a frog that had stuck up its head near the bank, and the tobacco stained the grass some distance short of the water. "My boys used to tell him that there was big nests of cottonmouths in creeks hereabouts. Told him, too, you never knew when one would crawl up a tree and hang over the water on a branch. Tompkins would get all cottony himself and rush out of the room when he heard that." Gibson laughed and spat again. This time he aimed at a big thistle but came up short once more. After a while, he asked again, "Ain't snakes neither?"

"No," Tull answered, "not snakes."

"Well," said Gibson, "I heard Tompkins got him a church now with a pond built right into it, a kind of stock tank up front, where he can baptize all day without ever a fear for snakes. That's what you need."

"River suits me fine," Tull said as he waded back to shore. "And when the rivers get low, I can make do with a pond like yours." He stood in his shorts, letting the air dry his legs, and looked out over the water. Gibson sat behind him working at his tobacco.

A tractor came toward them across the field.

"Looks like Fred," Gibson said after the tractor had pulled up to the barbed wire and everyone had recognized Gibson's youngest son.

"Got to do something with that sow," Fred called. "She's eating her litter."

"Well, hell," Gibson said. "Pigs never come when they ought. Got to go with Fred." He did not get up, and after a few minutes Fred shut off the tractor.

"How come you bother with them churches?" Gibson asked. "I mean, you never take one on except when they can't pay nobody else. Then, they get a little money, they bring in some out-of-state preacher, and you go back to the farm till that one either quits or dies or does whatever preachers do when they get ambitious or bored or whatever preachers get."

Fred put his head on the steering wheel and closed his eyes.

Tull picked up a flat stone and skipped it six times across the pond. "I ever come up with the answer to that, I'll be sure to let you know."

Gibson laughed, the chortle a horse makes when it smells

oats. He spat, but his laughter had used up his spitting power and the tobacco fell to his shirt. He wiped his chin on his sleeve. "I reckon you will at that," he said.

"Least they ain't 'fraid to have you baptize and bury 'em," he went on. "You should fix special rates for putting 'em in the water and in the ground, and you could quit doing anything 'cept drive around the country behind them fancy horses of yours." He started laughing again, choking and gasping. "Ain't it the damnedest thing, all them Baptists trusting you with their mortal remains and their immortal souls but not their god-damned money."

Tull smiled. "Don't let us keep you from those pigs," he said.

Fred raised his head. "If we go now, Pa, we might get the one she's saving for dessert."

Gibson pulled himself to his feet, stumbling before he could straighten up. He put his hands on his knees and pushed. "Damned pigs ain't worth the fuss. See, Preacher, I do things crazy as you. I got to tend to my own insignificant flock." He spat at the pond and hit it. "Why don't we both quit fretting for others and live on manna? Together we ought to get a good crop of manna in a year or two."

Fred started the tractor and Gibson wormed through the fence, snagging his shirt on the barbed wire. Lonnie ran over and released him.

"Thanks," Gibson said. Then he called to Tull, "Ain't no snakes in that pond. Leastways no mean ones."

After Gibson and his son had driven away, Lonnie stood beside Tull, both facing out over the water. "What were you checking?" he asked.

"Itchweed," Tull answered. "Nothing takes the spirit out of a baptism like itchweed."

The boy picked up a stone and threw it, sidearm, at the pond. The rocked splashed and sank.

"Pick a flatter one," Tull instructed. "And keep it lower, closer to the water."

Lonnie found another stone, and this time managed two

short hops. "Why come here?" he asked. "Isn't there some-place better?"

With a low, easy swing, Tull skipped a rock, in evenly spaced loops, the length of the pond where it disappeared in the cattails. He smiled. "You mean, why come to someone like Gibson who never hits the mark even with his chewing to-bacco?"

Lonnie threw another stone, but two skips were all he could manage.

"Curl your finger around the edge more," Tull said, as he took the boy's hand and moved the fingers into position. "Gib-son's not so bad," he continued. "No worse, anyway, than the rest of us, and he hasn't confused himself into thinking he's any better."

"I don't think Grandpa likes him much," Lonnie said. This time he skipped the stone three times.

Tull gathered up his overalls and began pulling them over his feet. "A long time ago Gibson had a dead elm that fell on the fence between his pasture and your grandpa's cornfield. Gibson didn't do anything about it, and the cattle ruined most of the corn before your grandpa found out. When he got there, Gibson wasn't anywhere to be seen, so he rounded up the cattle by himself and just as he got finished Gibson walked down from the house. Said he must have fallen asleep. That night, about midnight, your grandpa removed the elm from his cornfield with three sticks of dynamite. Managed to send most of the tree back to Gibson's side of the line. Gibson came running out in his nightshirt scared to death. He was yelling, and your grandpa complimented him on his nightshirt and said he came over at night because he was under the impression people at Gibson's slept during the day and he didn't want to wake anyone." Tull hooked the suspenders and sat down beside his shoes. "There's been something of a strain ever since."

The boy laughed and dropped down beside Tull. "Grandpa likes dynamiting," he said.

"An impatient man about some things," Tull said. "That's

the main difference between him and Gibson. Gibson would
have left that elm to rot over the next century or two, but your
grandpa blew the whole thing away in one night." Tull took the
socks from his shoes. He brushed the dirt off his feet, then
pulled on the socks.

"Uncle Ivan," Lonnie asked, "what did Gibson mean about
the manna?"

"He was just joking," Tull answered. "Teasing me for being
the kind of preacher that just fills in the gaps here and there
when someone needs me. He forgets that I'm a farmer as much
as a preacher." He unlaced his shoes.

"Does it bother you?" the boy asked.

"No," Tull said, "it's best this way. There aren't but a few
things need saying, and I get to say them. And I don't depend
on keeping folks happy. It works out all the way around, because people need novelty, new faces to keep them interested.
But they need me, too. Tull, who was here when most of them
were born and who keeps coming back till he buries them." He
laughed. "Gibson was right about one thing. I am a dirt-and-
water preacher."

"What's manna? Really?" Lonnie asked. "I mean, I know
it's in the Bible, but what is it?"

Tull tied his shoes and stood up. "The usual explanation is
a kind of bread that fell from Heaven. But I don't know for
certain what it really was. There were a lot of people and they
were starving, some wanting to go back to being slaves. Maybe
they just started picking up the hoarfrost and even while it
melted in their mouths, told themselves it was God's own bread
and started liking it better every morning. Try to skip one all
the way," he said.

The boy stooped for a stone that looked to be the right size
and shape. "Is it okay to baptize in a pond?" the boy asked.

Tull laughed. "It's all right anywhere. I prefer the river
because I like water that moves. And because snakes don't
bother me. But anywhere will do. I guess if we lived in a desert,
I'd use sand."

"Let me look," he said, and checked the boy's grip on the stone. "Loosen your hold a bit. Keep your fingers relaxed."

"The whole point with water," he went on, "isn't whether it's pond water or river water or even that it's water, but just you're doing something a way people have been doing it for hundreds of years. Like the water's been running all that time connecting you with all those who came before and, in time, with all those who come after."

The boy swung his arm and sailed the rock out over the water. It skipped four times, then curved to the side, its flight dying with one last faltering jump.

"Pretty good," Tull said. "You'll get it across one of these days. A few things get easier as you get older."

s e v e n

The children's beach towels, terrycloth bearing near human-sized pictures of superheroes, hung over the line we had strung from a spindly balsam to the corner of our storage shed. There, between official duties, and dried as much by the breeze off the lake as by the sun's warmth, they spent the entirety of a hot dry summer, great sheets of color rippling against the drab green of the balsam and the flat blue water.

First one hummingbird and then another, drawn by the reds and yellows on Wonder Woman's costume and Superman's cape, came to thrust their pointed beaks at the bodies of these comic book powers, to taste the richness so carelessly lavished on such perfect physiques. The birds, themselves extravagantly decked out, were fearless, unaware that here were powers beyond the ordinary, saw perhaps only fellow lovers of color and came to share the bounty. They hovered in front of the flapping cloth, adjusting instantly to every rise and fall of wind, changing directions more quickly than the gifted fliers whom they bedeviled.

Day after day they hung before the line, slashing toward their targets, braking, probing, then retreating to hover, once more, inches away. Despite the absence of nectar and the thinness of the illusion, something in the bright cloth brought them back, seemed to tease an

RESURRECTION
AND DEATH

Resurrection died." The woman called from the kitchen where she was sealing jars of strawberry preserves, the smell of paraffin mingling with that of the cooking fruit. The screen door, however, had slipped from her son's hand, and he and his father were still outside, unhearing, when she spoke.

Again Lonnie opened the door, then, on the inside, pried the spring from its hook. When his mother came from the kitchen, drying her hands on her apron, he was helping his father guide a baby crib over the threshold.

The woman looked at the crib and said nothing. Her son knew she was disappointed.

"Just a coat of paint, it'll look fine," her husband tried. "Maybe some decals. Swans would look good."

The bed frame was badly scarred, one of the side rails had split, then been splinted with metal strips and screws, and the mattress ticking had separated into widely spaced lumps. Lonnie and his father pushed the crib into the middle of the room, the metal wheels squealing in harsh complaint.

"Beats a dynamite box," the man said. "You won't have to fold Timmie like a road map when you put him to bed."

The woman turned toward the kitchen. "Come here," she called. "See what Daddy's brought you." She waited a moment, entered the kitchen, and returned with a jelly-smeared baby in her arms. She stood him in the crib. Clinging to the rail he began to jump up and down on fat bowed legs, looking like a child pumping a swing or a railroad man powering a hand-car. He did not laugh, did not even smile, just crouched and straightened with a profound determination.

A wheel gave way, twisted to the side and dropped its corner of the burden in a sudden lurch. The baby tumbled into the sunken corner with a shriek.

"Hell," the man said.

The woman lifted the howling infant from the broken crib as her husband sank to his knees beside the broken wheel.

"Just needs something to wedge it in place. Get a clothes-pin, Lonnie," he said to the boy. When the boy returned, the baby had quieted, pacified with more strawberry preserves. The father broke one leg from the clothespin and whittled at it with his pocket knife. When he was satisfied, he slid it into the socket and jammed the wheel into place. He stood and shook the crib from side to side. The wheel remained steady. The baby, his legs now curled beneath him, was returned to the crib, but he refused to let go and clung, whimpering, to his mother. At last he accepted his fate, put his legs down, grabbed the side rail, and began once more to pump away at his previous work.

"Resurrection died," the woman repeated.

"Well," the man replied.

"Last night," she added. "John Hanks found him this morn-ing. Went by to return Resurrection's harrow."

"Well," the man repeated.

"In the barn. He'd been milking. Just slid off his milking stool and was laying there on his side. John said the cow was still standing in the stall, a half-full milk bucket under her. Hadn't kicked it over or stepped in it or anything. Just stood there waiting for the job to be finished."

"Never heard of any female standing still that long," the man said. "Better buy her quick." He caught himself just as he started to grin. "Resurrection's dead," he said, shaking his head slowly. "But a good enough way to do it," he said, the grin still working at the corners of his mouth.

"A Guernsey, John said. An old Guernsey."

"Well," her husband said, the grin no longer concealed. "When I go, I want it to be alongside an old Guernsey, too." He put his arm around his wife's waist and pulled her next to him. She clicked her tongue against her teeth and shook her head in mock irritation, but she didn't pull away.

The baby slumped down in the crib. He rolled onto his stomach, knees pulled up, rump pushed high so that he sloped away in either direction like a hill with strawberries sprinkled on its lower slopes. With great slurping noises he sucked at his thumb, and his eyelids closed, not slowly but all at once like windows flung shut.

"How old was he this time?" the man asked. He was looking down at the baby. "How old do you reckon?"

The woman shrugged. "It's been forty years," she said, "and he was over thirty then. Seventy-five, I'd guess. Maybe more." She paused. "Anyway, he's older than the Owl Creek school-house, and that was built in 1885."

"How can you know that, Mom?" Lonnie asked.

She laughed. "That's not so hard when it's painted on the sign right below the name."

"I mean about his being older than the school," the boy persisted.

"Because once, when I was about the age you are now, he told me. It was at a box social and I remember he said he saw the schoolhouse built twice. The first time the walls blew down before they got the roof on, and he watched from his pony while the men put it back together again. It's only down the hill from his house. Same house he was born in." She looked at Lonnie for a long moment. "Funny how that just stuck some-where in my mind only to pop out right now." She shook her head. "After all these years."

"When's the funeral?" the man asked.

"Day after tomorrow. Velma's already called to see if I'll help clean the church."

"Well, fix it nice. Resurrection will draw a crowd. They'll come just on the outside chance he can do it again." He dropped his arm from around her waist and started toward the kitchen. "You finished already?"

"Nearly," she said, "but you stay out of it until this last batch is done. I want to see the job ended before you start opening jars." She pushed past him as though determined to protect the newly canned preserves. "You can have some at noon. That'll be your dinner."

"I'm going to Tull's before then. Promised to help Chet and Linc with the barn roof. Otherwise Tull will be doing it himself." He turned to the boy. "Want to come along?"

"Can I help?"

"Do the whole thing, be all right by me." He gave Lonnie a light push toward the door. "Go put a ripsaw and hammer in the car. And a nail apron."

The boy rushed out to the toolshed. His father followed to the door and stretched the spring back to the hook.

"I don't want him on any roof," the woman said. Her voice was firm. "I don't want him falling off a barn and breaking his neck."

"Don't worry." The man moved back beside her and returned his arm to her waist. "Boys belong on ladders and roofs. Men sure don't."

"Don't go telling me where men belong," she said, pushing him away. She sighed. "I'll go make the sandwiches." She started for the kitchen. "Take a couple of jars to Uncle Ivan." She poked her head back into the room. "And ask him how old Resurrection was."

When lightning split the big mulberry that stood west of Tull's barn, the half that grew next to the building fell, breaking the outer joists and crumpling the tin roofing like wastepaper. When Lonnie and his father arrived, Chet was at work chopping the broken section free from the rest of the trunk. His brother Linc had climbed up on the roof and was waiting to get at the damaged sheeting.

Tull's team, hooked to the upper limbs by a logging chain, pulled away from the barn as Chet swung the ax. With one last sigh the wood began to break, and the half tree, creaking and groaning, twisted as the team pulled out and away, then fell into the narrow space between the barn and the remaining section of the mulberry. When the chain had been reattached to the splintered trunk, Tull clucked to the huge horses, and they lifted their great hooves and with a slow, unfaltering pace dragged thirty-five feet of tree through the gate and into the pasture.

"Gee up," Tull called, more a request than a command, and the horses turned to the right, pulling the tree parallel to the fence, the leafy branches, still thick with berries, close by the gate.

"As long as we're at it, why don't we just take the rest down?" Linc called from the roof. "Only take a few minutes."

Tull unhooked the singletree hitch from behind the team, then rose slowly, his head no higher than the backs of the horses. "No need." The muscles of the roan, a huge Belgian, rippled across its hips in little waves, and it flicked its tail at a horsefly. "I'm used to a tree there. Half's better than none."

"I doubt it'll make it long in this shape," Linc persisted.

"We'll see," Tull said. "I know it won't survive if we cut it down." He removed the harness and closed the gate. The horses began to pick at the mulberries with a remarkable delicacy, lips pulled up, yellowed teeth purpled by the crushed berries. They seemed at once grinning and indifferent.

"Want up on Dan?" Tull asked. Without answering, Lonnie ran to the gate and, as soon as Tull had latched it, began climbing. At the top, steadied by Tull, he grasped the coarse mane in both hands and crawled still higher, hugging the warm, rich-smelling back of the roan. When at last he had pulled himself into place, it was more like sitting on a wide, reddish plateau than on a horse; his knees barely bent, his feet only slightly lowered. Dan lifted his head from the mulberry branches and, before moving back to the fruit, nodded as if to acknowledge the boy's presence.

Ben, the young Clydesdale, raised up and whinnied, then, sidling closer to Dan, stretched his head over the roan's neck, bringing his white forehead within range of the boy's hand. As Lonnie scratched, Ben moved his neck slowly up and down, occasionally nickering his pleasure, while the placid Dan continued munching.

Linc had already peeled away the old sheeting and together with the boy's father was replacing the outside rafter while Chet splinted over a crack in the next beam with pieces of two-by-six.

The roan's back provided a privileged view of the barn roof, lifting Lonnie nearly to the same level as the working men. Looking away he could see, to the south, the wheatfield and, beyond, a narrow strip of corn that backed against the line of timber on the distant river bottom. West of the barn stood Tull's house, an old frame building with white clapboard siding and, on the upper story, a widow's walk that faced toward the timber. Visible in the distance, except where the house and a pair of oak trees blocked the view, a thin line of elms and sycamores followed a creek down to the river. Northward rose high pastures, already showing the first white of Queen Anne's lace and the yellow of wild mustard. These were bounded to the northeast by a row of hedge apple trees, and a stock pond whose high-piled banks were thick with thistles and milkweed.

The Clydesdale, sufficiently scratched and petted, returned to the mulberries. Lonnie watched the men, but under the midday sun he eventually grew warm and sleepy. He leaned forward on Dan's broad back and closed his eyes, all the while listening to the hammers, the regular, rhythmic beat when it was his father or Chet, the erratic flurries when it was Linc. Because they often had nails clenched between their teeth, the younger men mumbled their talk. But Tull's voice, when he spoke, came strong and clear, not really an old voice but deep and layered, what Lonnie always heard as two voices perfectly tuned, one graveled with experience, the other smooth and young. His father had once said, with the joking seriousness that ran through so much of his talk, "If God were ever to speak to me, I'd probably take Him for Tull."

Tull remained on the ground, sawing boards to the dimensions called down from the roof and then lifting them from the sawhorses up to the men. The lumber, rough-cut sawmill wood, caught the light, became itself yellow light, as the old man raised each plank to the hands reaching down from the roof.

The sound of the saw, steady and unrushed, came in long rasping measures, rising on the outward thrust, dropping on the return pull. Sometimes amidst the solid thumping of the hammering, Linc's quick, shallower staccato sang out above the other two, the hammer blow glancing off into a metallic twang. Linc would cuss at the bent nail, and Chet or Lonnie's father would say under his breath, like a "Bless you" after a sneeze, "Pecker's still growing," and Linc would cuss some more.

After a while Dan quit feeding on the berries but seemed content beside the gate, taking the sun. He stood steady, his only movements the shuddering of muscles on hips, withers, and flanks as he shook off flies, the lazy swishing of his thick tail when he worked to dislodge his more accessible tormentors, or a barely perceptible snort when an insect found his nose.

The boy turned over, letting the sun warm his face, placing his spine against the broad sloping ridge of the horse's backbone. He dozed until he heard the men clambering down from the barn roof. Tull was coming from the house with a milk pail and a dipper.

"Had a long ride?" His father walked to the gate, the top of his head barely reaching to the boy's knees. "Thirsty? Tull's bringing some ice water."

Rolling to his belly, Lonnie swung his legs to the side and slid down into his father's arms. After his father dropped him to the ground, he brushed dust and horse dander from his shirt front. There was only a little; Tull's horses were clean.

Tull ladled up the ice water, passing the dipper to Lonnie and then, refilling it three times, handed it to each of the men. Linc had taken off his shirt, and sweat ran on his chest in stripes of sawdust and matted hair. His back and neck were pink. Chet still wore a blue chambray shirt—its long sleeves buttoned at the wrist, sweat stains dark under the arms—and he wore a broad-brimmed straw hat, curled up at the edges and pulled forward to shade his face. Lonnie's father had stripped to his undershirt. He had been planing the crown off one of the joists, and little gold shavings had caught here and there in the white cotton ribs. He had on a red baseball cap with a St. Louis ensignia on the front, and when he lifted it to wipe the sweat from his forehead, his hair glistened the same color as the wood shavings on his undershirt. As the water came to him, he drank deeply, then dashed the last few drops onto his face. "Seconds?" Tull asked. Like Chet, he too wore a long-sleeved shirt, but his was white and partially hidden by the bib of his overalls.

"I could use another round," Linc said.

Linc drained the second dipperful in a long gulp, his Adam's apple clicking up and down as the water slid by.

"Say, Tull," Lonnie's father asked—he was one of the few people the boy knew who called the preacher anything but "Uncle Ivan" or "Brother Tull," and yet he said it without any hint of disrespect—"how old was Resurrection?"

"He would have been eighty-one next week," Tull answered. "Ten years older than I am." The boy, who never thought of Tull as any particular age, looked up at the face which had tanned over the years to a leathery color and texture. Tull's hair was still dark, almost black. He stood straight, taller than the three young men beside him.

"Is he really dead this time?" Linc asked, chuckling.

"That's what the doctor and the undertaker say." Tull's face held no expression. "That's as much authority as a funeral requires."

Chet had taken the dipper and was drinking in little, widely spaced sips, as though he were savoring the flavor. He smacked his lips. "You were around the first time, weren't you? Whose authority was it then?" Linc had leaned back against the barn, resting. Lonnie's father worked at slivers in his palm, scratching them out with the small blade on his pocket knife. He, like Linc and the boy, listened, glancing up occasionally at Tull's impassive face.

"I was around," Tull agreed, "but I'm not sure who declared Elton dead. There was considerable dying at the time, and the main business was getting those who were gone into the ground as quickly as we could and then doing our best for the sick who were still alive." The Clydesdale lurched over the outer limbs of the mulberry, reaching higher into the branches for the remaining fruit. He whinnied, and branches cracked. Tull looked toward the pasture. "We weren't overly particular about whose authority was working then." He took the dipper from Chet, filled it, and lifted it to his own lips. When he had drunk as much as he wanted, he tilted the cup until the remaining water ran in a thin, clear stream into the dust at his feet. "Elton made us all a little more careful."

"Did it happen that way any other times?" Chet asked.

"Not that I ever heard," Tull said. "At least not around here. But later, when the epidemic was over and the doctors settled back into their regular work, Doc Bryant said it wasn't the flu but something peculiar to Elton, something that the flu brought on. A kind of epilepsy, he thought."

"I never heard of Resurrection rolling around on the ground and swallowing his tongue," Linc said.

"There's other kinds," Chet said. "I heard about it in the army. Some little kink or something in a fellow's brain. Can do a lot of different things."

"Sounds like the kind of fancy explaining you get after some doctor screws up. That's how I'd guess it," Linc said.

"More than doctor's screwing up if you put a man in the coffin," Lonnie's father said. He picked up a mulberry branch and began to whittle.

"All that 'in the coffin' and 'into church' sounds like fancifying to me," Linc said. "Did it get that far for sure, Uncle Ivan?"

"Not into the church but into the coffin. There were too many for church. We carried the dead directly to the cemetery, said a few words and a prayer before lowering the casket. The only reason Elton's coffin was open was his mother wanted everything said to his face. She wouldn't let the lid go on until the last amen."

"Are you sure?" Linc persisted. "It wasn't just talk?"

"I'm sure," Tull answered softly. He still watched Ben eating among the mulberry branches. "I was the one doing the praying."

The three younger men all looked at Tull more closely. "I never heard that," Chet said. "I mean I heard the story a hundred times, one way or another, but I never heard that you did the funeral."

"No reason you should have," Tull said. He bent and put the dipper into the milk bucket. A tiger swallowtail glided by, settling on the bucket rim, nearly brushing Tull's hand with a deliberate sweep of yellow and black wings that looked brand new. The old man slowly straightened. He looked up toward the barn roof as though inspecting the work. "Only ones there besides Elton and me were Elton's mother and his sister who was just coming down with the sickness. She died a week later."

A smile touched the corners of Tull's mouth, lightly like the butterfly on the bucket rim. "His mother wanted a regular preacher. I didn't have a church, and she didn't think my words would carry any weight. Her husband had died a deacon, and she thought they deserved better. It didn't matter to her that the only other preachers were someplace else or sick themselves. She probably never told anyone I was the one officiating." He looked toward the river. "For some reason Elton never seemed to remember I was there. He always told the story as though it was just him and his mother."

The butterfly lifted from its perch but remained, flitting above the bucket, sinking down nearly to the remaining water and then lifting up above the men's heads. The yellow of its wings caught the sun and its black stripes glowed like onyx.

"That was my first funeral, and I didn't get to finish it."

"Huh," Chet said. He shook his head. "That beats everything. When did he sit up?"

"He never sat up. Not in the coffin. That was invented later," Tull continued. "He moaned and fluttered his eyes. The sister, the dying sister, saw it and called out. I had just gotten to 'a time to mourn and a time to dance' when she broke in. I still had eleven more verses and a prayer to go when she interrupted."

The boy's father spoke so softly that only Lonnie and perhaps Tull could hear. "You were an Ecclesiastes man from the beginning. It figures."

"Well," Linc said, "this time you'll get to finish. Maybe say the same words since it's the same man and a different crowd."

Chet looked at his brother, seemed about to speak, and then looked away.

"Well," Lonnie's father said, "it doesn't seem quite right. Should be some kind of double jeopardy in graveyards, same as in courts." He grinned at Tull. "This time you should represent the accused and not the state."

"I thought that's what I did last time," Tull said with his voice soft and thoughtful. "What I always think I'm doing."

"That's so," the younger man answered. "The state wasn't what I had in mind exactly." His grin had disappeared.

"You meant the man rather than God," Tull said.

"I guess so. God, maybe, but—you're right—clearly not the state. You seem to go after the state more than any preacher I ever heard."

Tull was looking intently at Lonnie's father, and Lonnie saw the light smile edging back around his mouth. "Probably so, but that would argue I *am* representing man; I am the defense."

The younger man laughed and shook his head. "I thought preachers were supposed to be on God's side, not man's," he said.

Tull's eyes crinkled a little more at the corners than usual. "A preacher has to believe man's side and God's side are the same. Sometimes I think he's a go-between, always explaining one to the other but never himself understanding more than a little about either. It would be easy work otherwise. Everyone would want in on it." He looked over toward the horses, watching as the Clydesdale tried to work his way back over the limbs that had sprung up, trapping him while he ate. "You thinking about becoming a preacher, Will?" Tull asked quietly, his face serious once more.

The boy's father reddened. He shook his head quickly. "Not me. Too old, Tull. Too old and too dumb. I'll leave the preaching to you."

Ben thrashed among the mulberry limbs, gradually getting himself turned, crushing the branches with his huge hooves, his whinny changing from one of frustration to one of triumph as he lunged forward in escape.

"You don't mean dumb," Tull said. "We both know that. Maybe doubtful is the word you thought to say." His eyes softened but his lips held firm. "Or thought not to say."

Lonnie's father looked directly into Tull's face as though in search of something. He still grinned, but his eyes were intent. "Mostly I think you're the best preacher I ever heard because you sound like God." He spoke softly, intensely. "But maybe, Tull, it's because you listen like Him."

Chet had been silent during the exchange between Tull and Lonnie's father. He had listened attentively but looked slightly dazed, as though he couldn't quite get the two men in focus. Linc had grown restless and wandered to the corner of the barn, where he rubbed his back, catlike, against the building's sharp edge. Chet blinked his eyes and straightened.

"About time to get the tin up," he said, stretching. "You want to come check the rafters, Uncle Ivan?"

"No," the old man said, "you are as good a carpenter as I am. If you say it's ready, I'm satisfied."

Linc, followed by the boy's father, climbed to the roof and, standing on a crossbeam, crouched for the sheets of corrugated metal that Chet and Tull handed up one at a time.

"Not too many," Lonnie's father called down after the second sheet had been passed to the roof. "We're liable to kick them down again."

Chet looked at Tull. "Go on up. Lonnie and I can lift them to you." The boy rushed to help Tull as Chet started for the ladder. "Say," Chet asked as he began the climb, "is it true that after he came back, Resurrection danced in church?"

The boy looked at Tull and watched as a rare full smile broke across the old man's dark face. It was like a wave of light moving across deep water. Ben whinnied and tossed his head among the mulberry limbs.

"The next Easter," Tull said, his low voice wholly young and rippling, "people standing, singing 'Amazing Grace,' and when they came to 'that saved a wretch like me,' I heard a commotion towards the back and then I realized that Elton was moving around. At first I thought something was wrong. I could see his mother go pale and agitated as though he had died again. Then Elton rushed right into the aisle, in this stiff-legged little jig, and with everybody watching, he went out the door. I could see him sort of hopping and turning as he crossed the road. Everyone pushed to the windows, children crying to be lifted up to see what was going on. Then, when Elton got to where his grave had been dug, he jumped up and down and let out a long whoop that must have carried clear to the Ferguson place."

Tull's head was tilted back slightly and the afternoon sun set his face ablaze.

"I said 'amen' and that was it, the best Easter service I ever presided over."

"Reckon even Baptists can't stop you from dancing if you've come back from the dead," Lonnie's father said.

"It's hard to think of Resurrection that way," Chet said as he pulled himself onto the roof. "He sure never seemed the dancing type. I never even saw him talk to a woman, nor anyone else unless it was a kid."

"He was always a little awkward with people after his sickness," Tull said. "He thought they tended to look at him as though a part were still dead."

The hammering gave out a new sound as the men drove the large-headed roofing nails through the metal and into the rafters, and the vibrations sent a tinny falsetto that continued between blows. Through the afternoon the men worked their way upward, overlapping each lower sheet with a higher one, until in the late afternoon Chet had reached the ridge and nailed the last panel into place.

The temperature did not lessen, even when the sun slipped lower in the west, and the heat continued to send wavy shimmers up from the metal sheeting. Linc was already on the ground gathering up tools, and Lonnie's father was easing down the roof toward the ladder, picking his way gingerly over the hot tin. Tull, next to the sawhorses, worked on the bent weather vane. He had pounded flat the green copper horse, correcting the raised front hoof that had been bent to one side, and was now lightly hammering the rod, turning it slowly on the sawhorse as he beat it straight. Lonnie had returned to the real horses, carrying handfuls of red clover gathered from an alfalfa clump beside the barn.

High on the roof, Chet stopped to mop the sweat from his forehead. He braced himself on one knee, flinching at the first contact with the hot metal on the western side. He raised up and then, shading his eyes with the straw hat he held in his right hand, looked off in the distance to where the county road crossed the gravel that swung past Tull's farm.

"Something must be mighty wrong over at the Hawkins place," he called down.

The others, except Tull, turned to face him as he gazed over the barn ridge to where the gravel road curled like a snake between wooded hills.

"Leastways their truck is coming like a bat, lurching all over the road." He paused, still intent on the distant vehicle. "You've got company on the way, Uncle Ivan, and they're in some special kind of hurry."

Lonnie dropped the broken clover in front of Dan and Ben. Instinctively he hurried to the ladder as his father descended to stand beside him.

Tull did not look up. He was sighting with one eye closed down the rod of the weather vane. When he straightened himself, he did so unhurriedly; his face, unchanged, gave no evidence of curiosity. Slowly he walked to the barn and set the vane, with its horse and arrow, upright against the building. He dusted himself, then took his handkerchief, wet it in the little water that remained in the milk bucket, and cleaned his face and hands.

Lonnie wanted to hurry toward the road in case the truck rushed on by, but he did not. He stood beside his father, watching as Tull prepared himself. A golden shaving clung to the laces of one of Tull's cracked high-top shoes. Tull bent and lifted it free. The boy looked at the others and saw that Linc had moved to the edge of the road, and Chet still crouched at the roof ridge, looking, not so far now, from under the straw hat he held like a visor over his eyes. Lonnie saw that his father was watching Tull, the same concentration in his gaze as earlier, when he had questioned the preacher.

The truck, trailed by a long white cloud of billowing dust, barely slowed as it raced past Linc and swung in a wide gravel—spraying arc into the barn lot, braking hard at the very last and skidding to a halt. The door was thrown open with such force that it caromed against the truck body, then bounced back heavily toward the boy leaping from the cab.

At sixteen Johnny Hawkins was already tall, as tall as Tull, but still carried only a boy's weight. He came out of the truck crouched like a fighter and rushed toward the old man. Johnny's face, white as the dust drifting above the road, seemed both uncertain and angry. With a convulsive jerk he thrust himself upright but made no sound. His arms twitched like a daddy longlegs that has been picked up by one of its thin limbs.

"What has happened?" asked Tull, his voice gentle.

Johnny's whole body began to shake, and Lonnie thought he must be terribly sick. Lips moved, but no words came. The blue eyes, open wide, were lit by a feverish brightness. At last he cried out, "Richard," with a terrible, echoing sob.

Tull put a hand on Johnny's shoulder and the two stood

silently as though the old man were propping up the teenager.

"Which Richard?" Tull asked, his hand still holding Johnny's shoulder.

"My cousin Richard." It came in a shriek. The mouth twisted in anguish. Softer, he added, "Thompson, Richard Thompson."

"What has happened?" Tull asked again. "What has become of Richard?"

Johnny's entire body clenched and released, clenched and released in two wrenching contortions. Tull lifted his free hand and held the other shoulder, bracing Johnny with both arms now. The young boy watched the anguish on the older boy's face and was filled with fear and fascination. "He is dying," he thought. "This is what a death rattle must be." And a rattling did come from Johnny's body, but Lonnie couldn't tell whether from the shaking or the gurgling in his throat.

No one else moved. Linc, still for once, stood staring from the road, while across the way his brother looked down off the barn roof. Lonnie's father, whose own hand had lifted to his son's shoulder at the same moment as Tull's hand had lifted to Johnny's, remained rigid beside the boy.

There came a long shudder, a writhing of Johnny's whole body, and then a deep sigh like a dying wind. "He's cut his goddamned head off," Johnny said.

"Shit," Linc cried and turned to vomit in the drainage ditch behind him.

"Jesus," Chet whispered.

Johnny fell away from Tull's hands, slumped to the ground with his legs thrust in a big V. Head bowed, he sat in the dust. Tull knelt before him, holding both of his shoulders once more.

Johnny spoke, this time in a monotone, his flat voice so low that, standing beside his father, Lonnie had to listen intently.

"Rich was cutting in the timber, up towards the ridge. We were both cutting, but I went down to the bottom to get fence posts." The words, now that they came, were unhurried but inescapable, powered by an inevitability beyond the one who spoke them. "He cut oak all morning. I couldn't see him but I could hear the saw. Whenever I quit cutting, it always seemed to be going." Johnny wiped his mouth, and a long, thin string of spittle carried across his cheek. Tull brushed it lightly away with his fingertips.

"Then about an hour ago, I quit hearing it anymore. I listened for a long time, and I called out, but he didn't answer. And his saw didn't start up again, and I got to worrying."

Mud flaked with sawdust hung in a moist rim around Johnny's shoes. The tiger swallowtail drifted over from the well and flitted around his feet.

"He'd wired the throttle and fixed the saw, running wide open, between two wedges." Johnny's voice continued without inflection as though repeating something memorized but not fully understood.

"And he put his throat to it."

"Jesus," Chet repeated.

"It threw him to the side, but not before it went nearly clean through."

Linc threw up again, his retching a harsh accompaniment to Johnny's quiet voice. Chet looked down as though the world had fallen away before him and he was unable to take his eyes from the hole it had left. Lonnie's father clasped his son closer to his side as they watched Tull and Johnny.

"Has anyone seen to him?" Tull asked.

"I came straight here," Johnny answered. Tears slid from his eyes in big drops that drifted down through the wood and gravel dust upon his cheeks. "I came here," he repeated, his voice rising. "I couldn't touch him. He was dead." His eyes, intent on Tull, still burned in the chalky face. "It ran out of gas," he said. "That's why I didn't hear it no more."

A lock of Johnny's hair had fallen down almost to his eyebrows and in it a small fleck of greenish gold wood caught the light. "Elm," the boy thought to himself.

"Rich always kept his saw real sharp, carried two chains so as not to ever let it dull." The words went on, a litany to be recited till the end. "Nobody kept a saw in better tune," he said. "It went nearly clean through."

Suddenly he moved both arms and grabbed Tull above the elbows. Tull did not move, his hands still bracing Johnny's shoulders. "Can he be put back together?" It was a wail now. "Nobody should see Rich that way. Nobody, Uncle Ivan." The face began to move uncontrollably, and he threw his head back as though to see Tull more clearly. The fleck of gold slipped from his hair and drifted away in the afternoon light. "He's nearly in two pieces, lying where the saw throwed him, his head turned on one cheek, but with no throat, and all swung backwards. O Christ, Uncle Ivan!" His voice sounded like the rattling of a chain. "O Christ."

Johnny began to sob, his body rising and falling in long slow movements, ebbing and flowing with a rhythm beyond Johnny or even his grief. "I knew he was low"—he looked up at the preacher—"he got that way regular, but he always came out of it. I never thought . . ." and he began once more to weep.

Tull lifted Johnny gently to his feet and slowly, arms supporting him, guided the boy toward the house. From the back, as they walked away, they looked to Lonnie surprisingly alike; the same height and both dressed in overalls. But Tull's hands were noticeably larger and his body both thicker and straighter than Johnny's. Johnny's clothes were rumpled, laced with sweat and grime in contrast to the cleaner, straighter lines of the preacher's shirt and pants. Yet their gait seemed much the same, like that of men carrying lumber on their shoulders, and they leaned inward toward one another until their heads nearly touched.

"You've got to get him put together," Johnny repeated as he moved beside the old man.

Dan still stood, looming over the gate, watching the two figures enter the house. But the Clydesdale, neighing wildly, began to prance across the pasture; its great brown back gleamed in the late sun. As it moved, Lonnie could see the long white hair lifting above the dancing feet, could hear the thudding noise of the hooves, big as platters, as they struck the ground. Again and again Ben called to Dan, turning toward the roan and shaking his huge head in invitation. But Dan remained by the gate, his own head turned to the house. Above the mulberry branches, the swallowtail flitted in ever-expanding circles.

His appeal rejected by the older horse, the Clydesdale turned at last, his muscles wide, rolling bands beneath the brown coat, and galloped toward the distant hedge apple trees.

eight

Insects covered the window that fronted against the woods, drawn to the light either to batter themselves against the glass or to land on its hard surface and bask in the gas lamp's glow. Occasionally one of big moths, a cecropia or a luna, would flit cautiously in the surrounding shadows, but mostly it was the little bugs, mosquitoes, drakes, and midges, that came.

Then the tree frog would appear. Starting in the lower corner, he worked his way up from one pane to the next, harvesting the insects with his sticky tongue. No larger than a child's eraser, he moved with incredible delicacy on long tapering feet that rounded into little circles at the ends of his toes. From inside the cabin the soft white belly edged with light green could be seen unblemished, perfect.

By the time the frog had worked his way around the square, a new crop of bugs covered the glass, and he repeated his circuit, moving at the same easy pace up the pane and down, round and round, as long as the light shone through the window, a solitary mower scything his way through an endless harvest.

THE THREE TIMES
I SAW MY
FATHER RUN

My father was a runner. In high school he had been the best half-miler in Missouri, and though I never saw him compete in a regular race, my strongest recollection—or rather recollections, since there were three events, distinct in time and place—is of him running, and ironically, for all his speed, in each memory someone else is in the lead.

My father was stationed in Lincoln, Nebraska, for several months during World War II, and after a few weeks my mother and I joined him. Except, of course, he spent most of his nights on the base. We lived on the first floor of a house in town, and he came to us whenever he wasn't on duty. Another soldier's wife, Lois, and her son occupied the second floor so that even when my father couldn't come home, we weren't alone in the building.

Because I was very young and had already moved a great deal, Lincoln and the people who shared our house, even the war, are blurred in my mind. But I remember certain things vividly, almost perfectly, like the face of Jay, the upstairs boy, framed by red hair and smears of banana, and that of the teenager up the street who made elaborate airplanes from balsa wood and paper, and then, rubber band wound tight, set them on fire and launched them from a second-story window. And I remember the weekend my father came home on a pass, and my mother told him that Lois, without asking, had been taking our food.

We lived on different floors, but the house had only one kitchen, and a shared stove and refrigerator. Things went smoothly enough until food from our section of the refrigerator began to disappear. Because it had never happened before, my mother knew exactly when it began. On Thursday morning she had gotten up earlier than usual and had gone into the kitchen before anyone else was awake, and when she opened the refrigerator, she discovered half a bottle of milk where a whole one had been and none of the leftover meat loaf from our previous night's supper. The food budget was small and she resented the loss but decided maybe Lois had needed it at the last minute and would explain when she got the chance. The day passed, however, with no mention of the borrowed food, even when Mom went to the store and made a special point before leaving of asking Lois if she needed anything.

On Friday morning not only had more milk disappeared but with it nearly half a pound of bologna and a large dish of cottage cheese. This time my mother decided to raise the issue directly. Lois, however, seemed upset about something and so Mom decided to wait a little longer.

Friday evening my father came home on a weekend pass. We hadn't seen him for ten days, and in the excitement of having him back, nothing was said about the missing food. Snow had fallen that day, and after dinner I was bundled up and we went for a long walk. I had gotten tired and my father was carrying me when my mother said, "I think Lois is taking our food." He didn't understand what she meant and she repeated, "I think Lois is taking our food." She didn't sound angry so much as puzzled.

My father asked, "Are you sure?"

"About food I'm sure," she said.

"Probably just borrowing and will return it soon enough," he said. But my mother wasn't easily sidetracked.

"No, she had plenty of time to explain. And besides, something's bothering her. Could they be broke?"

"No, Andy got paid last week, same as me." If any further discussion took place, I missed it. My father carried me to my room, got me ready for bed, told me a tall tale about the year of the late flood and early freeze, when he and his brothers had harvested corn under ice—one of my regular Friday night stories—and pulled the covers up to my chin.

His yelling woke me at midnight. I could hear him in the kitchen, then on the basement stairs, and as I climbed out of bed and made my way toward the noise, I could hear him below my feet. He had an impressive, rich voice and it was at its best that night. When I got to the steps I could catch flashes of him as he ran around the furnace chasing a stranger. The furnace sat exactly in the center of the basement, a big round affair with four huge pipes that reached out in every direction and then bent up to the ceiling. My father, dressed only in boxer shorts and T-shirt, ran barefoot through the dark, around and around the furnace. Whenever he came close to the stairs, the light from the kitchen caught the flapping dog tags, his blond hair, and the butcher knife he carried in his right hand. Ahead of him a man wearing a dull blue shirt managed to keep about a ten-foot lead, never enough to allow a break for the stairs but sufficient to avoid the knife. All the time they ran, my father described in elaborate detail what he did to wife-scaring, food-stealing bastards whom he found in his kitchen. Whenever they reached one of the pipes, each man ducked so that the two looked as if they were riding horses on a merry-go-round, popping down and up, down and up. My father provided the music.

At some point my mother had come to stand behind me and at last, just as the front runner was tiring and maintaining his lead only through one final surge of effort, she called out, "Don't be a fool." The man in the blue clothes didn't look up,

but my father did. And that is why he didn't see the next pipe
and why, with a tremendous clang, he ended his tirade.

The man in blue took the stairs in three steps, barely brushing past me and hardly pausing as, dashing by my mother, he
said, "Thanks, lady." Then he was gone and my father lay on
the floor in his underwear, a great red welt forming on his
forehead.

The second race took place out of doors and put less emphasis on endurance. This time we lived in Missouri in a town we
shared with about a hundred other people. Because of the
town's size, it had only a one-house slum. We occupied that
house. Railroad tracks cut through the very edge of town,
severing half a dozen houses from the rest, and since most of
these were large, two-story affairs with fenced-in lawns, no one
thought of them as being on the wrong side of the tracks. Only
ours was referred to as the house on the tracks, and in fact it
sat so close to the rails that the weeds from the right-of-way
grew nearly to the building's foundation. And since the Santa
Fe people didn't see much point in mowing our side of the
tracks, the depot being across the way, the growth was always
high, taller in July than a grown man.

I was older, the war had ended, and my father no longer
wore a uniform, at least not the government-issue kind. He did,
however, wear a suit, something of an oddity in our community, but he was selling insurance and the suit went with his
territory. He hadn't been at this new job very long and his area
wasn't the most densely populated or the most prosperous that
a salesman ever worked, and that is why we lived in the house
on the tracks: that, and the fact that it was the only building in
town unoccupied after the war.

The house was a simple frame building, one large room with
a kerosene cookstove at one end and a sofa bed where my
parents slept at the other, and an afterthought of a tiny bedroom and bath tacked onto the back side. My baby brother and
I shared the bedroom. Whenever a train went through, the

place shook from the floor up, creating a tingly sensation, the way it might feel to sit on a tuning fork.

Since the railroad generated the only excitement in town, life on the tracks was not all that bad, and for a five-year-old there was much to recommend it. First, the trains themselves, hauling cars from different lines, provided color as well as movement, and when they stopped, which they sometimes did, or slowed for the big curve above town, which they always did, there were passengers in sleek metallic cars to wave at, and the contents of boxcars, flatcars, cattle cars, and tank cars to consider. Beside the depot, the stationmaster hung mail in a big canvas bag that mysteriously disappeared when a train passed by, or he put up a little red flag on those rare occasions when someone wanted to board.

And the thicket growing along the right-of-way made its contribution, too. Mornings and evenings rabbits came out of the long grass to feed in our yard. During the hottest hours of the afternoon, garter snakes emerged to unlimber in the sun, and all the while a constant drone of insects vibrated through the weeds, sometimes clouds of gnats with their thin whine, or shrill locusts bending the plants with their clumsy weight, and always bees threading their way in and out of the dense growth.

But the most exciting time to be living on the tracks was when the railroad gangs were in town. They lived in boxcars beside the depot for a week or two at a time, an exotic collection of men, Gypsy-like in complexion and rootlessness, who pumped their way in handcars, working the lines for miles in either direction. In the evening, when the workers—everyone called them gandy dancers—sat around the depot, townspeople passing the tracks would look away as if they hadn't noticed anyone there, and mothers would hurry their children to some suddenly urgent business on ahead. Living on the tracks, I saw and heard everything—from the tall skinny man who climbed on top of a boxcar and played his harmonica to the man with one ear who sang in a language I couldn't understand. Occasionally one of the gang would call out to me or talk across the tracks. When they were eating, they often offered me the apples or pears they got for dessert, and one time a man with a tattoo of a flag on his chest and a hula dancer on his right arm brought me an agate he had found in the gravel along the rails. After he handed me the stone, he flexed his muscles to let me see the flag wave and the hula dancer jump around on his bicep. One of the other men said I shouldn't be watching the dancer, so he quit.

On this particular occasion it was early July, and a railroad gang was in town. They had been around for a day or two but were working several miles to the north, leaving early and returning late, and I rarely saw any of them, only heard them arrive and depart in the summer dark. Then, on the second night, with my father out selling insurance and my mother doing dishes in the front room, someone scratched on the bedroom window above me. My little brother slept next to the wall in order not to roll out of bed, but he was sound asleep when the noise began. At first I ignored it, thinking a June bug had gotten caught between the screen and the window and was banging itself to pieces trying to escape. But then I knew the noise wasn't a June bug kind of sound but thinner and scratchier. So I stood up to investigate. The light coming through the bedroom door didn't hit the window directly, and at first I couldn't make out anything in the dark. Then, gradually, I saw the eyes and located the nose. Not frightened, I just slowly filled in all the blanks on what seemed a huge face.

The fact that the face was black did not bother me, though it heightened the excitement. I had seen black men on army bases, but except for one or two among the work gangs, had never seen any here. But there was nothing threatening about the face. On the whole it was a pleasant enough face, even smiling at me through the window. There was, however, the matter of the knife, a small pearl-handled penknife that he kept running across the screen. If that did not frighten me, it did worry my mother. She had heard the scratching from where she stood at the sink in the next room and had come to the doorway to investigate. The face did not show any awareness of her presence, and when she spoke, she drew back from the door and whispered. Her voice soft and reassuring—she told me not to turn but to keep calm while she went for help. I did not know why we might need help, but I knew I was being entrusted with my baby brother.

We had no phone but the next house did, and the distance from our door to their side entrance was only about a hundred feet. I heard my mother go out into the dark, heard the key as she locked the door behind her. The face in the window did not change expression, the smile remained, neither ingratiating nor frightening, just a slight, easy curve of mild amusement. And the scratching knife, for all its harshness, was steady like a bumblebee's hum as it followed the same circuit around and around the screen, never with sufficient pressure to cut the wire, as though the noise itself provided the only purpose, and only the repeated tracing of the same path caused the glow of metal that marked the knife's route.

I don't have any idea how long my mother was away or when she returned. Interruption came only when a car pulled up in front of our house, and somewhere in the dark beyond my view my father called out, asking what the man wanted, and finally the face in my window changed. The easy smile gave way to a startled expression, and the knife broke through the wire so that the blade gleamed brightly, inches away from me. My mother screamed, rushed to the bed, and tried to lift me away. I resisted, and so we both remained, looking out through the window.

My father yelled, and the face disappeared in the dark, the bright knife ripped free from the screen. Once more my father called out, his voice angry and shrill. A porch light went on at the next house, and I could barely see the two of them, my father rounding the far corner, wearing suit and tie as though he had gotten dressed especially for the occasion, holding a shotgun, the 20-gauge that had lain in the trunk since last quail season. He gripped it tightly, barrel up, for emphasis.

Four or five steps from the other side of my window stood the black man, several inches taller and many pounds heavier than my father. He raised his hand as though to shield himself from the neighbor's light, knife clenched in his dark fingers. And suddenly both men began to run. They took off at full speed as though someone had said "Go," tearing toward the high weeds of the railroad right-of-way. And at the exact moment the gandy dancer started down the slope where the weeds grew tallest, the gun went off and he dropped, crashing down into the ragweed and bluestem like a felled cottonwood. When I looked back at my father, he was standing absolutely still, his face dead pale against the night. The gun lay on the ground several feet away where he had thrown it.

Nothing moved for several moments. Then my mother, hugging me tightly to her, lifted me away from the window. She carried me to the other room, where she spread a quilt on the floor and made me lie down and then laid my brother down beside me. I tried to question her, to find out what had happened, but she answered me with hushing sounds. The fear in her face, now more pronounced than at any other time that evening, stopped my chatter. I was silent but did not sleep for a long time. I heard voices calling outside and several sets of footsteps around the house. And I heard a thrashing in the weeds as though harvesters were moving through the night.

Shortly after dawn, when I awoke, my father sat at the table already shaved and wearing his suit and tie. I dressed, waiting to ask my questions about the previous night. Then he called to me and we walked hand in hand toward the town. Along the railroad tracks the weeds were flattened, uncut but beaten down.

The work gang had not yet left for the day and a few of them still lounged beside the boxcars. Off to the side, apart, I saw the face from the night before. The man rose slowly, carefully, as though reluctant to surprise any part of his body with abrupt movement. When at last he stood full height, he looked to us, gazing unflinchingly at me with a familiar smile, as though we knew each other but he hadn't seen me for a long time and didn't know whether to speak or not.

My father tightened his grip on my hand.

"I'm sorry," the man said, his words accented in a way I'd never heard, a lilting, almost like singing. "I had too much to drink and wanted to see the baby. I meant no harm. Just wanted to see the child, wanted the little one to show me his face. I'm sorry."

"I could have killed you," my father said.

The black man looked toward the maple tree in our back-yard, its leaves riddled with tiny holes.

"You aimed a little high to hit a man," the stranger said.

Then, simultaneously, each man dropped his head toward the other, just a slight tilting forward, but at the time I thought they were bowing.

The next race occurred on the last day of class of my third-grade year. Report cards had been sent home the day before with instructions for our parents to look at them, sign them, and send them back to school. My card said that I had failed third grade.

After my mother and father had seen the card, they went for a long walk, just the two of them. My terror grew while they were gone, but when they returned and my father called me outside, they did not yell or threaten the way I assumed parents would when informed of such disgrace. Instead my father asked if I knew why I had failed.

"No," I said. And it was true. I had no idea because the teacher that year, Reverend Watkins, had so confused all the students that I had no idea what the point of going through the third grade might be.

My mother probed further. "I know from what you've been reading here that reading can't be the problem. Have you done your workbook assignments?"

The books I brought home had all come from the bookmo-bile that the school district sent to Mt. Canna every two weeks. "I don't have a workbook," I confessed.

"Well, what reader are you in?" she asked.

"I don't have a regular reader," I said. "I sort of borrow other kids' books when they aren't using them."

"What do you do for arithmetic?" my father asked, his words clipped, his anger starting to break through.

"The same thing," I said. I blinked my eyes trying to keep the tears from coming.

"What do you mean?" His voice was louder now.

My mother interrupted. "You don't have any books?"

"Not of my own," I answered. I felt deeply ashamed, as if I had just admitted some terrible sin. "I borrow, though. Sometimes."

We had moved back to my grandparents' farm during the winter after my father's work on the road crew had ended, and I had been promptly enrolled at Mt. Canna, where I had also finished the previous year. But there had been a different teacher the previous year. Reverend Watkins had not greeted my appearance with pleasure, and he had not ordered any textbooks for me, saying that I had come too late for that expense. Somehow I felt as if the fault were mine and I had never told my parents until the evening before the last day of school, when the information poured out with a torrent of tears. The shame and guilt were overwhelming, but relief at admitting the horrible truth grew as I talked. Finally I even confessed to having been whipped twice during the year. Since I had always been told that spanking was the ultimate humiliation—failing, up until this moment, had been beyond imagination—and that a spanking at school would mean another at home, this admission did not come easily.

"What for?" my father asked. His words came out like hammer blows on a spike, and I knew I lived in mortal danger.

"Once for getting my shoes wet at recess. The other time, I don't really know." Then as a desperate afterthought, as though it might lessen the offense, I added, "I didn't cry. Not really cry."

My mother looked at my father. After a while he said, "I

think I better go over to school tomorrow and have a talk with Watkins."

My father had another highway job and was to leave the following Saturday to join his construction crew. Before he left, my brother had to be taken to the doctor in Lewisville to get shots and a checkup. The next morning, after the three of them had driven away, I started for Mt. Canna. My grandfather, inventing a need to check fences, walked through the upper pasture with me, but the last mile I went alone, confused and uncertain. I had not been punished and did not know why. I also had no idea what would come from a confrontation between my father and Reverend Watkins, but I guessed it could only hold terrible consequences for me.

My friend Edward, the only person at school in whom I had confided my failure, met me as I came up the last hill. Sympathetic and curious, he asked, "Did your dad beat you?"

"Nope," I answered.

"Did he yell or what?"

"Yelled a little."

"I thought he would kill you at the very least." Edward seemed more disappointed than pleased.

"He might come see Watkins," I added.

Edward perked up. "Oh, my Gawd," he said.

But my father did not come, not all morning, and I began to feel reprieved. Perhaps the car had broken down. Or the baby had developed some interesting but not very serious disease that delayed them and made coming to school seem unimportant. When he hadn't arrived by lunchtime, hope moved from the bud to the blossom, since school would end at one-thirty. All morning we had cleaned and packed away books and papers, and convinced that Reverend Watkins would dismiss us as soon as everything had been cared for, I scurried around, rushing the process as much as possible. By lunch break everything seemed to be in order, and I prayed that we would be let go as soon as we finished eating.

At one o'clock, Reverend Watkins called us back into session and began a little talk about discipline and how judgment can be as much an act of kindness as any pat on the back. He looked at me and said how pleased he was that some people seemed to understand that. My morning's work had not gone unnoticed.

He had just warmed to his subject when I recognized the sound of our car pulling up at the bottom of the Mt. Canna hill. Edward, who sat next to the window, began to smile and shake with expectancy. I felt cold all through; for a moment I thought I had died and waited to see my body topple from the chair.

My father came to the open door wearing his church clothes and knocked on the frame. Reverend Watkins turned and with an annoyed look asked why he was being interrupted.

"Reverend Watkins, will you please step outside where we can talk?" my father asked.

Edward had started coughing to cover his excitement and had turned bright red.

"It will have to wait," Reverend Watkins said. "I am in the midst of my final instruction to this class." He sounded the way he did when reprimanding one of the younger kids, except that his voice wavered a little.

My father slowly rubbed his chin. "It will be now. Would you like me to come in or will you come out?"

"It cannot be now," Reverend Watkins began, but as my father stepped into the room, he changed his mind. "All right. I'll speak with you but only because I do not want these children disturbed further."

The two men went outside, shutting the door behind them. I sat paralyzed, fully expecting the door to open and to be bodily dragged from the room.

Lyle slipped to the front to eavesdrop but before he could hear anything, Edward called out, "Oh, my Gawd," and Reverend Watkins, wearing his black Montgomery Ward preacher's suit, went tearing past the window. In a few seconds my father, dressed in his brown church suit, went past. He looked a little bewildered. Reverend Watkins, oddly enough, looked both confident and determined, as though this race were in the bag.

Mt. Canna had four windows in each of the long walls but was blank on the ends. As the two men raced around the building, everyone inside the building watched, window by window, as they ran past and then waited for them to round the corners and reappear, framed on the opposite wall. Reverend Watkins screamed out things about my father and me and about my grandfather. My father no longer looked bewildered but now glowed with anger. Inside, the students began to cheer, urging my father on. Only Ernest and Patsy Goring called encouragement to Reverend Watkins. But the teacher kept his lead. While my father's anger was apparent enough, he seemed to be running easily, not going all out the way Reverend Watkins was. Lyle yelled, "He's throwing the damned race," but my father kept the same smooth pace while Reverend Watkins ran as hard as he could, all the time shouting out the iniquities of my family.

I had not moved from my seat. It seemed that the two men circled the building for hours, and the thing I now most wanted was what I had previously most dreaded: I wanted it to end. Finally they passed from the last window on the east wall. Everyone turned to the west wall and waited. No one appeared. We waited some more. At last Lyle yelled, "He's caught him. I'll bet he's beating him into a cow patty," and he ran for the door. There was a rush as everyone, even Ernest and Patsy— even I—followed.

When we got to the back of the building, we stopped and stood in silence. There was no fight. The two men remained several feet apart, looking away from each other. My father had not spoken through the entire event. He no longer looked angry, just sort of sad as he gazed toward the road and straightened his tie. Reverend Watkins faced away from us toward the Shockley farm. His back shook. At first I thought it was from exhaustion, but then I heard little sobs.

The two men, dressed in their best clothes, stood looking off in opposite directions, surrounded by twelve schoolchildren. Then my father turned to me and said, "Let's go," and we left. I don't remember him running after that.

The popple had fallen away from the river, upper limbs resting on the higher slope. It had been cut almost perfectly, chewed nearly through all the way around.

When a man cuts a tree, he undercuts in the direction he wants the tree to fall. Then, above that deep gash and from the opposite side, he cuts until the weight closes the undercut and the tree falls. Even then things do not always go right: the limbs hang up in surrounding trees, the trunk splits from the undercut and jumps off the stump upright rather than toppling in the expected direction, or a wind catches the upper branches and pushes the tree back toward the person felling it. But a beaver chews from all sides, sharpening the trunk like a pencil, until, with a large tree, its head is deep in the cut, teeth gnawing near the very heart.

This time the tree had broken early, and beneath the trunk, its head grotesquely twisted, the beaver had been caught at the point where the popple still clung to the stump with a few twisted splinters. Leaves, still green and healthy-looking, fluttered in the breeze, but the body stretching back from that huge head to the flat tail had already stiffened beneath the popple's weight, the broken skull caught in the vise of its own making. The dark eyes, dull but wide, gave no evidence of surprise, as though this were no more, after all, than might be expected.

MAY ICE

From his perch on the tractor, Lonnie watched the distant timber waving in the heat above the big engine, and to the east, over the Lawson place, two buzzards rippled through the distorted air, riding diesel fumes and a summer breeze down toward distant carrion. The idling engine enclosed him like a cocoon, blocking out all other sound. Then the screams tore free from the engine's roar.

"Kill it, for Christ's sake! Kill it!"

He started to turn toward his uncle, but then, instinctively, threw the ignition and silenced the diesel. In the quiet, the moans, the pain-filled curses, came to him in low waves, rolling up from where his uncle, on his knees, hunched over the power takeoff. With his left hand, the young man pulled at something twisted between the driveshaft and the housing, something that had been white but was turning red as Lonnie watched. It was the glove that had covered his uncle's right hand, the extra thumb sticking out to one side, like an unmoved observer.

When the shaft had rotated enough to release the glove, his uncle clutched at his hand, pulling it close to his chest. His eyes were closed, and he rocked on his knees, rhythmically, his lips moving soundlessly.

"Tom," Lonnie whispered. "Tom? Are you OK?"

No answer came.

"Tom, what should I do?"

His uncle opened his eyes. They were blue as ice and loomed large in the colorless face. He did not speak.

"I'll get help, Tom," Lonnie cried out. He was sobbing, and tears ran down his cheeks, falling to the drawbar, adding their dark stain beside the blotches of blood. "OK, Tom? I'll go to the house." He climbed over the huge tire, avoiding the power takeoff.

"It'll be all right, Tom. I'll hurry. I'll be right back, I promise."

He ran up the road, his tears drying as quickly as they came. At the top of the hill he fell, cutting his hands and knees on the gravel, but he did not feel the wounds and continued, as fast as he could run, toward the house.

The return trip took only a few minutes. Lonnie's mother had heard him call from the road and was in the car by the time he pushed through the gate. She held open the door on the passenger side; the wheels were already turning as he crawled in beside her. She accelerated quickly, letting the momentum slam shut his door as gravel sprayed out behind the car.

"Where?" she asked quietly.

"By the fence row. This end of the east forty." He continued crying softly.

"It was the power takeoff," he said. "He jumped down to pull something out, and it caught his glove."

They sat silently as the car topped the hill, lifting from the springs before dropping heavily again. Lonnie had braced for the descent, but it still carried him high off the seat. From this side of the hill, they could see the tractor and hay bales and the boy-man who knelt beside them. Heat still shivered over the engine, and something dark still rode easy circles in the distance.

"He's done it before," Lonnie said, appealing to some abstract justice. "Lots of times. He's quick. There's never any problem." He wiped his nose. "He doesn't like to kill the diesel just for something jammed in the machinery."

The woman did not speak. She braked the car quickly and was through the fence, running to her brother before Lonnie could get through his door. She lifted Tom from the ground, her arm under his arm and around his back, and her son realized for the first time that she was the taller of the two. Lonnie held the top strand of barbed wire as high as he could, crushing down the rest of the fence beneath his feet, while his mother guided his uncle through. Tom still clutched the broken hand to his chest. He did not speak but seemed to be pulling inside of himself, willing himself physically smaller, everything about him absorbed in that diminishment. Lonnie opened the car door while his mother eased his wounded uncle onto the back seat.

No one spoke till they reached the farm. The woman looked quickly at the bloody hand, then ran for the house. At the gate, she stopped and turned back to Lonnie. He stood hesitantly beside the car.

"Get all the ice we've got into a milk bucket," she called to him, and he raced after her toward the porch.

As he dumped freezer trays of ice into the galvanized bucket, he heard her, inside the house, giving directions to her mother. "Call Lewisville and tell them we're on our way. There's no time to get hold of anyone first. By the time Dad and Will get home we can be at the hospital." While she talked she scorched sheet rags over the stove.

Further away, the boy heard his grandmother hurrying someone off the party line. Then his mother came rushing onto the porch. She grabbed the bucket of ice. He hesitated again. "Come on," she said. "I need you."

He rode in the back, crouched on the floor beside his uncle, holding an old army blanket that had been behind the seat, unsure of whether it was needed or not. As he watched the face of the uncle whose boyhood had overlapped with his own, he thought that in spite of its gray color and its tautness, it still looked much like his own. Gently he wrapped the green blanket over Tom's legs and chest.

"What should I do with the ice?" he whispered.

"Tom," she called, "put your hand in the ice. It will hurt for a while, but it will help things keep until we get to the hospital."

The figure on the back seat did not stir.

"Help him," she said softly to the boy. "See if you can wrap some of the rags around the hand. Be as gentle as you can."

He took his uncle's forearm well above the injured hand and pulled it toward him. "Reach over here, Tom," he whispered. Tom's eyes remained closed, his face expressionless, but he did not resist, and the arm responded to the boy's pull. At last, when it was straight, the wrist resting on the seat, the boy wound the strips of scorched cloth around the bloodstained glove and the exposed flesh.

"Put it on top of the ice," his mother said.

He once more took hold of the forearm, lifting the bandaged hand over the bucket of ice. Then, sliding across the hump of the car's driveshaft, he lifted the bucket, slowly, onto his lap until the rag-covered hand rested on the ice. He looked up into the staring eyes of his uncle. Tom made no sound, but his face had tightened around parted lips, and he looked like someone who had just finished screaming. Then slowly, like shades being drawn, his lids came down once more over the pale blue eyes.

Lonnie rode, holding the bucket and watching the bandages dampen from the melting ice. His uncle did not stir. When the boy looked upward through the rear window, he saw only a midafternoon sky, cloudless, blue as deep water. Once a flock of crows blackened this patch of light, but only for a moment, and then there was nothing save the depth of the summer blue.

One hip rested against the hump in the floor, and amid the rattle of flying rocks he felt the vibration of machinery beneath his body. He knew from the way the car glided over the gravel that his mother was driving very fast, and when she topped one of the sharp ridges, he felt the car, then his stomach, lift, and even as the muscles in his throat tensed, he adjusted the bucket to keep his uncle's hand from jarring against the ice as the car dropped once more. When they turned onto the blacktop of the state highway and swung to the south, the ride smoothed, and his mother drove even faster. The driveshaft still hummed against his hip, and he felt the first thin needles of sleep beneath the skin and shifted his weight to the other side. In the rear window, in spite of the hour, the sliver of a new moon hung sadly against the blue.

They drove on for a long time. The water from the melting ice had moved up through the bandages and into the glove. Streaks of purple eddied into the bucket and then diffused, tingeing everything pink. The weight of the water pulled at the rags, and they sagged in a lumpy mass, deeper and deeper into the bucket.

"His hand's getting wet!" Lonnie's voice held an edge of hysteria as he suddenly became aware of what was taking place before his eyes.

"It's OK," his mother said. "It will still keep the hand cool. We're nearly there now."

As they entered the city, his mother slowed only slightly. She turned in to the hospital, and the boy could see the roof that covered the driveway above the emergency entrance. His mother flung her door open and ran toward the building. Immediately two men in green hospital clothes were pulling Tom, eyes suddenly wide open, from the car. No one spoke to Lonnie, and in an instant they had all gone. He did not know whether to follow or to remain. At last he pulled himself from the floor, straightening cramped legs, and crawled into the front seat.

When his mother came back to move the car, she brought a bottle of Coke, and they shared it as she drove to the lot across the street and parked.

"Is he going to be all right?" Lonnie asked.

"The doctors are checking him now," his mother said. "They've given him a shot for the pain, and they're looking at the hand."

"Is it bad?" he asked.

"I don't know. I expect so," she answered. "We better go in. I've got to call the farm."

Inside the long bright corridors of the hospital, Lonnie sat on a bench, leaning back against the wall while his mother called from a telephone around the corner. Something in the hospital smell made him sick to his stomach, and he looked for a door where he could escape into the air. But he remained seated, watching the people rush back and forth, some in white uniforms, some in green. At first there seemed so many, but after a while he realized he was often seeing the same persons passing repeatedly before him, as though they were plowing the same row over and over. Lonnie was confused by the way in which everything seemed clean and dirty at the same time. Men mopped at the floors but it was as though something here could not be scrubbed away, some odor the disinfectant could not conceal. At the end of Lonnie's bench a pile of hospital gowns rose in a small mound. One, child-sized, was blotched with blood.

His mother came to the bench. "Will you be OK for a while? I've got to find out what's happening."

"Sure," he answered, but he didn't feel as confident as he tried to sound. "I'll stay here."

After she rushed away, he began to feel very lonely and misplaced as strangers milled around him, absorbed in their own urgency. He had never seen the inside of a hospital before and was surprised to discover that it made him feel a kind of homesickness. He hoped his mother would return quickly. At last she came around a distant corner, talking to a doctor. He could not hear them, but he could tell she was being stern, and that the doctor, though resistant, was yielding.

The doctor said one last thing, then walked briskly away. Lonnie waited for his mother. She came slowly, as though very tired, and slumped down beside him. Neither spoke for some time. Then, at last, she said, "They're taking the finger off; the index finger." She sighed. "It could have been worse."

The boy looked at his own hand, tried to fold under his own index finger and to imagine it gone. It seemed to him the hardest finger to live without. He could not even bend it completely out of sight.

His mother saw. "Down to the second knuckle," she said,

and straightened his fingers gently with her own. "It will be all right," she said. "He's got the rest of his hand, which is luck enough."

"Are they doing it now?" he asked.

"Yes." Her voice seemed to be coming from somewhere far away. "They should be done in a little while."

"Will he have to stay here?" he asked, wondering if he must spend the night on this bench.

"No," she said, a defiance in her voice. "We'll be taking him home when the anesthetic wears off, and we'll have to bring him back in two days for the doctors to examine." Then, again, as though further explanation were necessary, "He belongs at home."

When Lonnie and his mother had brought the car to the hsopital door, the boy sat in the front passenger seat, turning as two men wheeled his uncle through the oversized doors. He watched as the wheelchair rolled over the sidewalk to the curb. The fresh bandage on Tom's right hand caught the glare of the lights shining above the emergency entrance, dazzling as the men approached the darkness of the car. One of them opened the door, and they eased their passenger inside. Lonnie saw the crooked grin and the glazed blue eyes and thought his uncle looked drunk. Tom was dressed in the same jeans and work boots he had worn all day, but in place of the bloody twill shirt he had arrived in, and which his sister now carried in her pocketbook, he wore a green surgical top.

One of the men handed a package through the open front window.

"He'll start feeling it in a while and will need two of these pills every hour. The first time, if it's bad, he can have two more on the half hour. But only the first time." The man massaged his neck as he talked, as though it had stiffened in the air outside the hospital doors. After he handed over the pills, he waited.

Lonnie's mother looked up, briefly, and said, "Thank you."

"Do you have far to go?" he asked. "He won't be a very

good passenger if it's more than an hour, hour and a half." He twisted his neck, still trying to get at the stiffness. "Usually they stay, you know."

"Thank you," she repeated. "We'd better be going then."

Outside of town, the headlights pushed back the dark to the fence rows and the top of the next hill. The sky had become overcast, and the moon, visible in the clear afternoon, had disappeared. No stars were to be seen, and in the valleys between the hills, patches of fog hung, ragged, above the black-top. An occasional rabbit, its feeding interrupted, would freeze in the lights, then break for the darkness. And, once, the yellow gleam of eyes Lonnie mistook for a cat's settled into the pointed face of a fox as the car sped by.

No one spoke. The woman, intent on her driving, did not look away from her work, leaving it to Lonnie, seated beside her, to glance back regularly and check on Tom. The boy watched, as well, the surrounding darkness, looking for some landmark by which to locate himself. When they came to the Salt River bridge he recognized where they were. The sign, obviously a favorite for target practice, once had read "This bridge may ice in cold weather," but had been so thoroughly shot up that the top and bottom lines had virtually been erased, the message reduced simply to "may ice."

What Tom watched, Lonnie could not tell, for though the blue eyes were open, they did not focus on any single thing but drifted aimlessly. Even in the dark, the shiny bandages were brightly visible, and for a while all the boy could see inside the car was his mother's head silhouetted by the dashboard light, his uncle's eyes, and the bandaged hand.

At last Tom broke the silence. He laughed. At first, only a short, low laugh, but after a few seconds, it returned and continued for what seemed a long time.

"It's all right, Tom," the woman said. "We're headed home." Her voice was strained.

But the laughter began again. This time when it stopped, the uncle asked in a husky, slurred voice, "Where are we?"

"Not quite to Hawkston," his sister said. "Rest quiet now. We're on our way home."

"Are we now?" he said and began to laugh again.

The woman and boy remained silent, and in a while the laughter died. Lonnie had never heard his uncle laugh that way and was glad when it ended. Against the darkness ahead, the lights of Hawkston began to appear.

"I'm hungry," Tom said.

"We'll be home in another hour," the woman told him, trying to sound reassuring.

"Stop here," her brother demanded. "I've got money and I'm hungry."

The woman hesitated. "I don't think you should eat yet, Tom." The doctors hadn't said anything about food, and she was uncertain about what to do.

Tom's tone softened, the demand fading from it. "Ah, come on, Sis. I haven't eaten all day. It'll be all right."

Gratefully, she gave in to the familiar tone and stopped before a café with a neon EAT sign above the entrance. She helped her brother from the car, staying at his side as he walked falteringly toward the building. Lonnie ran ahead and held the door. Inside, a jukebox was playing "Your Cheatin' Heart," and a man wearing a cowboy hat fed it more nickels and punched at the selection buttons.

They crawled into a booth, Tom on one side, Lonnie and his mother on the other. A girl, chewing gum and wearing a checkered apron, came to take their orders.

"I'll have a grilled cheese and a cherry Coke," the uncle said. Then, showing her the hand, "But I think you'll have to feed me." He smiled in flirtation.

"All customers gotta feed themselves here," she answered. She did not smile. All of her energy was devoted to the gum.

"A Coke for the boy and a glass of water for me," the woman said.

The girl did not speak, just turned abruptly and went behind the counter. She put the food on the grill and ran their drinks from the soda fountain. After carrying the glasses to the table, she brought a napkin and silver for Tom. As she carelessly dropped his place setting on the table, he patted the seat beside him. "Sure you won't come over and help me?" He opened his eyes wide in appeal, the crooked grin declaring his good nature. "After all," he continued, "I suffered this serving my country."

"I can't sit with customers," she said, her voice flat with boredom. Then she hesitated and looked down at the bandaged hand. "We ain't in no war," she said, making it clear how difficult it would be to outwit her.

Tom laughed a soft, teasing laugh. "I was serving my country in the fields," he said, "but not of battle."

The girl looked at him suspiciously.

"But," he went on, "my hand doesn't know the difference."

She shook her head. The bored look returned to her face, and she went back toward the counter. Tom laughed.

When the sandwich came, he ate the first few bites quickly, joking about the lengths he had to go for a night on the town. But then he slowed, chewing deliberately as if it had a suspicious taste, and then he seemed to develop difficulty swallowing. He looked across at Lonnie.

"I'm sorry," he said. "I forgot you didn't get anything to eat. Help me with this." Awkwardly, he divided his food and passed the larger portion to the boy.

Hank Williams continued to sing "Your Cheatin' Heart," and the same man in the cowboy hat kept punching the button that played it again and again.

Lonnie offered part of the sandwich to his mother, but she shook her head without looking away from Tom on the other side of the table. As the boy ate, he too watched the lines deepen in his uncle's face and the mouth tighten at the corners until Tom laid down the remainder of his grilled cheese and looked up at his sister.

"It's getting pretty bad, Sis," he said. He tried to laugh, but all that came out was a rusty squeak.

She pulled an envelope from her purse and removed two white pills. "Take these," she said softly. "They'll help."

Tom grabbed the pills, put them in his mouth, and swallowed hard. He closed his eyes and leaned against the back of the booth.

As Lonnie finished the last bite, his mother went to the counter and paid the girl. The man at the jukebox put in another nickel and pushed the same number he'd been pushing all evening.

Back in the car, Lonnie watched as his uncle sagged heavily into the seat. Tom leaned sideways, his eyes closed now, his lips clamped shut.

The fog had thickened, and the woman had to watch intently as they came over each rise and descended into the gray below. Each time the road dipped, they dropped into a dense pool that sent the light splashing up around them, and then, as the road lifted upward once more, they again broke free into the night.

t e n

A sliver of moon broke the tree line shortly before eleven o'clock. In the deep timber the owl began to hunt, swinging its vast darkness between hemlocks and maples, banking through the maze, its harsh call rolling over the woods, echoing back from across the lake, old cries crossing newer ones in midpassage. Relentlessly it worked the night, following the forest furrows, its hooting surging, unhurried, unresisted.

At last the pattern broke. The shriek of a snowshoe rabbit—too shrill to echo—sliced through the dark, a fingernail on slate: the scream of the prey at last more awesome than the cries of the hunter.

THE FROG AND
THE KING

The way I remember it—and I remember it clearly and in great detail, though I can't say how accurately—begins with me, as I picture myself when I was a child, walking from the milk shed to the house, and I am midway between two pools of light that break the summer dark. The first spills from the barn's big double doors onto the path I walked nightly, a journey that began on the far side of the building where the cows, warm and listless, ignored the stanchions around their necks and the hands pulling milk from their udders and fed on hay strewn loosely in the manger. Like its successor, this break in the dark serves as a milestone, designating a third of my passage toward the house and the cream separator on the side porch. The second pool, a hundred feet beyond the first, spreads in a perfect circle beneath the yard light. Every evening I make two trips, and each trip I carry a half-filled five-gallon milk bucket, stopping to shift hands only when I arrive at the exact center of each flood of light.

On the night I am recalling, somewhere between the second circle and the porch, a tree frog, green as oak leaves, fell into my bucket. Unfroglike in its delicate beauty, it shimmered, an emerald island in a sea of milk, its color just starting to fade under the dazzling light the pail gathered and magnified. Slowly the frog swam to the metal side; with the tiny suction cups on its front feet it clung to the concave surface, back legs still awash in milk.

I dipped it up, clean and shiny, and held it like a precious stone cupped loosely between my hands, and it perched so lightly on my palm that I repeatedly peeked between my fingers, convinced it had slipped away. There was no panic, no desperate thrashing against flesh. It sat calmly, aloof or resigned, with a dignity marvelous in a thing so small. At last, when it had turned to the dull, chalkish green of cottonwood leaves, I carried the frog to the big mulberry from which the dinner bell hung, and on tiptoes carefully placed it on the highest leaf I could reach.

It is odd but in all my recollections of boyhood, excluding adolescence, I appear the same, always the same size, usually in the same clothes, even though common sense tells me the remembered events are often several years removed from one another. No matter, there is one and only one version of me, repeated in every memory, and looking at him now—and going by rather fuzzy appearances—I would say he is somewhere between five and nine. Official family chronology, however, indicates that I was older. Probably eleven.

Whatever my age, it is clear in this story that I already knew something about the fact of death, knew at least that on a special bed in the front room my grandfather was engaged in the slow business of dying. But despite all this compelling evidence, the idea of death had never become overwhelmingly real until I thought of the tree frog floating in the white abyss. Inexplicably adrift in a milky pool, it could see no more than its own distorted image in the burnished surface of the pail. Why that seemed to me like death, or rather dying, I do not know; but that is what I took it to resemble.

Abandoning the frog on a single leaf of a mulberry full of leaves, I ran back to the light, left the milk for my uncle to pour into the separator, and hurried to my grandfather's bedside. The cancer had found his bones, and when one or another of us walked across the living room floor the movement would

sometimes be transmitted to the bed and increase the dying
man's agony. But I loved my grandfather sufficiently to endure
the pain I caused him, and even as others approached his
bedside with growing reluctance, I went often to talk and to
read and, unconsciously, to share the life that remained to both
of us. This night I went to him, and because his eyes were
closed, sat for a long time without speaking. After a while my
grandfather, eyes still shut, asked me if I would read to him,
and since he asked this of me regularly, and always with the
same primer in mind, I took the Bible from the nightstand and
turned to the passage he requested. On this occasion the text
he called for was the book of Samuel, chapter twenty-eight. I
turned the pages until I found the place, a story unfamiliar to
me, and read:

> Now Samuel was dead, and all Israel had lamented him,
> and buried him in Ramah, even in his own city. And Saul
> had put away those that had familiar spirits, and the wizards,
> out of the land. And the Philistines gathered themselves
> together, and came and pitched in Shunem: and Saul gath-
> ered all Israel together, and they pitched in Gilboa. And
> when Saul saw the host of the Philistines, he was afraid, and
> his heart greatly trembled. And when Saul inquired of the
> Lord, the Lord answered him not, neither by dreams, nor by
> Urim, nor by prophets.
>
> Then said Saul unto his servants, Seek me a woman that
> hath a familiar spirit, that I may go to her, and inquire of
> her. And his servants said to him, Behold, there is a woman
> that hath a familiar spirit at Endor. And Saul disguised
> himself, and put on other raiment, and he went, and two
> men with him, and they came to the woman by night: and
> he said, I pray thee, divine unto me by the familiar spirit, and
> bring me him up, whom I shall name unto thee. And the
> woman said unto him, Behold, thou knowest what Saul hath
> done, how he hath cut off those that have familiar spirits,
> and the wizards, out of the land: wherefore then layest thou

a snare for my life, to cause me to die? And Saul sware to her
by the Lord, saying, As the Lord liveth, there shall no punishment happen to thee for this thing.

Then said the woman, Whom shall I bring up unto thee?
And he said, Bring me up Samuel. And when the woman
saw Samuel, she cried with a loud voice: and the woman
spake to Saul, saying, Why hast thou deceived me? for thou
art Saul. And the king said unto her, Be not afraid: for what
sawest thou? And the woman said unto Saul, I saw gods
ascending out of the earth. And he said unto her, What form
is he of? And she said, An old man cometh up; and he is
covered with a mantle. And Saul perceived that it was Samuel, and he stooped with his face to the ground, and bowed
himself.

And Samuel said to Saul, Why hast thou disquieted me,
to bring me up? And Saul answered, I am sore distressed; for
the Philistines make war against me, and God is departed
from me, and answereth me no more, neither by prophets,
nor by dreams: therefore I have called thee, that thou mayest
make known unto me what I shall do. Then said Samuel,
Wherefore then dost thou ask of me, seeing the Lord is
departed from thee, and is become thine enemy? And the
Lord hath done to him, as he spake by me: for the Lord hath
rent the kingdom out of thine hand, and given it to thy
neighbor, even to David: Because thou obeyedst not the
voice of the Lord, nor executedst his fierce wrath upon
Amalek, therefore hath the Lord done this thing unto thee
this day. Moreover the Lord will also deliver Israel with thee
into the hand of the Philistines: and to-morrow shalt thou
and thy sons be with me: the Lord also shall deliver the host
of Israel into the hand of the Philistines.

Then Saul fell straightway all along on the earth, and was
sore afraid, because of the words of Samuel; and there was
no strength in him; for he had eaten no bread all the day, nor
all the night. And the woman came unto Saul, and saw that
he was sore troubled, and said unto him, Behold, thine
handmaid hath obeyed thy voice, and I have put my life in

my hand, and have hearkened unto thy words which thou
spakest unto me. Now therefore, I pray thee, hearken thou
also unto the voice of thine handmaid, and let me set a
morsel of bread before thee; and eat, that thou mayest have
strength, when thou goest on thy way. But he refused, and
said, I will not eat. But his servants, together with the
woman, compelled him; and he hearkened unto their voice.
So he arose from the earth, and sat upon the bed.

And the woman had a fat calf in the house; and she
hasted, and killed it, and took flour, and kneaded it, and did
bake unleavened bread thereof: And she brought it before
Saul, and before his servants; and they did eat. Then they
rose up, and went away that night.

I remember thinking this an especially strange story, not the
kind of passage my grandfather usually chose, but I read it
without too many stumbles, and those only with the more
exotic place names. I knew the Bible relatively well, having had
it read to me from infancy as a storybook by my mother and
father, and so I knew about Saul and Samuel generally, but I
associated witches—I knew she was a witch because my grandmother on the other side complemented my literary education
with tales of ghosts and familiars—with a different sort of story.
In fact I was surprised to find such talk in the Bible, thought
witches and ghosts to be vaguely blasphemous subjects for
Christians—apart, that is, from a few privileged souls like my
father's mother. So I was puzzled both as to what I had just
read and the reason for my reading it.

After the story was finished, the two of us remained in silence
for a while. Despite the fact that my grandfather had still not
opened his eyes, I could tell by his breathing that he was awake
and, by his color, that he was not enduring one of the "bad
spells" that made it impossible for him to carry on a conversation. "He died, didn't he?" I said.

"Of course," he answered, his voice surprisingly strong.
"They all died a long time ago."

"He died the next day, though."

"Yes."

"And his sons?"

"Yes."

"Jonathan, too?" Jonathan was the only one of Saul's sons whose name I knew. Bible storybooks were big on the story of David and Jonathan, always putting it right next to the story of Goliath.

"Yes. Jonathan and his brothers." His eyelids flickered slightly but did not open. "Raise the bed for me," he said.

The bed had been hauled from town by my uncle, a loan from the local chapter of the American Cancer Society—it had "American Cancer Society" painted on the side in big red letters just so no one would forget—and the head of the bed could be elevated with a crank. I turned the handle as smoothly and gently as I could until my grandfather's upper body had been raised several inches.

"Thank you," he said when he wanted me to stop.

We fell silent again. Then I asked, "What are witches doing in the Bible? I thought stuff like that was just in fairy tales."

"I reckon there's not much in fairy tales that isn't in the Bible too."

"But there's no such things as witches and ghosts," I persisted. "Why would the Bible say there was?"

My grandfather's changes in expression had grown so subtle with his disease that an outsider would not have seen the smile. But I saw it and was encouraged. "Lots of things have got their names mixed up, things that are real enough if the name is understood, but we no longer know what they are rightly applied to." He paused as though surprised not to be out of breath. "I figure what Saul ran into was real enough, even if our dime-store ghosts and witches aren't."

He licked his lips, then asked, "Would you get the water for me?" I held the glass, adding the long curved straw so that he did not have to raise his head, and he sipped small, thin sips, then with the slightest of nods had me take it away.

"Why did she make him eat? She said he was going to die,

why make him eat?" I was afraid of tiring him, but he seemed
to get stronger as we talked, and so I pushed on.

"Everyone dies. You don't expect them to stop eating, do
you?"

"But he was going to die the next day. That's different."

"I suspect most people eat the day before they die. Don't
you?"

"Yes, but they don't know they are going to die, at least they
don't know it will be tomorrow. That's different."

"It seems different, but what if Samuel had said to Saul, 'You
will die the day after tomorrow or late next week'? Would he
quit eating then?"

"Yes, I think so. Next week would be too soon, not much
more than tomorrow."

"But so is next year and the year after that. When is far
enough off that it doesn't hurt your appetite?"

My grandfather seemed, to most people, a stern man, but
there was about him a profound—albeit complicated—sense of
fun. He often teased, but in a manner that was not readily
understood as teasing even by some who knew him well. He
took his amusements with an extravagant seriousness, whether
it was the mail order fireworks he bought for the local Fourth
of July display (always in large enough quantities to ensure a
year-round supply) or religion or inventions. He pursued such
matters, when they caught his fancy, with an intensity that folks
around him thought incompatible with fun, and often as not,
they had trouble recognizing how easily amused he actually
was. Once, when he had gone to Quincy to buy a part for the
baler, he came home with a vacuum cleaner, had purchased it
not as an aid for housecleaning but because he liked the effect
when he reversed the hose and had it balance an inflatable
beach ball in the air. "Just like having your own seal," he said,
"and without the fish smell."

I knew, as soon as he began the discussion of how far away
one's death has to be in order to maintain an appetite, that my
grandfather, a few weeks removed from his own grave, was

teasing me. I also knew that all his expressions of play were, simultaneously, serious. And so I considered his question carefully, happy that our conversation could bring him this double pleasure.

Next year seemed to me far away compared to tomorrow, and yet it did not seem so far away where dying was concerned. Still there was something awful about Saul's knowing, knowing so certainly that no matter what he did, *it* would be the next day. As I pondered this matter, I thought of the tree frog plunged into a milky waste, suddenly alone, removed from all that was familiar and reassuring; and I thought of Saul hearing that he would be dead within a day, and felt an emptiness float up inside as I thought as well of my grandfather. And of myself. I became frightened in an unfamiliar way.

"Grandpa." My voice cracked, caught in my throat. "Grandpa, why did you have me read this instead of . . . of . . ." I searched for a more appropriate passage.

"Instead of the Twenty-third Psalm?" he asked, and for the first time he opened his eyes, not all the way, but enough so that I could see them. He smiled, this time a smile that anyone could recognize. "You think one of those 'Yea though I walk' texts would be easier to digest than the witch of Endor's bread?" He almost laughed but coughed a small raspy cough instead.

It had been several days since he had been in such a good mood, and I thought this a good sign—perhaps he was not so terribly ill after all—and yet I remained upset, frightened by whatever it was I had glimpsed in that image of the tree frog and the story of Saul and my grandfather's cancer. He saw the fear. "Could you give me a little more water?" he asked. When he had finished drinking, he closed his eyes again and swallowed hard to clear his throat. His Adam's apple looked enormous protruding from his shrunken neck.

"You came in at the middle of things," he began. "There's a lot more to the story." He liked doing this, plopping me down somewhere in midstream and then, after I floundered around for a while, breaking in to tell me there was more to it all than

I had realized and backtracking to set the record straight. He sighed. "And it's a good story, too, when you get the whole of it."

He hesitated. Worried that our talk had taken away whatever strength he had left, I hurriedly said, "Maybe you better rest some." I started to leave.

His eyes jumped open and the lines in his face tightened. "Is this boring you?" My grandfather never had much patience with anyone who didn't show sufficient appreciation for a subject he himself was interested in. Even cancer hadn't mellowed him as much as you might think. But he saw my concern, realized what had motivated me, and a small grimace of regret broke through before he caught it and closed his eyes once more.

His bed was next to the window, and over him and through the glass, I could see the Big Dipper. "I feel like talking," he said. "Listen or not, as you like." That was the way my grandfather apologized on those rare occasions when he went to the trouble.

"I sort of like old Saul," he said, and his voice sounded strong, not at all like he was dying. I even thought maybe I should run and get the others to listen, but I stayed right there instead. "I could never think of me and, say, King David as having much in common. Never me and Solomon. But Saul is different. He is the biggest jackass in the Bible, or at least the biggest jackass I find likable. Saul hadn't any idea what he wanted. Here he was king, but he was always worried or jealous, and being king just wasn't the pleasureful thing he'd expected. He had some decent children, but he didn't know what for; he just wanted to keep on being Saul when Saul wasn't Saul anymore." He liked these kinds of preacherly turns, like repeating a word in an interesting way or using one, like "pleasureful," that could seem common and unusual at the same time. He'd never admit to such a pride, but it was there, as real as the gift.

"I see Saul," he continued, "as just a farmer that one day

Samuel came to and told, 'You're a king now.' There wasn't any training for the job. Just all of a sudden there it was, and he had to make do. And it was a bad job to start with: God didn't want Israel to have a king, mistrusted the whole idea, and Samuel would get angry every time people said they needed one. Finally God said, 'OK, have a king, you've earned one.' But nobody likes a king once they've got him, and right away they started looking for new candidates." He paused for breath, paused for a full minute but nodded "no" as though he suspected I might start to leave again.

"There Saul was, no experience in such things, no notion at all of what was happening to him, so he reacted like any farmer: he got angry, angry at everyone, and worked himself deeper into trouble every day. Then, at last—where you came in—it was just about over. Samuel was dead, the Philistines were ready for battle, and Israel was divided. Saul was still angry but now he was more scared than angry. Worst of all he felt alone, felt even God had left him."

He sighed, rustled his arms just a little beneath the sheet. Again he went at least a minute without speaking, but I remained, leaning in toward him, because his voice had started to weaken.

"I imagine Saul hated Samuel—hated him for making him king, hated him for not letting him be king—but now he had to talk to somebody, and after years of mocking fortune tellers, of chasing them out of his kingdom, and after years of fighting with prophets, he had to find a witch who could conjure up Samuel's ghost." A sort of rattling sound came from his throat, alarming me until I realized it was all he could manage of a chuckle. "Saul had been desperate to have a prophet tell him that what he knew was happening wasn't happening. Instead Samuel said, 'Tomorrow you are dead,' and Saul fell to the ground as though he had decided he might as well be dead today."

This time the pause lasted several minutes. Outside I could see the hollyhocks as the moonlight hit them for the first time, their colors breaking out of the night but paler than they appeared by day. I suspected he had fallen asleep but stayed in my place, nevertheless. In a while, he stirred and said, "I'd like another taste of that water." After another sip, he got his narrative going again. "That witch, after her magic or whatever was through, all of a sudden became just another old woman. She pried Saul up off the ground and told him she knew all this was a shock but that he wasn't dead yet. So she fed him, because the fact that he was going to be dead didn't change the fact that he wasn't yet."

He stopped again, and this time I looked at him as he lay there, stretched out on somebody else's bed with the word *cancer* written boldly on the frame. He was so thin his bones were visible, yet his white hair was trimmed and combed, his face, sharpened by disease, freshly shaven.

"Grandpa." I hesitated because I had never before said the word in his presence. "Dying—what is dying like?" I tried to stop the question but it slipped out before I could get my teeth clenched. He remained silent for a moment, but nodded a little so that I knew it was OK.

Finally he answered, "It's hard, the hardest work I've ever done." He sighed. "It hurts an inconvenient amount. There's that, but I think the hardest part is living through it. You've got no choice, not really." The words were more labored now, and fatigue was showing on his already haggard face. "Pretty soon, even if the witch had simply gone on about her chores, Saul would have felt kind of funny just lying there on the ground. Oh, he might have tried to convince himself he couldn't or wouldn't ever stand again, but after a while his leg muscles would've started twitching or his head begun to hurt from the roughness underneath, or he would've had to relieve himself, and he would have peeked around to see if anybody was looking; and eventually he'd have gotten up and gone on toward the next day—out of embarrassment if nothing else."

He took a couple of deeper breaths before going on. "You get impatient at not being dead yet. And if nothing else, that impatience forces you to get back to living what life is left."

My grandmother tiptoed to the door, looked in on us, and

then retreated toward the kitchen. I don't think he saw her; anyway he continued as if he hadn't, but he was always good at not seeing things when he was attending to something else. "Dying is a strange business once you know you're employed at it. While you're going along not knowing, you don't see the curious part of it, but once the witch or the prophet or the doctor has told you that it's going full speed, and when you've learned you can't stay on the floor until it's done, then you have to set to work living and dying all at the same time." He moved his head weakly. His voice had hoarsened to a loud whisper. I offered him more water but he shook his head no.

"The next day Saul was in battle swinging his sword, all excited and sweaty—probably just happy at last to be doing something he was good at. And all the while he was thinking, 'Here is all this life in me and yet in a few minutes I'm going to be dead.'" He hesitated, then opened his eyes to look at me. "What confused me at first was the idea that there was this thing in me that was growing and was going to kill me. How could death 'grow'?—that's what I wondered. Could death be a living thing? I haven't got that worked out yet, but I've come to find the idea comforting for some strange reason. Maybe, if he still had any of the farmer in him, Saul came to feel that too. But likely not. He had a different disease."

He stopped there, his eyes once more closed, and looking at him I could see the depth of his exhaustion. In a moment I got up quietly to leave. This time he made no effort to detain me but said, very quietly in his now raspy voice, "Whatever Saul made of it, it's a good story. Remember it."

I went to the kitchen where my mother and grandmother were making bread. My father stood drinking coffee, and I moved to his side. I felt oddly bold, grown up, perhaps because I had spoken what seemed unspeakable and had become older and stronger for having done so. But I welcomed the kitchen and the comforting smell of yeast and dough. My uncle walked in carrying the parts of the separator for washing. He put them in the sink, then went into the living room. When he returned he said, softly, "Dad's asleep."

Somewhere in the dark, where the previous week's rain had left large puddles, spring peepers forgot what season it was and began their mating chirp. I confused them with my frog, the one I had lifted onto the mulberry, and thought of the evening's strangeness, of kings outstretched on the dirt and frogs singing in the trees.

eleven

The loons began shrieking just after dawn. The pair that lived on the lake had been joined by two others, and their cries came from all the little coves around the shore. Not a single, drawn-out call whose echo is allowed to rebound and die before it is answered, but screams edged with hysteria, intersecting and overlapping one another.

Above the lake, gliding with smooth, deliberate strokes, the eagle circled. When it soared above the trees on the eastern shore, its enormous silhouette made a shadow against the sun. Against the pines to the west only the white head and leg feathers could be seen. The screams below did not trouble its flight as it rose and fell effortlessly, circling the lake again and again. At last, wings folded, it plummeted to the water, lifting slightly just above the surface. Then, with a rocking motion, it swung its legs backward, setting the talons in a large perch.

The shrieking stopped. While the eagle devoured his meal in a tall maple at the end of the lake, the visiting loons cautiously took flight until only the resident pair remained. And they, after the intruder had finished dining and had gone, swam out together, diving and calling back and forth in playful crescendos. With them was the baby, practicing its cries in clumsy parody of the parents. But not diving. It still could not dive and so had to stay on the surface, vulnerable to any predator that would not be diverted.

CICADA SEASON

It was nearly dark when the phone rang. Lonnie sat on the front porch waiting for a breeze to break through the late summer heat and watching thunderheads build in the west. The air did not stir. The evening sky wore a greenish cast, the sickly hue that precedes violent weather. Lonnie heard the phone and recognized the series of rings that meant the call was for them, but he did not get up. His mother answered, then called her father from the side porch. At last Lonnie moved, but slowly and with little interest, as though he were sleepwalking, and then only as far as the door, where he sat once more, leaning against the frame. Everything seemed far away, the telephone, his mother's voice; the heat had become a barrier separating him from the surrounding world.

But more even than the heat, the constant whine of locusts oppressed him, their noise so penetrating and relentless that he could not tell for sure if it came from the grass or the shrubs or inside himself. They had been a part of all his summers, their raspy drone drifting through the evenings, underlining the calls of whippoorwills and bobwhites. But this was the season when, after seventeen dormant years, they awakened in swarms, pulling themselves up out of the earth in unthinkable numbers. Just a few at first, their amber husks—split neatly down the back— clinging everywhere, until by mid-August the throbbing insects weighed down branches of lilacs and bent over the two young peach trees beside the house. No longer the invisible presences of their dormancy, they had come alive with a vengeance, crawling over windows and screens and swirling up out of the grass to land on flesh and clothing. Their black-green bodies, half blunt heads with thick, protruding eyes, lumbered like huge scarabs over every surface, irresistibly crawling over anything in their path, all the while vibrating with some unstoppable engine deep inside. And the whine had gradually become an incessant scream, cutting through the day as well as the night, unwavering in a pitch that approached the threshold of pain.

Everything the boy saw was buried in the August heat, everything he heard was entrapped in the droning cries of locusts. Lights had gone on in the house, and from his new post beside the front door, he could see his grandfather rush in and take the phone, could hear the old man yell above static on the line.

The thunderheads had bypassed the farm, and though clouds still blotted out the southwestern sky a star appeared on the eastern horizon. The lightning that flashed now was only heat lightning. The evening offered no relief.

Lonnie's mother opened the screen door just as a locust landed on the boy's shoulder and began to crawl across his bare back. He leaped up, slapping frantically with both hands, trying desperately to reach the insect. He felt another hand brush the locust away.

"I hate them," he cried.

His mother put her arm around him. "They'll be gone soon."

"Grandpa says not till there's a frost, there are so many. That could be forever."

She laughed. "This is the worst. Believe me, they'll be gone soon. Grandpa exaggerates." She watched the heat lightning, her arm still around Lonnie. Her touch felt cool to him, and he did not pull away.

"It's bedtime," she said. "Do you want to sleep out here?"

"Not with the locusts," he said.

"I'll get a sheet. It will be cooler than inside."

She brought out a throw rug and put it on the porch floor

along with a pillow. Then, after he had taken off his pants, she covered him with a sheet and sat down beside him. In the house his grandfather was still on the phone, making calls, sometimes speaking excitedly and at other times with great weariness.

"What's wrong?" Lonnie asked. More stars were visible now, and his mother watched them with him.

"I'm not sure," she said. "Grandpa's still got calls to make, but it has to do with Uncle Franklin." A shooting star flared to the north. "Did you see?" she asked.

"Yes."

She was silent again. Lonnie knew about Franklin, at least what there had been to know. Franklin was his mother's uncle but she had never seen him. He had run away from home when Lonnie's grandfather was the age Lonnie was now. Franklin and his new stepmother did not get along; he left and the younger brother had awaited his return for sixty years.

"Is he coming back?" Lonnie asked.

"Yes, I think so," his mother said. She lifted a locust from the sheet and tossed it into the night. "He's dead."

After a while Lonnie's mother leaned over and kissed him; then she rose and went back into the house. He rolled over onto his back. A hard sliver of moon had risen, and he could see the Big Dipper. He tried to find the Archer or the Bear, but without his father or grandfather to trace the patterns, the constellations eluded him. In the house his grandfather was still talking on the phone when Lonnie fell asleep.

The day before the funeral Lonnie rode to the church with his uncle and father. Two other men, half-nephews of his grandfather, were standing beside the graveyard. They had been mowing, and the air was heavy with the smell of new-cut grass. Locusts moved beneath the cuttings so that the cemetery seemed strangely alive.

"Looks good," Lonnie's father said. "It'd been let go a long while."

"We just did the yard and along the road," Chet, the taller

of the two men, said. The two were brothers. "Linwood mows the cemetery pretty regular. Even trims around the stones."

"You open the church yet?" Lonnie's uncle Tom asked.

"No," Chet answered. "Neither of us has a key."

"Probably could have gone through a window easy enough," his brother, Linc, added.

"We got the key," Lonnie's father said. "How long since it was used?"

"Not since Mom died last fall," Chet said. "The Hawkins baby was buried here in April but they didn't use the church. Had the funeral at Maple Grove and just came here for the burying." A bobwhite called from the corner of the cemetery.

"It should be OK, though," Chet continued. "They were considering having Bible school here in June, and I think the women cleaned it up then."

The men leaned against the pickup, looking toward the church. It was a frame building with lap siding; white paint had weathered away and the grain of the boards, gray and bare, showed through. Every few feet a locust husk held to the wall. The small steeple remained intact, but the bell had been removed, and the empty metal mounting was visible through the opening.

"Might as well start airing it out," Tom said, and they all trailed across the gravel and weeds that separated the cemetery from the church. Two enormous oaks grew in front, shading the steps and much of the yard. As the men and boy approached the trees, the whine of locusts grew louder. An oriole had built a nest that hung like a cradle from one of the lower limbs.

When they unlocked the double doors, one side pulled loose from its lower hinge and had to be lifted and carried into an open position. "I got some long screws in the toolbox," Chet said, and he crossed to the tractor parked beside the road.

The others went inside, where the air was hot and stale. Lonnie had been here before for other funerals and, when he was very young, for Sunday worship. The smallness of the building surprised him; he had thought it much larger, but only six rows of pews faced the pulpit, with room for two more rows of folding chairs behind that. The bulletin board on the front wall still announced, in numbers that had curled but not fallen, an attendance of twenty-seven, an offering of $8.90, and the page numbers for the hymns of that long-ago service.

"Not too bad," Linc said. "Just needs a little dusting. Knock down a few cobwebs."

"What about light?" the boy's father asked.

"Nothing but the window light," Linc answered. "Unless you think we need a kerosene lamp by the pulpit."

"Not for Uncle Ivan," Tom said.

"I reckon not," Lonnie's father agreed.

Linc laughed. "Goring declared once that Uncle Ivan was always being visited by the Holy Ghost when he preached, and that's why he never used any notes. But Uncle Ivan said, no, he just thought things through while he drove his team, and he couldn't fit a writing desk behind the horses. Goring's lacked enthusiasm for Uncle Ivan ever since."

Chet finished repairing the hinge, then straightened, turning his body as though working kinks from his spine and neck, then stopped, head twisted upward, and pointed to the ceiling, where two bats hung from a beam. A third, a few feet away from the others, moved along the wood in jerky little movements, all quivery as its body alternately contracted and stretched, but it did not drop from the beam. "Suppose we ought to get rid of them?" Chet asked.

The others looked up. "I don't see how without a ladder," Lonnie's father said.

"When we still had regular services there was at least one up there often as not," Linc said. "People will just ignore them."

"Will your dad mind?" Chet asked.

Tom looked at Lonnie's father. "I better go get a ladder," Tom said. "Do we need anything else?"

"Did you bring something to dig with?" Chet asked.

"Spade and a couple of long-handled shovels," Lonnie's

father answered. "We won't need any more unless we decide
to bury a baseball team."

Chet turned to Tom. "Velma and some of the other women
are coming to clean this afternoon. We ought to check out these
windows and get to digging."

Tom left and the other three men began opening windows
while Lonnie sat on a back pew and watched the bats. Whenever a window could not be broken loose, Linc would pry at it
with his brother's screwdriver and curse the uncooperating
wood.

"We better close these back up once we get them working,"
Lonnie's father said. There were no screens. "Place will fill up
with locusts before tomorrow, otherwise."

"They're going to come in during services," Linc said.

"Can't be helped. It's not likely to get cool enough to keep
the windows closed unless we wait till Christmas to have the
funeral," Lonnie's father replied.

When they had finished with the windows, they went back
out. The heat did not lessen as they walked under the oaks, the
air outdoors no less oppressive than that inside. Lonnie followed the men, his father in the lead, across the gravel to the
pickup where they each took a shovel, and then through the
grass of the cemetery. All around them locusts lumbered into
the air only to drop heavily a few moments later to the ground.
The men and boy walked single file around the stones to a
corner of the cemetery where family members were buried.
Here the grave markers bore familiar names, names of people
Lonnie vaguely remembered along with names from other
people's stories. He passed the stones for his grandfather's
half-sister and the baby, his aunt, lost to typhoid three decades
before his own birth. There was room for more graves beside
hers, but the men went further down the row to a vacancy
beside a second cousin, twenty years removed.

"Franklin goes here beside Wesley," Lonnie's father said.

Chet carefully stepped off three long strides from Wesley's
stone and stuck the spade in the ground. Then he stepped two

more strides from the mound above the spade to the point where this line intercepted the one he'd previously marked.

"That's a child's grave. Did you allow for enough to keep the rows straight?" the boy's father asked.

"That was the extra step," Chet said. "One yard for the boy and two for the man."

Both men stood back to line up the spade with the other graves. Then, while Chet watched to make sure they did not lose their alignment, Lonnie's father took the spade and cut the outline of a grave in the cemetery turf. When he had marked all the sides he began to dig. As he cut away the sod in neat pieces Linc carried them over to the fence row and stacked them carelessly. Then, when all the sod in the marked area had been cut away, Chet took a shovel, and Lonnie's father, sweat running down his face, sat down on the grass.

The boy watched as Chet cut down through the dark topsoil and into the reddish clay underneath. After a while Linc took Chet's place, and Chet sat down on the grass beside Lonnie's father.

"Must be mighty peculiar," Chet said, "to have a brother show up after fifty years and not know anything about where he's been or what he's done. All you're allowed is just a look and a burying." He shook his head. "Some strange old man you've never seen before instead of the boy that ran away."

Lonnie's father nodded.

"I remember when John was still alive, they hired a St. Louis detective and everything. I was a kid. Must have been twenty-five years ago. Can you remember that, Linc?" Chet called to his brother.

"No," Linc answered. "Before my time. Back in the good old days, when older brothers had the good sense to run away." He had taken off his shirt and his chest was streaked with sweat and clay.

"It cost a fair amount," Chet said, refusing to be baited, "and the detective came up dry."

"Well," said Lonnie's father, "they don't know much more

now. He's worked for some outfit in Houston the last fifteen years, done all right there, but nobody knows much before that. He lived alone and never said where he'd been, least not to anyone who seems to remember." He stood up and crossed to the grave to take Linc's place. "The police found a slip of paper with John's name on it in the apartment. Franklin and John had been close, more like brothers than cousins, and somehow Franklin knew John lived in St. Louis because that was on the paper too. That's how come they called the house. John's widow told them to call up here." He took the shovel. "Wonder what's keeping Tom?"

"Probably had to go to Webster's for a long enough stepladder," Chet said.

Linc got out of the hole, and then Lonnie's father stepped in. It came above his knees now. Lonnie watched for a while and then wandered away to read the names and dates on the stones. He recognized nearly all the last names but only some of the first ones. He decided to hunt for the oldest grave, and did, then set out to find the newest, but he tired of bending over the stones and switched to amusing himself by walking the outer boundaries of the cemetery. The side closest to where the men were digging Franklin's grave bordered on an alfalfa field, and he saw a young rabbit hiding in the clover. He crept toward it, but the rabbit caught sight of him and hopped into the deeper grass. Lonnie picked an alfalfa blossom and chewed at its sweetness. Bees explored nearly every plant but their buzzing was lost in the whine of locusts.

The side of the cemetery farthest from the church and the end that ran along the road were bounded by a high hedge, so dense Lonnie could not see through it. The hedge was throbbing with locusts, seemed a thing wholly of insects, packed thickly one on another by the millions, and the boy hurried away toward the churchyard and the oriole nest.

Lonnie spent a long time watching the swinging pouch the bird had made, tried to figure out just how it had been woven. He even put two long weed stems into his mouth and tried to

wind them together with his tongue in imitation of what he
thought the oriole must have done. Failing at that he decided
to clean all the locust husks from the front of the church,
picking the lowest off with his fingers, batting the higher ones
with a long branch. The husks crumpled, but the hooked legs
clung tenaciously, often remaining behind after the body was
gone. He had nearly finished when he heard Linc's yell and
turned to see the man scrambling out of the hole. Lonnie ran
to the grave.

"It's Wesley's coffin, clear over here, and I damned near put
the shovel through it." He walked quickly toward the church.

Lonnie's father slipped down into the hole, moving lightly,
trying not to break loose any more dirt than necessary. Chet
bent down, inspecting the side where Linc had been digging.
The edge of something smooth and square-cornered barely
broke through the dirt wall. Lonnie's father spat on his hand
and rubbed at the finished surface.

"It's pine all right," he said. "Linc didn't break the wood,
though."

"How in hell did it get clear over here?" Chet asked.

"Maybe it moved some. I don't know. The stone's newer
than the grave; they probably just got it in the wrong place."

"Will you have to dig another hole?" the boy asked.

"No," his father answered. "There's room enough, and nobody will notice it from up there."

"Smear a little clay on it to make sure," Chet said.

"What got to Linc so bad?" Lonnie's father asked.

"Smells," Chet said. "He's real sensitive to smells and no
other smell's quite the same. Ever since we found Sam, he's
worried about catching that stink again."

"Wesley's beyond all that, I expect," the father said.

"Sure," Chet said, "but for Linc the idea is as bad as the
smell. Sam had been gone for two weeks and was pretty ripe.
Cats had got to him too."

"Nothing to worry about here," Lonnie's father said. He
squared the corners of the grave and cleaned loose dirt from the

bottom. "This look OK from up there?" Linc had taken most of the grave down to six feet on his last shift and was digging out the remaining corner when he'd hit Wesley's coffin.

"Fine," Chet said. "Probably be full of locusts tomorrow." Several of the insects had already fallen into the hole and were crawling clumsily on the bottom.

"Girst will put a tent over it this afternoon, in case it rains," Lonnie's father said. "But that's not going to keep out locusts. More likely just make it more inviting for them." Gripping the blade, he stuck the shovel handle up for Chet to grab, and then, bracing his feet and legs, in two crablike bounds came up out of the grave while Chet pulled against his weight. Just then Lonnie heard the pickup beyond the hedge. "Good timing," his father said, as the truck turned in beside the tractor.

The two men scraped together the loose dirt that had fallen close to the grave and added it to the main pile a few feet farther back. While they tidied up, Lonnie crept to the grave's edge and looked down. It had been neatly dug and only a few small clods, broken loose when his father had climbed out, littered the bottom, a few clods and a growing number of locusts. He could not see Wesley's coffin but exposed on the far side, barely visible in the dark earth, he saw a fat grub, star-tlingly white. He wondered how the shovel could have passed so closely and still not have disturbed the creature.

"Let's go," his father said. It surprised Lonnie to find his father beside him. "You want to carry the spade?"

"Sure," Lonnie said.

The two men and the boy walked to the pickup, once more holding to the straight lines that separated the graves. Linc came out of the church carrying Chet's screwdriver. They could hear Tom inside.

"Here, I'll clean those shovels," Linc said. He took the spade and the shovels and scraped the mud off with his screwdriver.

"That's pretty much everything," Chet said. "Sounds like Tom's having a good time with those bats." They could hear something banging against the ceiling and Tom's voice swearing.

"Can I go in and help Uncle Tom?" Lonnie asked.

"Just a minute and we'll both go," his father answered.

"He got the first two all right, but the third one's worked itself back in a crack," Linc said.

"Wouldn't be any fun if they were all easy," Lonnie's father said. "What took him so long finding a ladder?"

"Had to go to town and get some registered mail. I don't know. Needed some signatures," Linc answered. "What time's the train due?"

"Not till late tonight, and Girst is going to be there with the hearse."

"Sounds real poetic," Linc said. "Don't let Girst hear it or we'll have to listen to the Andrews Sisters singing it on the radio. That's all we need around here, an undertaker with a jingle."

"Will Grandpa be on the train?" Lonnie asked.

"Yes," his father answered. "Your mother will pick him up." He turned to Chet and Linc. "No need for you two to waste the rest of your day hanging around here. We'll go in and see what Tom needs, but you feel free to go."

"Velma'll be coming in a while," Chet said. "I'll take the car, then pick her up when the mopping's finished. Anyway, I like to watch other people chase bats."

They all went inside the church. Tom had gotten the bat out of the crack, and from his perch on the ladder was swinging a broom in long, erratic arcs as the bat dipped and turned in the air.

"No need to sweep up there, Tom," Linc said.

Tom's face glowed with sweat and irritation as he swung the broom whenever the bat passed close to him, every thrust a little more awkward than the last.

"I got two windows and the door open, but the damned thing won't go out and it won't land," he said.

"Maybe the locusts have him confused," Chet said. "All that buzzing at the windows."

"Well, I can't kill him if he won't land," Tom said.

The bat dipped low over their heads and then veered toward

the west wall but did not find the window. Instead it soared back up under the beam and then swooped over the pulpit.

"No use worrying him with that broom," Chet said. "He's confused enough already. Leave him and I'll take care of it this afternoon when I come after Velma."

Tom came down the ladder. "The ladder goes over to Webster's if you can spare the extra time."

"No trouble," Chet answered.

They all went outside. Chet and Linc watched as Lonnie, his father, and Tom climbed into the pickup.

"Sure you don't want a ride?" the father asked.

"Velma'll be here any minute," Chet said.

"Well," the father said.

"Thanks," Tom called out. "Dad'll appreciate all you've done."

"It's nothing," Chet said. "We owe him."

As they drove toward the farm, gravel dust swelled up behind them, filled the air and hung for a long time, reluctant to settle back down, and even in the fields away from the road, everything had turned white. Inside the pickup a dirty film covered the dashboard and the windows. At least here, Lonnie thought, you can't hear the locusts.

The heat and the locusts—an hour before the service Chet had shoveled out two wheelbarrow loads—persisted throughout the funeral but thunderheads had returned to the western horizon, and as Tull preached, accompanied by the shrill chorus coming in through the windows, the clouds moved overhead. By the time the pallbearers carried the casket to the grave, the sky had completely darkened and thunder rumbled toward them. As the weather turned, the locusts changed their whine, rising to an even higher pitch, one that Lonnie felt more than heard, like an electric tingle throughout his body. The heavy air seemed to drive them to a hysterical fury. The branches of the hedge shook, and they rose up from the cemetery grass whenever a breeze stirred. The air tasted of ozone.

After Tull's prayer, Girst and his son slowly lowered the

coffin on wide belts, carefully keeping it level until it rested, safely, on the bottom. People drifted away, some walking among the stones to look up friends and relatives, others hurrying to their cars before the rain could begin. Chet and Linc changed clothes and returned with shovels to fill the grave. Lonnie watched them while his parents and grandparents stood under the trees, talking to neighbors who had helped the family bury a stranger, a stranger who had also been an uncle and a brother.

A single locust was now visible in the grave, and Lonnie watched as it escaped one shovelful of dirt after another. He wondered if it could live under all that dirt, if it could remember a time before it had split its amber shell, when the earth had previously held it fast. Then it was gone. It had struggled upward, bumping against the side of the grave, only to be carried down beneath the weight of dirt Chet pitched into the hole.

Everyone, except the two men filling the grave, was gone. Even Lonnie's parents had disappeared, though he knew they must be on the other side of the hedge where his father had parked. But he stood in the cemetery, the lone observer, as Chet and Linc hurried to finish their work before the storm hit. When drops of rain began to darken the dirt pile, Lonnie started for the car. He walked to the hedge seeking a shortcut through the bushes. But the whine of locusts, suddenly subdued elsewhere, filled every gap, and he was reluctant to feel the brush of their heavy bodies against his face and hands. He stood for a moment beside the hedge, gazing up at its height. As he stood, the thunderhead, much closer now, rumbled and flashed with lightning. Beyond the bushes his mother called his name. He was amazed at how far away she seemed, her voice rising above the thunder and the whine of locusts. She called again and his father's voice echoed the call, but Lonnie delayed on his own side of the thicket, trying to remember what his mother was wearing and to picture his father's face.

When the rain began to fall more heavily, the car horn

honked, and Lonnie ran through the quickening storm to the end of the hedge, unaware that with the downpour Chet and Linc had finished filling the grave and the cries of the cicadas had ceased.

twelve

In August, the month of meteor showers, the second act in the late-night light show offers dramatic contrast to the short-lived brilliance of shooting stars. The meteors, always a surprise even when anticipated, flash into view where least expected and pass back into darkness before their presence has been fully realized. But northern lights build slowly, deliberately, announcing their coming from afar with a glow on the horizon like that seen on an after-dark approach to a Midwestern city, when the prairie darkness is lifted up, displaced by some irresistible lower power. But the north woods is not Kansas or Nebraska; its sky has not been welded flat to the ground, is instead spiked by trees black against the light, uneven as the ragged tracings of a charted heart.

Sometimes that is as far as things get, just this illuminated preface. But often the show continues, and after a time flumes of white surge upward, sometimes in shimmering columns, sometimes in fountains that splash against the black sky, flow back downward, then leap up again and again.

Most often in the wooded dark, far from towns and people, the muted light offers pleasant entertainment, a pale diversion watched from a distance—across a lake—like some old movie, enjoyed for its comfortable familiarity. But on occasion the performance be-

comes disturbing; the gentle light grows wilder, more electric, its upward surges break outward in harsh configurations that, rather than keeping their distance, ripple threateningly toward the viewer. The ghostly paradigm yields to more erratic forms; dull, flickering white gives way to slightly lurid shades, streaks of yellows, pinks, and greens that charge the sky and the reflecting water with unbearable contradiction, a liquid opal, an icy flame.

This is the Aurora Borealis, the arctic fire that hints of things to come, the incinerating frost whose very prologue drives us inward on August nights, turns us to a welcome dark where we defer so hard a light.

AMONG THE WOMEN

The men left, not all together but one at a time, each with a differing urgency, though similar, too, in that all three were acting in response to something that had to do with their being men. And so they set off in their various directions, grandfather, father, uncle, until only the women remained, the women and the baby and a boy, a boy too young to head for town but old enough to know he was excluded from whatever it was that occupied the women. Lonnie climbed to the fork in the big mulberry and there, partially hidden by leaves, fifteen feet above the sweet-potato beds, he waited.

The day had begun in the usual way with milking and the other morning chores, then breakfast. His Aunt Leah was there, but she had been all week, come home from her apartment in Clarksville and her job as a telephone operator to get ready for the wedding. She was a tall, thin woman only a year younger than Lonnie's mother and more impressive for seriousness than beauty. "Your mother's got ways intense enough for anyone," his father once told him, "but her sister can think holes in a barn joist."

It was unusual for the father to be there during the summer, but he had been working on a road job in northern Iowa and the state's eminent domain had been challenged by a corn farmer who preferred his field to a highway and had held up progress in court. So Lonnie's father had come to the farm, earning their keep by overhauling his father-in-law's faltering combine. That Saturday morning, while the family still sat at the breakfast table, the first time the phone rang it had been to call him back to work. The highway would start moving again the following Wednesday.

Lonnie's mother, eight months pregnant, had returned from Iowa in May, along with her two boys, to await the baby's birth. Lonnie had noted his mother's unhappiness during the summer's early weeks, a kind of tired anger that had worked in her since they had left Iowa and that only partially lifted when his father had rejoined them. During the past week, as her mother and sister sewed the wedding gown, she sat apart, somewhat awkwardly, working at her own tasks, removed from the nuptial preparations. There was a race between the baby and the wedding. If the baby came first, Lonnie's mother would not, in all likelihood, be much a part of the wedding. And even if the wedding won, she was reluctant to be forever pictured, huge with pregnancy, in attendance for the sister-bride. Lonnie sensed the impossibility of any satisfactory conclusion to events, knew that his father's efforts to humor her through her unhappiness had not only failed but, in the last day or two, provided yet another irritant. Perhaps the growing tension between Lonnie's parents added to the pleasure with which his father received working orders that would require his absence from both wedding and birth. But the boy could see how heavily the news had settled on his mother, could see the despair outgrowing even the anger as she listened to her husband's half of the phone conversation. When the man returned to the table, joking about earning an honest living again, all the while avoiding any direct glance toward his wife, she rose awkwardly and began silently to gather up the dishes.

Lonnie's father went to town immediately after breakfast, declaring that if he was going to leave for Iowa on Tuesday, he'd better pick up the new parts for the combine and get the machine in running order before he left. He said all this lightly, as though he was in a very good mood, but his words came more rapidly than usual and he seemed in more of a hurry than the situation required.

While Lonnie's mother washed dishes in the kitchen, his grandmother and aunt returned to the front room where the bridal gown was taking shape. His mother wore a dress she had made for herself from the gingham feed sacks that had collected during last year's experiment with turkey raising. The fowl had tested her father's limited patience and in the end turned out to be better at dying than at turning a profit. Good, too, at eating before they got around to dying, and so their legacy was a surplus of big cotton squares, variously dyed and decorated, that the turkey meal had come in. Having outgrown all her regular clothes, Lonnie's mother had sewn a dress, swarming with purple paisley, that would accommodate her ever-increasing bulk.

For a while the boy watched, perched on a step stool beside the back door, watched with an increasing unease as his mother carried a large kettle, two handed, from the black cookstove to the sink, watched as she wiped the sweat from her forehead then stopped in midmotion to look through the window toward the pickup pulling out of the barn lot and headed for town. As the truck disappeared in the distance, she dropped her hands to the sink edge and, bracing with both arms, lowered her head to stare into the soapy water. She was still in this position when Lonnie slipped quietly from the stool and left the room.

He glanced in to where his grandmother, her face clamped in a pin-clutching grimace, was fitting the sleeves. His aunt stood, arms outstretched to either side, the gown slipped over her everyday cotton dress like a white robe—Christmas pageant costuming for an especially high-ranking angel. The contrast between the austere women and the bright garment with all its frivolous folds and decorations bewildered the boy. His grandmother had always covered herself with a kind of dowdiness that went beyond financial limitations or the distance from city stores. It seemed a plainness rooted in conviction rather than necessity, an instinct for drabness that hinted at superiority rather than humbleness. A frugal woman, beige in taste and appearance, she had nonetheless put into her second daughter's wedding dress a luxury of embellishment, a fanciful mix of white-on-white lilies of the valley embroidered at the throat and highlighted with two tiny mother-of-pearl buttons, and an elaborate series of small pleats at the waist that spread into luxurious folds at the floor-level hem. The ultimate extravagance was an intricate lace collar that fitted over the bride-to-be's head, surrounding her neck and hanging down in the front like a broad necklace. The needlework, a tightly woven fantasy of flowers and leaves, had been brought by Lonnie's great-grandmother from Ireland, the most valuable item, other than her own person, she had carried out of the old country, carried it to give to her oldest daughter who now gave it to the first of her daughters to be married at home. This fragile yoke could, after the wedding, be put on with other dresses, a mother's gift to be worn long after the gown had been packed away.

The dress, even the boy realized, was an impressive creation but one so out of character and out of place for the two severe women whose work it represented that it made him uncomfortable in its presence. A thick wooden dowel stretched over the opening between the dining room and the parlor, the rod from which a divider curtain hung. At night the gown was suspended here, in the center of the doorway, and in the dark its ghostly shimmer frightened Lonnie, as though a large spirit were passing through the house; and during the day, when his aunt was wearing the garment, it took a kind of control over her, mocking her plainness, giving a vaguely threatening look to her normally kind, if somber, countenance. It seemed to Lonnie a sort of disguise but one that called into question the very nature of its wearer.

When the gown had once more been removed and his grandmother had begun to stitch the sleeves into place, Lonnie left the house. His grandfather had already gone to check the patch of late corn below the farm. He was eager to get on with the season, to start cultivating. After losing a first planting of beans to late spring floods and having watched a midsummer drought cut deeply into last year's corn crop, he wanted to claim as much as possible from his land this year. He knew the corn could wait, knew there was little urgency given the lateness of everything else, and yet he grew restless at not being able to hurry his work, at not being able to force the corn's growth with his own impatience.

When Lonnie went outside, a dog rose from the shade of the big mulberry beside the smokehouse and ambled lazily over to its master, then followed as the boy crossed to where the fence for the upper pasture joined the barn. His uncle Tom was repairing the gate, had it off its hinges and flat on the ground.

"You get tired of watching all that sewing?" his uncle asked.

"Not much to watch," Lonnie said. "Aunt Leah just stands there like a statue and Grandma pins the arms back on. She's put those sleeves on three times, I bet. And Mom seems . . ." He paused. "I don't know, just real strange."

His uncle laughed. "You being the oldest, you'll never know how strange older sisters can be. And mothers too, sometimes."

"Don't they want Aunt Leah to get married?"

"Sure they do. At least I think so."

Tom was bolting a salvaged piece of angle iron the length of the gate in order to correct a sag. Two orange and white cows, looking dusty and tired, eyed the opening in the fence as though vaguely contemplating escape but without any visible enthusiasm for the adventure. Behind them storm clouds were beginning to build, coming up over the horizon like huge pillars, white and gray tinged with glints of gaudier shades still concealed from view. The dog lay in the dust watching the cows.

"Well, they don't seem very happy about it all to me. None of them." Lonnie shook his head. "And why all the fuss about a dress, a big ugly dress?"

"Don't let your grandmother hear you say such a thing," his uncle warned. "She's put everything she knows about sewing into that thing. And let her garden go to hell in the meantime." He liked to say "hell" whenever he was alone with his nephew. "I guess not getting a chance to do one for your mom, she's putting twice as much into Leah's. Besides, women just seem to act as though getting married were unnatural or something." He also liked to talk knowingly of women.

"Why didn't she make a dress for Mom?"

"Because she and your dad eloped is why. You don't get a wedding dress for that." He felt under the gate, working a bolt up from the other side, then fitted a washer and nut into place. "What you get for that is six months of nothing from your parents, and a whole lot of hell for your younger brother since there's nobody else to give hell to."

Lonnie was confused. "Grandma and Grandpa yelled at you?"

His uncle straightened and twisted his shoulders slowly. "Nope," he answered, "your grandparents raise hell by shutting up. Like living in a tomb except for getting the daylights worked out of you. No talk at all except, when you finished one job, to send you directly to another." He raised the gate into an upright position, Lonnie grabbing hold as well to help set it in place. They lifted it up and onto the two big pins that came out at right angles from the gate post. "If Leah had eloped, I would have left the country. You only put up with one of those kind of experiences, I'll tell you." He squinted at the gate, then checked its swing a time or two.

"Well," Lonnie said, "I wish she'd done something different, something that didn't need that dress."

Tom laughed. "It'll be over soon. And the baby will come and everything will get back to the way it was."

Lonnie looked doubtful. His uncle ruffled his hair. "You'll see."

"I don't like Walter," Lonnie said, "and I don't think Grandpa likes him either."

Tom shrugged. One of the orange cows ambled over to the gate to inspect their work. "It's hard to say. Likely not, I guess. Walter's not serious enough for your grandpa." He shrugged. "God knows how he's serious enough for Leah. Or maybe that's why she likes him. Maybe she's had enough seriousness.

Maybe she wants some of that 'don't give a damn' foolishness
Walter specializes in. Maybe. Dad, on the other hand, can't get
his fill of seriousness." They started walking toward the house.
"But then it took him a while to figure out there was more to
your father than his banty rooster ways, and now they get along
fine."

The phone rang the second time, their ring—the two short
bursts followed by a longer ring cranked out over the party
line—as Lonnie and Tom arrived at the house. Lonnie stopped
on the porch while his uncle went in to get some iced tea. The
boy didn't want to face the dress if he could avoid it. When he
realized the call was for them, he stood and looked in to where
the telephone hung on the dining room wall. Lonnie's two-
year-old brother sat in the center of the room building a wall
of lettered blocks, and through the gray haze of the screen
Lonnie saw the others, his mother in the kitchen door, Tom
leaning forward, arms braced on a ladder-back chair, Leah—
the wedding gown clutched before her like a shield—beside the
table, his grandmother facing the wall, phone in hand. His
grandfather, who had returned while the gate was being repaired, stood to the side, and though his face was concealed
from Lonnie's view, something in his posture and the tilt of his
head made him seem out of place, embarrassed in his own
house. Puzzled, the boy turned away from the adults, walked
away from the door, and began throwing a stick for the dog to
retrieve.

The dog was willing but unenthusiastic, loping to the spot
where the stick had fallen, then walking back with the prize in
his mouth, and—after a long hesitation—dropping it so that
the game could continue.

Lonnie's grandfather came out first, his face rigid, not quite
his face but a mask of his face done in plaster. He walked
directly to the fence at the front of the yard, stood with one
hand on the wire and the other at his side, and stared past the
lower barn out at nothing in particular. In a while he returned
to the house, stopped at the porch door, stood for several

minutes, and then walked back to the fence. He stopped again in the same position and posture as before, his back to the boy, who had risen to follow when the old man made his first trip to the road, but who, sensing his exclusion from things, went back to his seat on the porch steps.

The next time his grandfather returned to the house, Lonnie saw him hesitate, hand on the screen door, then say in a low, tired voice that he was driving over to Tull's. He moved more slowly to the Chevrolet parked at the edge of the barn lot and then drove away. A wind had started to build in the south and it whipped through the car's train, whirling the dust in ugly funnels, then tearing the funnels into shards that flew out toward the cornfield.

Next came Tom, his face crimson.

"What is it?" Lonnie asked, hurrying to keep up. "What's happening?"

"It's that son-of-a-bitch Walter," his uncle answered.

"What's he done?"

"Got drunk and taken off with some woman he'd just met. Some whore from Quincy."

"Some what?" Lonnie asked.

Tom ignored him, rushed to where the Chevrolet had been parked, then, realizing it was gone, stomped his feet in rage. "I'll kill that bastard. I'll kill him. Everybody listening in—that son-of-a-bitch, I'll kill him."

"Grandpa took the car," Lonnie said.

"Yeah, I know. He's gone to tell Uncle Ivan. No need for a preacher now. That dumb son-of-a-bitch woke up married to some bitch whose name he couldn't even remember." He lifted his fists next to his ears, then shook them hard. "That son-of-a-bitch." Then it was as though all the rage left him, just ran out somewhere, and he sat down on the ground, pulling his legs up in front of him, hugging his knees tightly. "I can't believe it. I can't believe any of it." He seemed far younger in his confusion than nineteen, and when Lonnie dropped down beside him, drawing his legs up in exact imitation of the teenager, they seemed more like brothers than uncle and nephew.

"Who called?" Lonnie asked.

"Walter's sister. Teresa, the older one." The uncle had his chin balanced on his knees. "She was as mad as anybody, as likely to kill the fool as Dad or me. Walter called her this morning, crazy and wanting to know how to get out of it all."

"Will Grandpa go after Walter?" The idea troubled Lonnie.

"No. I sort of wish he would, but that's not his way. My guess, he'll talk to Uncle Ivan, then go all quiet and not speak to anybody for a while. Least not to me or Leah or your mom or even my mom. He talks more to you than anybody but Uncle Ivan." This last was said matter-of-factly, without jealousy. "No. He'll just act like it never happened, and if he ever runs into Walter he'll treat him like he isn't there, sort of invisible or dead or something. And in the meantime he'll just work the hell out of you-know-who."

"I'm glad Aunt Leah isn't marrying Walter."

"Yeah, I guess I am too. But I don't know what she's going to do. She's not likely to beg back her job with the phone company, and I can't see her hanging on here." He shook his head and the anger seeped back into his voice, but he seemed more frustrated than anything else. He got up quickly. "Look, Lonnie," he said, "I got to go somewhere. I can't just hang around here. Your dad took the truck so tell your mom I borrowed your car." He started toward the coupe at the far corner of the yard.

"Can I go?" Lonnie asked. "Let me come with you."

"You stay," Tom said, his voice no longer so boyish, deeper now with an edge of hoarseness. "You stay. Watch over things here."

As the last car and the last man drove away from the farm, Lonnie climbed the mulberry tree. The dog watched his ascent, then settled to the ground, head on his paws, looking toward the house.

The wind was picking up, and it moaned through the wide mulberry leaves, a low trembly sound but with an occasional high whistle that was only barely audible. To the south the clouds had broken free of the horizon and were now rolling in great tumbling rotations toward the farm, hard-colored, the gray shot with purple and everything vaguely green. Here and there lightning showed through the garish mass like a distant lamp flashing off and on behind a curtained window. Lonnie gripped a smaller limb that hung above his head and watched the door to the house. He felt alone, but did not consider climbing down to go inside, only wished his father would come home.

After another twenty minutes, when the entire sky was hidden behind the greenish-gray clouds that continued to careen recklessly in from the south, Leah came out of the house. Her head was uncovered and the long hair she normally kept in a tight braid was loose, hanging to her waist. She walked quickly, body straight and, except for her legs, nearly rigid. Her arms were locked to her sides, her neck erect, head lifted slightly to the wind. At the high end of the garden, where the rows of vegetables ran uphill to the fenced-off pasture, she stopped beside the oil drum in which they burned their garbage. There was paper already in the barrel, and to this she added some dried apple limbs that had been piled by the fence. Then she struck a match on the inside of the drum and ignited the paper.

Lonnie watched her through a latticework of wind-tossed leaves as the flames shot up from the mouth of the incinerator, saw the shimmer of heat that distorted the distant clouds, watched with the woman who stood unmoving an arm's length from the fire, her hair driven in whirling black streamers behind her. Lonnie did not see his grandmother until she was halfway up the row of pole beans staked high and green on either side, her own hair blowing wildly, and the skirt of the newly finished wedding gown billowing up from her arms.

Leah did not take her eyes from the flames until her mother stood beside her, then, moving stiffly with a kind of ceremonial formality, she turned to the side, facing toward the old woman, who had taken out a paring knife and begun picking at threads, carving away at the seams.

Lonnie's mother appeared at the downhill end of the garden,

stopping short of the cultivated rows. The wind blew her dress
tight around her swollen stomach, surrounding her pregnancy
with a thicket of purple figures and whipping the skirt behind
her in a truncated train. She, too, watched the far end of the
garden, her arms folded over her stomach, unaware of her
leaf-hidden son perched in the mulberry.

As the first drops of rain drummed into the leaves and
thunder began to break through the noise of the wind, Lonnie's
grandmother handed the amputated sleeves to her youngest
daughter who, in turn, threw them onto the fire, then piece by
piece, a garden length away from the pregnant mother and her
tree-borne child, the old woman tore out every stitch, even the
embroidery and the tiny white buttons, handing each piece to
be cast into the flames by the daughter, who waited unyield-
ingly, furiously, at her side, going about their work with a
terrible deliberateness. Inside the house, barely audible above
the wind, Lonnie's brother began to cry, but no one in the
garden seemed to hear.

When the necklace of Irish lace had been thrown into the
fire, it disappeared briefly below the barrel's rim, then lifted up,
a filigree writhing on the green wind, carried high above the
women and the burning they tended, carried in slowly realized
patterns like some wonderfully shaped kite dancing on a March
breeze. As the boy watched the fretwork tossing in the air, he
could see it blacken until all the white had fled, leaving at either
end a crimson tongue of flame that leapt out with every turning
of the mother's gift.

thirteen

There were several of us, chasing one another up the nearly dry creek bed, jumping the stream in its narrowest places, grabbing after frogs and crawdads—just boys horsing around.

We had seen the rounded, chalk-colored rocks but not really noticed them. They looked like badly shaped softballs, all lumpy and lopsided, and that is why we finally started picking them up—to throw. They littered the place, like the clumsy products of a kindergarten pottery experiment, crude and ugly but with sufficient shape to indicate an intention, no matter how partially realized. We lobbed them overhand into the trees and into the water, at anything that seemed an appropriate target.

When the first one broke, we gathered round the pieces and were dumbfounded. In our easy carelessness we had no idea what we were tossing about, simply assumed that things so mudlike were common, without any inherent value, and so when one opened before us, we were amazed by the miscalculation. For a while we simply stood and marveled, but only for a while. Then we went on a binge, more presumptuous than Moses, striking rock on rock until each split into rough-edged halves, dividing—once we knew their secret—with surprising ease onto a hollow center lined with delicate crystals.

Here was Aladdin's cave. The spars of quartz—mostly clear but sometimes softly tinted with pastels—catching their first light, gleaming in gemlike fineness after an age of patient darkness. Sometimes they were still beaded with the ancient water that had parted around them, the water that had turned their shell like an artist working an indifferent wheel.

We broke them by the score, quitting only when our arms gave out and leaving a trail of splendor an emperor could covet.

THE NEXT ROOM:

A GROWNUP'S STORY

Old man Himmel built a big-as-hell house. Not that it was much to start with, but it kept growing through an old man's lifetime, spreading in every direction like a strawberry plant. The first three rooms—a kitchen, parlor, and bedroom, all square and small—he built by himself in 1910, just before he got married. Then, years later, Mrs. Himmel had their first child, Edith Louise, and Himmel decided, all of a sudden, that the baby had to have its own room. He cut trees, traded part of the lumber for the milling, and built on next to his and Mrs. Himmel's bedroom. It was a hurry-up job, the idea having come to him so late, and when he finished he swore he would never get caught short again, since you can't always count on having decent timber. The next month he loaded every stick of the Bear Creek schoolhouse that the tornado didn't bend and brought it through twelve miles of mud to stack behind his barn.

And from then on he gathered any other piece of planed wood that time or disaster or fashion made expendable to others. Everything got used sooner or later. Mrs. Himmel gave birth four times after Edith, and as soon as each child started to show, Himmel tied on a nail apron and pulled the best lumber out from behind the barn. During the war Milton Ferguson had a fight with his father and went to Burlington to

work in a munitions plant and didn't come home until 1924.
When he drove back to his father's farm, he went past the
Himmel place and there was Himmel putting the first studs
together, singing "Bringing in the Sheaves" so loud it drowned
out the hammering. Milton hollered from the road to ask if
another baby was on the way, and though it was the fourth,
Himmel blushed, grinned, and pumped his head up and down.
He was more for building than he was for talk.

That baby was Robert Lawrence, the last one, but the collecting of lumber and the construction of rooms didn't stop.
Himmel had it in his head that the only proper way for a man
to celebrate was to build a room; so, soon as something good
happened, he would start eyeing over the old creation to see
where he could hang his next addition. Another room came
when Edith Louise got over pneumonia after Doc Reynolds
said she didn't have much hope. That time Himmel built the
biggest room to date, using half the old Gadsden depot. Mrs.
Himmel never completely succeeded in scrubbing out the smell
of coal smoke, and years later people going into that room
would start thinking about taking a trip and never know why.

When Roosevelt beat Hoover in '32, except for some two-by-
fours out of an old henhouse, Himmel had no lumber set aside.
His wife and neighbors told him to wait for spring; something
would turn up; November was no time to celebrate. But Providence provided and there was a train wreck over by Monroe
the very next week, and before the smoke cleared, Himmel had
scavenged the sheeting from two Santa Fe boxcars. They became the walls of what the kids always called the Presidential
Suite, since Hoover had been on the Santa Fe when he passed
through town during the campaign. The part of the wreck
Himmel packed home was brand new, the paint still perfect.
He kept a whole side intact and put it up so that the wall facing
the road, painted orange and black, had "Atchison, Topeka,
and Santa Fe" written across it in big letters. One night, shortly
after that addition was completed, Billy Raymonds ran off the
blacktop below the Himmel place and wrapped a year-old

pickup around a honey locust tree. He couldn't open either door, and while they were prying him out he kept ranting that no man ought to have a house that looked like it was about to cross the road.

Not much building went on in the years after that. Six dry summers yielded six poor crops and one wet year brought hail late in August, wiping out all the corn in Jefferson County. Himmel didn't complain, but he didn't build either.

The day after Pearl Harbor, the oldest son, John William, joined the army. He was twenty-eight but hadn't married and was still sleeping in the same room his father had built during Mrs. Himmel's second pregnancy. The next year Robert Lawrence graduated, and he enlisted as soon as he kissed his mother and the oldest Miller girl and turned in his robe at the back door of the high school.

It wasn't like both boys had to go, since Himmel needed help in the fields and farming was an industry "vital" to the war effort, meaning that at least one of them could have excused himself from the fighting. But they went and the youngest girl quit her job with the phone company and moved back to the farm for the duration. She and Mrs. Himmel plowed and planted alongside the old man. John William wound up in airplanes: a tail gunner on a B-17 flying raids across the English Channel. He got wounded during the summer of 1944, hurt bad enough to spend nearly a year in a London hospital. But they had barely heard about the injury when John wrote home that no one should worry, he would be as good as ever. Old man Himmel believed him and he believed the war reports from Europe, where Robert Lawrence was still fighting in an infantry unit.

Once more lumber, neatly stacked, began to appear behind the barn. The Hurley auction building blew down in August and Himmel was there the next day to help clean up the mess and reclaim any boards that the owners didn't want. In fact, despite the extra work at home, he managed to be on hand to pick up loose scraps of wood all over the county. When Walter

Girst tore out a wall in his funeral home so that the viewing room could accommodate the larger crowds he somehow expected, he burned everything as soon as it was carted out the back door because he didn't want Himmel hanging around. Girst claimed Himmel was bad for business, but most people thought it a little persnickety for a man who conscientiously inquired after every sick person within twenty miles, sometimes making a special trip in his black Ford to see if the patient might have turned into a customer. Tom Willet, at the Co-op, said Girst just didn't like for anybody else to get leftovers, and Milton Ferguson said at least old man Himmel didn't charge for what he carted off.

Except for the undertaker, no one ever resented Himmel's scavenging. He gave more in work, cleaning up a mess, than he took in lumber, and he always made sure he took only what wasn't wanted. So Milton and Tom and nearly every other farmer in the area decided to pitch in and build the kind of monument appropriate for the end of a war. They started their own lumber piles so that, soon as armistice came, they could help Himmel put up a room big enough for a lord. They couldn't get away with such frivolity at home so they seized on the opportunity the old man provided.

Things rarely work out the way you plan them. In the fall everyone thought the Germans were finished, but in December the Battle of the Bulge put the lie to that. Robert Lawrence wasn't coming home. A Snyder boy died, too, and the same week word came that the Baptist preacher's son had been killed in the Pacific. Telegrams about all three arrived on the same Saturday morning; nearly a quarter of the death notices sent by the War Department to Jefferson County came that one day.

About nine-thirty Saturday night phones started ringing and word spread that there was a fire at the Himmel place. Milton Ferguson, whose house sets just east of Himmel's, called the switchboard to say no buildings were burning. The fire was behind the barn. Neighbors stood in their yards watching and when they realized what was happening, they dragged clear the lumber they had collected and set it ablaze. By ten o'clock, everywhere you looked, flames leaped up and a fire burned against the snow of every hill in Jefferson County.

Then Himmel stopped all building. It wasn't that in later years he seemed particularly unhappy, though Mrs. Himmel let slip that the night of the fire he'd nailed shut the door to Robert Lawrence's room and that he did the same with their middle girl's room when she died in childbirth two years later. But as he got older he just didn't seem to feel any need to celebrate, and most people forgot that he'd had such a habit in the first place. No one thought of him as anything more than a quiet old man who smiled a lot and lived in a peculiar house—neither of which made him particularly noteworthy in that part of the world.

Which is why it came as such a big surprise when, in the middle of April 1958, he began to build again. Lilacs were blooming along the west end of the house, and there in the middle of it all Himmel could be seen laying out the most elaborate room of his life. He must have been better than seventy, but he went at it like a yearling beaver with his first dam. And this time, he used new lumber, oak from the woods over by Ferguson's, and cedar siding from the creek bottoms east of town. Where all the other rooms had been simple in design, with only a casual effort at keeping things plumb, this one he squared and leveled at every step. And it wasn't any basic four-cornered affair either. First it went due west about eight feet, then it took a turn of a few degrees, and kept on working its way north until, after seven sections of wall and six corners, it had turned back east and struck the main house again. The roof was just as complicated, radiating out to each of those corners like sections of an umbrella, only the slightest hip joining one part to the next.

In his previous construction Himmel hadn't been much for glass. He had saved it all for this time around. Every stretch of wall had its own window—big ones with mullions—and the fourth section, the one running due north and south, was filled by a huge bay that took up nearly the entire wall. And this last wasn't a regular, clear house window. It was stained glass with a bouquet of Easter lilies and a big gold sun coming up in the back. For the first time in twenty years you could see the window that used to look out from the old Harp's Ferry Methodist Church. Under a shake roof and framed by cedar siding, that glass looked better than it ever did when the Methodists owned it.

While Himmel worked away—the better part of summer and fall—neighbors paraded by to see how the thing had progressed. In fact more than neighbors; as word spread people came clear from Monroe and Lewisville and once Arthur Ferguson claimed to have seen two Iowa license plates on the same afternoon. Cars lined up some weekends like the parade for a rich man's funeral when the cemetery's close to town, and all the while old man Himmel kept working away, whistling or singing or, at the very least, smiling.

But the proceedings troubled Mrs. Himmel. She didn't mind the fun it provided others or the pleasure it gave her husband; she just didn't know the why of it all. All the previous rooms Himmel constructed had clear explanations. They were untouched by mystery. But when he set to work this time, after so long a retirement, she couldn't see the point. Nothing special had happened in years. She told Ella Whitehead that she thought they were too old for special happenings. She brooded for several weeks until she thought, at last, she knew the cause of it. The Hammond widow lived about ten miles north of the Himmels, and Jim wasn't dead a year when she lost twenty pounds, bought a corset and a lot of catalogue dresses, and took to seeing a beautician as regular as a deacon's prayers. She was forty. She was ripe. And she was Mrs. Himmel's explanation.

Mrs. Himmel worried into September, clear up to the day the widow married a drummer from Farmington. When Himmel kept on working, she stopped fretting, stopped even speculating. Of course Mrs. Ferguson and the other neighbors went right on guessing, but they eventually ran out of widows, too.

By first snowfall people had come to take old man Himmel's extraordinary room for granted. And by the time—late in January—when Himmel died, no one thought much about the building anymore.

fourteen

For days the baby vireos had stayed in the tiny nest, at first comfortably, despite the smallness of their home, but as they got larger, gorged by doting parents, they seemed virtually to grow into one another, become one body with four heads. Of course all this was relative. Seen in any other context vireos are not imposing birds, but their nests are small, the size of a cupped hand, built in the fork of the slenderest of branches.

This nest was wedged in a maple shoot no more than four feet off the ground, easily visible except none of us saw it for the first week or so even though we walked past it several times a day, and even then only by accident when I cut off a nearby limb for a marshmallow roasting stick. But after we found it, there was no way to pass by without stopping to look and be amazed by the elegance, both of engineering and construction, that the nest represented.

Eventually the four hatchlings feathered out and left their crowded nursery, the first three quickly, gone before any of us took note. But the fourth, once out of the nest, lost its nerve, froze inches away from where it began, thin toes clamped to the branch, body hunkered down belly-tight to feet and wood. It remained there one entire day like a miniature penguin—long white belly, short dark wings—its wizened vireo face scrunched up over a wide, flat beak

and its black, triangular eyes outlined with white so that it looked
like an undersized and not very pleased highwayman. Wispy white
tufts lifted from the back of its head, suggesting more an old man
than an outlaw, one who has taken a position he will never relin-
quish and who glares out angrily at more adventuresome passers-
by.

Convincing in sternness and grip, the vireo held his place even
into the evening, but sometime during the night he yielded, took
flight after the siblings who had themselves, perhaps, not gotten so
very far away.

OF THEM, MUCH
IS REQUIRED

Lonnie sat under the maple that grew at the edge of the chicken yard. The trunk leaned northward and cast its shade beyond the fence, over the patch of lawn where the boy, chin resting on knees, watched the frantic movement of bees, a great swarming mound suspended from the lower branch of the cedar that grew by the road. The bees clumped, beardlike, in a continuously shifting mass, occasionally falling to the ground in small bundles that writhed briefly in the grass, then broke apart into dark, frantic pieces, each rising in turn to the seething community from which it had so recently separated.

The boy's skin itched and tingled, as though the buzzing of the swarm was being conducted down the tree, along the ground, and up into his own body. And despite the July heat, he sometimes shivered, abrupt, body-shaking convulsions that erupted out of the bees' unrelenting vibration. He had been watching for half an hour, held by the terrifying claustrophobia of the swarm, his shivers due as much to the thought of so many individuals in such close proximity as to the skin-crawling throb of wings and bodies.

His grandfather crossed the yard from the house and stood unspeaking beside him, and the boy, still seated, knees pulled up before him, raised his head to observe the old man from the corner of his eye, even as he continued to watch the bees.

"It's time," his grandfather said, then, noting the boy's questioning glance, added "for the bees," and turned toward the barn. Lonnie jumped to his feet and followed. His dog, black coat dulled with dust and cobwebs, crawled out from under the porch, where he had taken refuge from the oppression of both heat and bees, and trotted alongside.

From a dark corner beneath the workbench, the man dug down toward a chalky white box that sat buried under a pile of old harness. He lifted cracked traces and bridles onto the bench before dragging out the box for inspection. It was a wooden cube, one side of which had sprung outward, its nails drawn nearly free of the adjoining end, and when he could find no hammer on the bench, the grandfather muttered in disgust, picked up a rusty horseshoe, and banged away awkwardly until the corner had been restored. He reexamined the box, shoving it around with his foot until he had checked all four sides. Then he lifted off the top, peered into the emptiness, and closed it up once again.

"No great shakes," he muttered, "but it will do. Get the wheelbarrow." Lonnie crossed to where the barrow leaned against the corncrib, wrestled it down, and, with all his weight leaning forward, pushed it on a wobbly course across the barn.

Once the hive had been wheeled next to the cedar and its top removed, the old man pulled a pair of six-fingered gloves from the hip pocket of his overalls. He always wore long-sleeved shirts—either because of his own odd sense of decorum or the psoriasis that scaled his arms with red and white blotches—and the tops of the gloves covered his wrists up to the shirt's blue chambray, the extra thumb sticking up behind, crumpled and out of place. With his right hand he grasped the limb just above the swarm and began to chew at the wood with a dull keyhole saw. The dog watched warily from a distance, ears up, head alert, his black coat rising and falling with each panting breath, then grew bored and retreated once more beneath the porch.

When the branch had been cut nearly through, the grandfather dropped his saw and, using both hands, twisted until the remaining bark gave way, then lowered the bees gently into the hive.

The boy was amazed that his grandfather handled the bees so casually, watched in frightened expectation, imagining the swarm suddenly dissolved into a thousand angry, stinging insects that could attack with the same terrible intensity with which they held so fiercely to one another. But they paid no heed to the man who sat them in the hive and scraped them from their former perch. Not even the small seething bunch that had dropped when the branch gave way and fallen heavily onto the toe of his left shoe took any note of the human presence.

When the lid was lowered into place and the hum contained and deepened by the wooden box, Lonnie asked, "Why didn't they sting you, Grandpa?"

The old man shrugged. "It just seems to be the way of things. They were too busy with their own affairs, I guess." He tossed the cedar branch over the fence and into the chicken yard. Two speckled gray hens ran over to investigate. "When they get like this, they don't take much note of anything so insignificant as you and me."

"But why not?" the boy persisted.

His grandfather looked down at him. "They have their reasons, I reckon, but they've never let me in on them." He paused. "I guess it has something to do with their need for one another, with some sense that nothing matters but keeping the swarm together, keeping it alive and holding onto its queen. It has to do with how they keep life going, with making sure the queen lays more eggs, with making way for another generation." He stepped between the handles of the wheelbarrow. "The work of carrying on that just takes over and makes everything else—including you and me—unimportant." He lifted and, carefully balancing his load, wheeled through the gate and across the road to a mowed spot beside the fencerow.

He lowered his burden and stripped off the gloves. "Put these on and help me get this hive on the ground." The boy

looked at the gloves skeptically, then took them and shoved his
hands inside. His grandfather's habitual stern look softened
slightly. "We do this right and neither of us will get stung. I
promise." Lonnie was less than convinced, but he took a corner
of the box, its inner life surging through the gloves and into his
fingers, and he helped lower it into place.

"I'll have to borrow some combs from Ivan," the man said.
"We'll let them settle in for a while, then make sure they get to
work."

Lonnie's grandmother did not ring the dinner bell at noon,
came rather to the side door and called them to the table. They
had been in the machine shed since hiving the bees, the man
repairing twisted tines on the hay rake while the boy watched
or handed over appropriate wrenches from the toolbox. Little
was said, and what was unsaid weighed heavily on both of
them. Each knew what troubled the other, but neither spoke,
both vaguely convinced that to voice their fears could only,
somehow, make matters worse. Before entering the dining
room the man and boy washed at a basin on the porch, scrubbing hands and faces, then combing their hair in front of the
round mirror that hung next to the cream separator. Lonnie
replaced the comb in the metal comb box and took his place
at the table. His little brother was already perched on the stack
of mail order catalogues which, added to a regular chair, allowed him to reach the table.

"I want Mommy," the toddler said. "I want Mommy.
Mommy here," he said, thrusting his finger at the chair next to
him.

A tired voice finally answered from the front bedroom.
"Mommy can't come to the table. Let Lonnie tend to you."
And Lonnie, eager to quiet the child, reached for a biscuit, but
seeing his grandfather's disapproving look, withdrew his hand,
dropping it back to his side. "Shh," he said and winked at his
brother, who actually did hush and squinched his eyes in a
full-faced winking effort of his own, lowering both lids at once
then springing them wide before crunching them tight shut
again.

After the blessing the food was passed from the grandfather to the grandmother to Lonnie, who served his brother and himself. There was little talk, and in the quiet the sound of hard breathing came from the front bedroom.

Lonnie's father was working two hundred miles away. He'd been back the previous weekend but had to return to his job that Sunday night. In his father's absence Lonnie spent much of his time following his grandfather and uncle Tom as they did their chores, sometimes going to the field where they were harvesting soybeans, but more often he wandered the yard and barn lot and the pasture below the road, accompanied by his dog. His brother stayed in the house near their mother, who for the past two weeks had been ordered to bed by Doc Little.

Today the combine was down, for the second time that summer, its cutting blade damaged by a piece of pipe that had somehow gotten into the field and flipped up between the teeth of the machine.

Tom had gone to town to get the blade welded, and though the grandfather had stayed home to work on the rake, he had spent more time around the house than in the machine shed. Lonnie stayed outdoors, away from the troubled breathing of his mother and the unusual agitation that seemed at work in his grandmother, spending much of the morning watching the progress of the swarm.

After dinner he climbed the walnut tree behind the house, hoping the shade would bring relief from the heat, but even perched in the main fork ten feet above the ground, he noticed no improvement. The dog had, much earlier, given up on the tree's shade and crawled under a lilac bush where he scratched up the dirt in search of a cooler bed.

Lonnie's uncle returned from town, parking the pickup at the yard gate and going directly to the house. In a few minutes he came around the corner and called to Lonnie, "I'm taking your brother to your aunt Ella's. Want to ride along?" Aunt Ella was his father's aunt, a woman no older than Lonnie's grandfather but who seemed elderly in her dark house with its doily-covered furniture. She professed to love children with an enthusiasm that Lonnie had never found convincing, and he could not imagine why his little brother was being trusted to her care, especially since his mother's family usually avoided any contact with the woman.

"I'll stay here," he said, "in case Mom needs me."

Yet he did not stay close to the house but wandered out to the barn and climbed into the hayloft. The dog lay down at the foot of the ladder to await his return.

The air between the bales of hay was heavy, full of dust and the scent of dry alfalfa, and the boy felt even more listless than on his perch in the walnut tree. He climbed to the opening at the end of the loft in search of a breeze, and seated there, where in haying season the bales, lifted by rope and pulleys, made their entrance into the mow, he caught the slightest stirring of the air. Once a silo had stood at this end of the barn, but it had long ago been taken down and now a hog wallow marked its former site, a dusty depression where two fat-bellied sows lay, only the rise and fall of their heavy sides indicating they were still alive. Lonnie had come here to think (he often came to the hayloft when he was troubled or confused) but he found the sows distracting. He was—on the ground—afraid of them and hated both the fear and the beasts that caused it. They seemed cunning, would lie in wait whenever he tried to cross behind the barn on his way to the north pasture or the pond, threatening him with low angry squeals when he was midway between fences, rising quickly and then eyeing him as though poised to charge. Only rarely did they actually pursue him, and then they pulled up after a few yards, but stories of sow attacks were common and the arrogance with which they claimed their territory, even the way their rooting despoiled the hog lot, kept his fear alive.

Now, suddenly, he smiled with pleasure. A week ago, constructing a fort of hay bales, he had found a nest left by an escaped setting hen that had been carted back to the chicken house before she had completed her work. She had left half a dozen eggs to rot in a makeshift nest at the mow's edge, and

Lonnie now carefully gathered and transported them to the opening above the hogs.

After the twenty-foot drop the eggs exploded on the heads and sides of the sows with spectacular effect, speckling backs and flanks with bits of shell and yolk. And the sulfurous stench carried all the way up to the boy, thickening the already heavy air. The first hog snorted in surprise after the initial bombing, heaving her wobbling body into a half-stance, front legs up, rear legs still sprawled in the dirt. She was quickly joined by her companion after the second egg crashed just behind that pig's jaw, but once the surprise had passed, their attitudes changed. Thrusting their snouts into the rotten splatter, they seemed pleased with this unanticipated gift, and snuffled down the mess with a stomach-churning disregard for its stink.

Lonnie was disappointed at the response his attack provoked, and threw the remaining eggs with as much force as he could manage and still maintain his balance; but the result was the same: the sows found no indignity in his efforts and ate the rotten eggs with a swinish enthusiasm.

When in his restlessness he returned to the front yard, he sat on the steps to the porch. From behind him his mother's moaning came in a steady litany of anguish, just loud enough to be heard over the clatter of the floor fan his grandfather had placed at the foot of her bed. After a while Lonnie entered the house and went to the bedroom door, but there he met his grandmother hurrying in with a wet washcloth. "I want to see Mom," he said. Tom had returned, and Lonnie could hear him whistling in the kitchen.

"Not now," his grandmother said. "Later, when she is feeling better. Doc Little will be here soon, so don't bother her now."

He returned to the porch. Somewhere near the maple tree a cicada had started its low, sharp-edged whine, and down the road a quail was calling, "Bob White, Bob White." Lonnie crossed the yard and mimicked the cry and in a while the quail answered. They continued whistling to one another until the boy tired of the game and returned to the porch.

His uncle Tom came from the house chewing on a chicken wing. He jumped over the porch steps, brushing his nephew's hair as he soared past. He finished his snack and threw the bones over the fence to three hens who fought for the remains, scuffling after one another with their beaks, thrusting out their wings in ragged shows of force. The winner was a thick-chested red-and-black chicken with a badly twisted tail feather that stuck out at a right angle.

"What's up?" he asked Lonnie.

"Nothing," the boy replied.

"I've got to water the cattle. Want to come along?"

They took the tractor, Lonnie standing on the drawbar and holding on to the back of the seat. Tom opened up to full throttle and laughed as they bounced over thinly graveled ruts. The house and the barn disappeared first in dust and then behind a hill. A bull snake made a thick dark line as it crossed the road, reaching the grass just moments before the tractor swerved in its direction.

"Damn, it got away." The boy could just make out his uncle's words above the roar of the engine. He knew the snake was in no danger, because killing hognosed snakes, except in the chicken house, was forbidden on his grandfather's farm. "Better mouse killers than a barn full of cats," the old man declared, "and unlike a barn full of cats, they never bother you when you're milking." But his uncle, whether on the tractor or in the pickup truck, always pretended an attempt on the life of every road-crossing snake, and always just missed with a curse.

When the tractor pulled up to the lower pasture, Lonnie jumped down and opened the gate. He waited until his uncle had driven through and then reclosed the gap in the fence. They rode to the well, the cattle—bawling and shaking their heads—rushing from across the pasture toward the same destination and kicking up puffs of dust with every hoof fall.

It took a while for the pump to draw water, working in long dry gasps for more than a minute before it produced a thin trickle into the stock tank. The animals grew more agitated at the water's slowness, frustrated by the slightness of the stream, and milled around, tongues lolling. They pressed in on Lonnie and Tom, who were seated on the well cap beside the wheezing pump. The boy looked at his uncle and saw that he was untroubled by the surrounding turmoil, but Lonnie remained uneasy, worried at the moment for the two calves that, wide-eyed with panic, fought against the surrounding crush of adult bodies.

It took half an hour to water the cattle, and even then their thirst seemed undiminished. "That's enough for today," Tom said, as though to the complaining animals, and climbed back onto the tractor seat.

Halfway to the house, when the road dipped between two hills, Tom pulled the tractor over to the side and stopped. Dusk was settling in and purple martins dipped and soared, cutting through clouds of insects that hovered over a field full of alfalfa stubble. A breeze lifted ever so slightly out of the west, unburdened with dust and carrying no particular smells, touching softly on skin, promising some small relief from the day's unyielding heat.

"Got to take a leak," Tom said as he swung to the ground. He faced the ditch and unzipped his pants. "You're worried about your mother." It was not a question but the boy nodded, hesitantly, yes.

"It's pretty scary," the uncle continued, his words carrying over his shoulder. "I remember the day you were born. She was in that very same room." The matter-of-fact tone yielded abruptly to one of awe, the nineteen-year-old's voice suddenly softened into greater youthfulness. "Jeez, I was your age." He caught himself, forced his voice back down to a serious, adult pitch. "I was worried. My sister in there crying and all the while Mom keeping everybody outside, nobody telling me what was going on or what I should do." He shook his head as though in bewilderment, then bent over slightly as he rezipped his pants. He returned to the tractor. "And that turned out OK, didn't it? I mean, your mother came through all right and even if we got stuck with you, it could have been worse, right?"

Lonnie tried to smile, but the result was unconvincing. "Why does she sound so sick and so unhappy?" he asked. "Is she going to die?"

"Did she die when you were born?" Tom answered. "Of course she isn't going to die. She's going to have a baby and it hurts a lot." He ruffled his nephew's hair. "When I went in to see you, you know, right after you got here and Doc Little had cleaned you up and everything, your mom was holding you and smiling, all happy, and just a little earlier she had been moaning and calling out like nothing was ever going to be OK again. It's just the way it is, I guess." He shook his head in wonder. "When I was little, I thought she was the strongest person I knew except maybe for my dad. She could work all day bucking bales or driving the tractor and never take a rest, never complain. At school none of the older boys ever picked on me, because they were always a little afraid of her. So when I heard her crying—and when you were trying to be born was the first time I'd ever heard her cry—I was as afraid for her as you are now. But afterwards it was all OK." He turned back around in the tractor seat, looked up the road toward the house, and took hold of the starter. "And that's how it will be this time. Wait and see."

After dinner Lonnie went to the barn to help with the milking. The cows filed in, moving to their usual places with slow, plodding tread, then standing while the men closed the stanchions around their necks. Lonnie threw hay into the manger and the animals began to chew, moving their heads slowly up and down, lower jaws thrusting sideways then grinding back flatly against the upper teeth. They did not eat with the greedy rooting of the hogs or the frantic darting of the chickens, but methodically, deliberately, as though from resignation as much as hunger.

The boy did not take his customary milking spot beside the gentle Brown Swiss that tolerated his clumsy squeezing and pulling with only an occasional complaint, slipped instead away from the cow-warm stalls and returned to his post on the front porch. He waited there while the sky darkened and the first lightning bugs appeared, blinking gently in the gathering night.

Sometimes he tried to pray, pray for the safety of his mother and the child that was trying to be born, but no appropriate words were forthcoming. Inside the house his mother called out, often for his father, sometimes angrily. In the grass below the road a whippoorwill cried out sadly, the rise and fall of its lament counterpoint to that of the woman's. Once Lonnie heard his mother, weeping, confess that she did not want another child, heard her sob that there was not enough for the two she already had, heard the bitterness and anguish as she rejected her own mother's comforting efforts.

The men carried the buckets of milk to the side porch, and Lonnie could hear the sounds of the milk being emptied into the cream separator and then the low whine of the machine as it began its dividing work.

When at last the woman screamed a long terrible scream, he knew it was not only the hurt of the new child but of his little brother and himself, that they too were hurting her. He wanted to rush to her bedside, to tell her it was all right, that they would help her, would—somehow—make it up, but he kept his vigil, held steadfast by the fear and sadness he shared with his mother.

After a time, Dr. Little, rolling down the sleeves to her blouse and straightening her collar, came to him. Lonnie looked up at her face, searching for some sign, some foreshadowing of the news she brought.

"Well, young man," the doctor said, "you have another little brother." Her voice was low and husky and she laughed with a horsy chortle. He had heard the baby's first harsh cries and had guessed it was a boy. "Your mother's named him Joseph." She chortled again, shaking her bobbed hair. "A dangerous name, I told her, for a younger son, but Joseph is what she wanted, so Joseph it is. You can see him shortly." She turned back toward the door, then looked once more at Lonnie. "Take good care of him," and she reentered the house.

He walked across the yard to the fence beyond the now quiet cedar, then stopped and looked up at the Big Dipper, lining his way to the pole star. Below the road the swarm continued to hum in their faded white home, muted by the wooden walls but quieted too, perhaps, by exhaustion from the intense effort of their day. In the milk room his uncle switched off the cream separator. The only sound that came from the chicken yard was a low rustle of restless sleepers and an occasional soft clucking that drifted out of the henhouse.

He accepted Dr. Little's charge, accepted it willingly and wholly. "Joseph," he whispered, "I will look after you. I promise." He said it formally despite the softness of his voice, as though he were standing in a courtroom before a black-robed judge. And he added, "I understand. I'll keep him safe."

And in the darkness behind him the bees continued their relentless labor and the whippoorwill repeated its sad complaint.

fifteen

Between the cabin and our storage shed, wood, split and carefully stacked, fills the eight-foot interval that separates a youngish spruce from an old birch, wood cut long ago by a man dead a decade before we took possession. His fine diligence has rotted to a slumping heap, his intention still apparent, yet no stick can be removed without crumbling to ruin, falling to fibrous clumps of compost.

The snake, however, knows the inner routes, the secret seams of this decay, and daily works its dark body through the pile, emerging at one place then curling slowly to disappear within another crack. So it hunts day after day some inner life invisible to us outsiders, stalks its prey with a terrible patience, curving in and out of the debris, caressing that dark bulk, first here, then there, but in time embracing all that remains of what once we thought protection against the coming cold.

Sometimes when the head eases out in that unhurried slide, its black eyes catch the recovered light and gleam like obsidian before returning to the tangled wood. The thick body follows slowly, slowly, diminishing to nothing before we know it's gone.

QUILTING

I t's me," I told her. "Me, Lonnie," I said, using the name no one but she still called me.

"You're not Lonnie," she insisted, rising suddenly in her hospital bed, her head cocked birdlike to one side, eyes squinted against the half-light of the room. Her hair, still tinged with yellow after eighty-three years, stuck out in frizzy clumps, and her skin—so deeply wrinkled that when she slept the lines of her eyes and mouth disappeared in an elaborate skein— tightened into isinglass. Her eyes glinted with a knowing, more a cunning, which nothing would escape.

"You're not Lonnie," she repeated. She slumped back down, looking past me at the ceiling, but her tone contained more of defiance than resignation. "Lonnie's better-looking. Better-looking." She sighed, her eyes shut, bored even with the ceiling. "And younger."

When I was a boy, when everyone called me Lonnie, my grandmother, this grandmother, told me stories. She endured a difficult life, always on the edge of poverty, sometimes on the farm, sometimes in towns or cities, and she acted and spoke with a boldness that others took, at its worst, as arrogant and opinionated conceit or, at its best, as courage. She could be harsh and vindictive one moment and extravagantly generous the next, and since she spoke her views on every subject force- fully and at great length, she was not a person about whom one could be indifferent. Stories about her abound, tall-tale ac- counts of her strength working in the fields or her anger on such occasions as the time she broke up a Ku Klux Klan cross burning, chasing the hooded riders from a neighboring house because their riot was disturbing the sleep of her babies. But these are not the stories for which I remember her. Working around the house or in the garden or collecting eggs or topping onions, she sustained an unbroken narrative chain. Her stamina was such that she could establish a steady—and punishing—work pace and still speak as evenly and clearly as if she were seated by a fireside.

She got her material everywhere, stealing from radio soap operas, fairy tales, pulp magazines, other people's lives, from anything and everything that had come her way in a lifetime of frequent moves and strange encounters. The odd part is that I do not recall her ever listening to the programs from which she borrowed or reading the books and magazines that she plagiarized. I just never saw her do such things. But during my life I have encountered time and again and in the least likely of places stories I had always taken to belong exclusively to my grandmother, to be the stuff of her life. In my college literature class, I discovered to my considerable surprise that the life of a remote ancestor had been shared with Nathaniel Hawthorne's Roger Malvin, that whole sections of Sinclair Lewis duplicated episodes from my grandmother's past. Once, when I was nineteen and in a New Delhi movie house, halfway through a terrible American film starring one of those interchangeable fifties actors with a name like Tab or Troy, I realized the whole plot was familiar, that it had all happened to a cousin or aunt or some other relation of my grandmother's.

"Lonnie?" she called.

"Yes, Grandma."

"Where am I? Just where am I?"

"The hospital, Grandma. Remember, I drove you here this afternoon? Remember? You were sick."

"This isn't my place," she said, an accusation. "I should be at my place. Where's Dad?"

"He's resting, Grandma. He'll be here in the morning."

"Tell him to take me home. Tell him now."

I said nothing. After a while, anger and fear conjoined in her voice. "They won't help me. And they mustn't touch my breast. I won't allow it."

"Try to rest, Grandma. They won't bother your breast; it's your stomach they're going to treat. Remember? You've been sick? No one will hurt you. Now rest. I'll be right here."

Again she raised up on one elbow, eyes pinched into hard, thin slits. "Just who are you?" Her tone was threatening, and her eyes, a cold translucent blue, were filled with belligerence as she stared at me, an intruder in this unfamiliar room.

"It's me," I cried out. Then, calmer, "It's me, Lonnie, Grandma. Remember? Lonnie?"

I had brought her here—despite my grandfather's warning that she would not cooperate—because of her stories, my inheritance, granted me years earlier. I had long ago stopped fretting about their origins, had learned there are, at the most, only a few stories and these are common property, these belong to all of us. Besides, my own narratives have come to bear a striking resemblance to hers and any judgment would cut both ways.

She had already been hospitalized twice in smaller medical centers closer to the farm, and twice she had checked herself out, much to the relief of the abused staff. But her pain continued to worsen, and she cried out against it even as she made treatment impossible. My grandfather was in a terrible dilemma; he had for fifty-some years of marriage deferred to her wishes, and yet he was now entrusted, by virtue of his own good health, with her well-being. My father had relayed all this to me on the phone, and eager to make payment on old debts, I drove to the farm, carried her to the car, and brought her to a hospital near my home, one where I knew the doctors. It had been, as well as a display of familial responsibility, evidence of my maturity that I could care for those who once took care of me. To calm her fears, I had promised to stay with her the first night, and as the night progressed I found myself answering to a childhood name and becoming increasingly confused about my relation to this woman and my own past.

She lay quiet for a long time. Then she said, her voice far away and not speaking to anyone in particular, "Better-looking. He wouldn't have let this happen. Wouldn't have let them bring me here."

She pulled up on her elbows, looked intently at me, then slowly lay back down. "You're not Lonnie," she said, no longer angry or frightened, just disappointed. "You don't even look like him. Not even in the dark."

In the hall nurses were making rounds and down the corridor someone laughed.

"Do you hear those kids?" my grandmother asked. "Do you hear those girls—out there in the yard, and at night?"

"It's the nurses, Grandma. In the hall."

"Dad and I never let our girls run around after dark. Turn on the yard light. See who's there."

"It's the nurses, Grandma. Remember?"

"Call them in. Tell them decent girls don't run around in the dark. Where's Dad now? Where did that old fool go?" Her voice had grown lighter, younger, and she chuckled. "Dad, are you popping corn for those kids? You know it's too late. Tell them to get to bed."

She was silent, and then in a different voice, full of pain and years, "My little girl." She spoke wistfully, then after a long pause, cried out, "What's become of my little girl?" Tears worked their way from the corners of her eyes and slid unchecked down her cheeks and onto her pillow, but she did not move, just lay there with her eyes closed. Then, with a stronger voice but hollow, like someone speaking in a cellar, "Do you know my little girl?"

"Remember, I'm Lonnie, Grandma."

"She's a sweet child. I love all my children"—she opened her eyes abruptly—"and you're not to repeat this." She had always been inclined to such confidences and warnings. "But she's the sweetest. She's always needed to be loved more than

the others. There are eight others and they've all grown up,"
now soft and confiding, "but she's the sweetest."

"What do you mean, Grandma?" I asked. "You only had
eight children." Even as I spoke, I knew the question ill advised,
knew I was being taken in the way I could be tempted as a
child.

She had been fully coherent when I had picked her up at the
farm, had chided me for going to so much trouble, trivialized
herself and her condition, but also basked in the unexpected
attention. She had joked and gossiped as she always did, but as
we drew closer to the hospital, she had lapsed into anger and
confusion, not remembering how she had gotten in the car,
declaring herself kidnapped, and demanding her return. My
grandfather, from the back seat, had at first tried to reassure
her, bring her back to our reality, but she turned on him
venomously and drove him into silence. That was why once she
was in the hospital he had stayed away: to avoid her accusations and demands. "She gets this way some," he'd said, as
though in apology for her. "I understand," I'd lied.

"You don't know my little girl? So pretty with blond curly
hair and blue eyes. Why did so many of my children turn out
so dark? She's how I thought all of them would look. And all
the grandchildren—even their children—dark, like Dad and
like Lonnie." And then, remembering, "But not as dark as
you."

"Who is the little girl?" I asked, but she lay silent and I think
she slept.

I dozed for a while in the big vinyl chair beside her bed and
when I awoke she was talking, not to me but in the voice and
cadence so familiar to me from my childhood. And I found
myself giving into it just as I had back then, letting everything
else drift away as she told the story.

"I always worked as hard as any man. Even when I was little,
my dad said I was a better hand than any boy he had. And he
wouldn't have said it if it wasn't the truth. My dad was an awful
good man. He worked hard, in the field before light, and lots

of days didn't come back till dark. He never had much, but he worked hard. And there wasn't any work he was too proud to do. Not like some. I've seen him shell corn till those big rough hands of his would bleed so as to make me want to cry. And when my granddad, mom's dad, stayed with us, dying from a cancer in his stomach, my dad would pick him up just as gentle and nurse him better than any woman, even if it wasn't his own father. That old man loved Dad better than he loved his own sons. He told me so before he died.

"And Dad took care of my mother. You don't know how some folks mistreat their women. Why, Selby, who lived down the road from us, wouldn't let his wife give birth in her own bed. Said it ruined good bedding. And so he brought in straw, and that's what she lay on with each child she birthed. Just like some old dog. My mother wasn't strong, not like me, and Dad took care of her."

Her face did not change expression, her eyes did not open, and her voice drifted on in soft undulation. "That's why Dad gave me the pony. Said I worked better than the boys and should have something to ride. I loved that pony—Patch. He had a big white square on his right side. Rode him to school and to church sometimes—times when Mom was sick and Dad stayed with her. Otherwise we all rode together in the wagon on Sunday mornings. But if Mom was sick and Dad stayed home too, I'd ride on Patch. Dad didn't miss often, only when Mom was poorly. He was a good Christian, but he wouldn't ever be a deacon; wouldn't even take collection, for being so humble, but he was regular in attendance."

Her fingers fidgeted with the hospital bedding. They looked almost translucent in the night light's glow, and it seemed impossible that they'd ever wrung the necks of chickens or twisted tight the lids on canning jars. Finally she opened her eyes and looked at the blue cotton blanket. "I wonder what I've done with that quilt?" she said. She laughed. "I'll bet my little girl took it, she loves my quilts so. Well, there's plenty in the closet. No shortage of quilts in this house." She laughed again

and her eyes closed. Her breathing, so short and shallow earlier, came more regularly now. I thought she had fallen asleep,
but after several minutes she continued. "Eight children leave
you with an almighty-sized pile of patching. I guess I can lose
a quilt now and again if I want." She chuckled softly.

"All those patches. I saved everything. What didn't go into
quilts went into braid rugs." Her voice was changing, a subtle
uneasiness tingeing her words. "All those patches," she repeated. "Remnants, pieces of this and that, accumulating like
dirt, and so hard to use them all, to keep from getting smoth-
ered in rags." She sighed. "I did the best I knew how. Found
a place for most of them, put them together the best I could.
Regular patterns at first, starbursts and sunflowers and such
when I had the right material, but usually not." She spoke
defensively now, as though in response to some accusation.
"Regular Dorcas Society patterns need lots of the same material, and there's waste. After a while I made up patterns of my
own, did the best I could with the material I had. Let somebody
else do better if they can. I did the best I could with what I
had."

I remembered all the quilts but none of the quilting. Sewing
always seemed too domestic an activity for my grandmother,
who despite her claims to the contrary was a poor housekeeper
and who left much of the care of her babies to her husband. He,
often as not, was also the one who cleaned house. In memory
I tend to picture my grandmother out of doors. But there they
were, all those quilts, tangible evidence of the time and energy
she had given this craft.

"As I got older, things got all mixed together. There were
rags from the first years of my family right beside the latest
scraps. Sometimes I saved a piece for twenty years until I found
the right place for it, a spot needing just that color. I never
forgot a patch either, but could tell you that the yellow piece
was from my wedding dress and that heavy black wool came
out of the suit Dad wore to Uncle Billy's funeral. And over in
the far corner, that blue scrap"—she was pointing now, eyes

still closed—"that came from Lonnie's first overalls. Most of the pink came from my little girl's dresses. She loved pink so."

Her eyes flew open like those of an uplifted China doll, and she looked toward the large plate-glass window that, in the night, revealed nothing but the reflection of her room. "That's why I came here. To see my little girl. She's been in the hospital so long now, and she wanted her mother with her. That's why I came. I am poorly myself, but I came." She saw me in the chair. "Do you know my little girl?"

"Yes, Grandma, I knew her," I said.

"It's so odd. Why can't I say her name?" she asked, not so much sad as puzzled. "It just won't come."

"Rebecca, Grandma. Her name was Rebecca."

"Why, Rebecca is a woman, a grown woman and strong like me. The little girl," and then with a sob, "the one we lost, I know her name as well as my own—better, 'cause I've said it more. I don't know what's come over me, not knowing my own sweet little girl's name."

"Becky, Grandma," I said.

"She was such a sweet child. I miss her so. Why can't I remember? It's like my mouth's forgot how to say it. But it'll come to me if I sleep. I'll know it when I wake up. I can tell you then."

She was quiet once more, as though willing herself to sleep, but her fingers moved constantly, smoothing her hospital blanket or the remembered quilt. This time, however, she did not close her eyes and after a while her gaze returned to the window. It was like a great mirror with only occasional car lights on the distant highway to indicate that it was a window at all.

"See that lady over there," she whispered, waving her hand toward the glass. "She isn't very friendly. While you slept, I talked to her, but she just looked at me. Wouldn't say a word."

I hesitated for a moment. "Grandma, that's you. Your reflection in the glass."

She laughed. "Well, I knew she had to be a good soul

because she kept smiling back at me. Wouldn't talk but didn't turn away either." And she laughed again, a strong and happy laugh.

The door opened, cautiously, and my grandmother's laughter stopped. A nurse came in with tentative steps. "Are you awake?" she called. My grandmother didn't answer. "I've come to check your blood pressure. I'll just be a minute and you can go back to sleep."

"I'm not sleeping, and you will do no such thing. I won't have any of your kind poking around at me. Just get that thing out of here and leave me be." Her voice was shrill, excited.

The nurse had a stethoscope around her neck and was readying a Velcro band to wrap around my grandmother's arm, deciding now to be more assertive about it all.

"You're not to touch me," Grandma hissed.

"Now, ma'am, this won't take but a minute." The nurse had slowed but continued, warily, with her work.

"Is this necessary?" I asked. "I thought Dr. Williams had decided to let her rest tonight, let her get used to being here before he did any testing."

"This isn't a test," said the nurse. "All patients have their vital signs checked when we come on duty. Now, dear, just let me put this around your arm."

"Don't dear me and don't touch me. I told that doctor"—thrusting an accusing finger in my direction—"I would leave, and you're not touching my breast."

"Grandma . . ." I tried to hold her hand but she jerked away and glared at me, a look full of anger and fear. "It just goes around your arm," I said.

"I don't care how many of you there are, you'll not touch me. You can't keep me here against my will."

I turned to the nurse, pleading, "Can't we let it go until tomorrow, when the doctor comes in? She's confused and excited. When they came for the EKG this afternoon she didn't know where she was or what they were doing. I'm sure the doctor doesn't want her upset again."

But the nurse seized the nearest arm and was intent on wrapping the wide belt around it when the other arm swung up from the bed, landing a slap on her cheek that staggered her. She jumped back, the mark of my grandmother's hand red on her face. The nurse stood rigid, anger and panic competing in her eyes.

The blow had carried my grandmother over on her side and she glared up at the frightened nurse. "When an old woman says leave her be, you've got no right to ignore her. You'll not be touching me, girl."

I hurried between them, facing the nurse. "Please try to understand," I said. "She's confused. Her daughter just died of breast cancer and she's confused." But the nurse rushed from the room without speaking.

Across the valley the sky had grown pink. "Rebecca's gone now," the old woman said, her voice quiet and steady. "My Becky's gone." She paused, but I could hear her breath like the rustle of ripe wheat. "Just the scraps of pink. The bits and pieces they can't cut away from me." She was looking out the window and I, too, had turned to watch the growing light. Outside, on the edge of a large ravine, a dead sycamore reached with broken limbs into the brightening sky. Beyond, where the valley flattened, a four-lane highway ran north and south in front of wooded hills. As the light grew stronger behind the hills, the stream of cars steadily increased and, made insignificant by the distance, crossed from one edge of the window to the other.

She spoke, softly now, not to me directly, but aware of my presence. "When I was a girl my dad gave me a pony because I worked so hard. I could ride better than the boys. I would carry tools to him in the fields and bring him lunch. It was me went for the wagon when Joe cut his leg on the scythe. A deep, nasty wound, but we cared for him and it healed. In those days we knew what had to be done and we did it ourselves. Who else was there? That pony did whatever I asked, and I cared for it just like, later, I cared for my own children.

"Once when Mother was sick and the boys were off at my

grandfather's helping him get his crop in, I rode that pony to church. Dad stayed with Mother, but he said for me to go, to leave early, so that I could stop over at Webster's and tell the old man we couldn't help him in the field until midweek. It was a considerable ride, and so I left before light. I had a new dress Mother had made for me, pink-and-white gingham with a kind of apron front, a bib all surrounded with white lace. Oh, I wore pants underneath, because of the ride, but I'd do that most times I wore dresses, rolled them up out of sight when I got where I was going or took them off if there was a private place. And I rode slow, to keep from getting mussed. Still I got to Webster's in good time and delivered the message. Mrs. Webster asked me for breakfast but I wanted plenty of time to get to church.

"When I got to the hill above the river, the sun was just breaking over the trees. Everything smelled good, and the long grass, all dew-wet and shiny, rolled in waves clear down to the water. I sat in my new dress and looked across that valley, full to the other side, and thought of how I'd never been in that particular place before and might never be again, at least not on Patch and not wearing a new dress. And I had the queerest thought that someday maybe I'd be over on that other ridge, on the other side of that river, a grown woman, and I'd be looking for this spot, looking for that girl in a new dress on a pony that was long dead. Even then I thought such things, and I looked across for that woman and wondered what she would look like, and if she'd be happy."

She pulled to a sitting position and leaned toward the glass. "See across that valley, clear yonder past the river? See that ridge? I've been watching since first light, thinking that girl could be over there, sitting all young and fresh on her pony. But it's too far. I can't see a thing over there but that fool old woman too proud to answer."

"That's your reflection," I said. And then, "You're in the hospital and that's a highway out there, not a river. Remember?" I asked.

She turned to me slowly. "What right have you to call me to

remembering? You don't know the first thing about remembering." She shook her head almost in resignation, but irritably, too. "When you're young and you think of a lifetime, you think of all those years stretching out ahead. And you think a year's a fixed thing, regular like a pound or a mile, regular and reliable. But after a while you learn that's not the way of it at all. A year's just a part of your life, a portion. When you're ten, a year is a tenth of a lifetime and seems awful long. Even at twenty, it seems a lot to wait through, and so many of them still ahead. But at eighty a year's nothing. Less than a child's week. One eightieth of a life."

She spoke without the anger now but with the resignation still intact, as though to a child too young for comprehending.

I raised her bed, and she lay for a long time, her eyes closed, but still facing the window. It was fully light now and two finches fluttered around the dead sycamore, landing, then flying away and returning again, wings gleaming in the sun.

"That tree out there is a danger," she said behind me. "I won't have dead trees falling on people in my yard. Lonnie, you and Dad get the saw and take that down. Do it now, before you forget. Hear?"

Later that day my grandfather, despite his own reluctance, came to see her. Holding his hat in both hands, his head bowed, he listened as she berated him for his betrayal, as she accused him of trying to get her money. And after a while he checked her out, and we drove her home. She did not recognize me again but she lived for five years after that, though often thinking my grandfather an intruder in the house where he cared for her. But she always knew where she was, that she was home, under one of her own quilts, and talked incessantly, repeating the entire litany of her life, one in which I am always a little boy with a child's name and where all her children are alive, and we are all better than any of us turned out.

The sound had frozen, and when at last it began to thaw, the tide lifted up great white blocks along the shore. Water formed dark canals in the crevasses and swans came to glide between the walls of ice.

One night beneath a full moon I watched my children, their faces bright against the dark of sky and sea, leap from one glistening mound to the next as huge white birds drifted contentedly beneath their feet.

More Than the
Watchman for
the Morning

He cussed out Dolan the first time. He was ten and the one who had last opened the hutch, opened it to toss in handfuls of red clover. But he must not have fastened the cage securely, because when he heard the dog yapping and looked out the back window, the door stood open, and the rabbit had disappeared. Convinced that the dog—in spite of being half blind and so ratty-looking it was hardly a dog at all—had dragged the rabbit from the cage and killed it, he ran up the road cursing dog and owner alike. Dolan came to the screen in a T-shirt, chewing a Mississippi crook cigar, and with a faint smile listened while the boy screamed in rage and sorrow.

Lonnie, in fact, had never liked the rabbit, not since the first time it nipped his hand when he offered it clover. It belonged to his little brother Timmie, not to him. One day, a year or so before Dolan's dog stood yapping outside the empty hutch, when Lonnie's family had been living in a cabin in a trailer court, one of the men from his father's road crew—a man with the same first name as his brother's—came to the door, drunk and hollering for "the kid." The man had a cardboard box in his arms, and when Lonnie came to the door he said, "No, not you. The little kid." Timmie was not yet four and looked two, and when he came to the door the man said, "For you," and set the box on the step. The child pulled the package into the room, tugging the top open as soon as the screen door closed, and found inside a very large white rabbit with a reddish spot around one eye. It looked at Timmie, then leaped from the box, hopped to the nearest lamp, and bit through the cord. The next day, a Sunday, the boys' father built a small cage from screen wire and two-by-twos, and for the next year the rabbit moved with them wherever they went.

But now Lonnie's family had settled down, had lived in the same three-room house at the end of First Street for the better part of a school year. His father had quit the road gang and the constant moves that ended in one-room cabins smelling of stale cooking and rotting linoleum, and, for Lonnie, a new school every few weeks. Not that First Street was much. It ended in front of Dolan's house, just as the land dropped off to the river's flood plain. And the house they rented had been built on street sweepings, so that the yard contained only the hardiest of weeds—and most of them sandburs. But Lonnie had spent seven months in one school, a personal record, and there was, not far from the house, a tree, albeit a scraggly apricot, that he daily climbed in order to watch airplanes approaching the municipal airport northeast of town.

The house had a kitchen joined to a small living room where Lonnie shared a sofabed with his brothers—in addition to the five-year-old, there was Timmie, a toddler nearly two. Their parents slept in a third room next to a closet-sized bath. Behind the house, at the rear of the lot, where nothing, not even sandburs, would grow among the cinders and gravel, stood a padlocked shed filled with junk, and often—especially in the first weeks—Lonnie slipped inside through an open window to poke among the litter. It was like visiting a museum. In one corner plaster figures and birdbaths, all maimed in one way or another, had been crowded together, and in another stood an old wooden icebox. But most of all there were boxes, large cardboard boxes with "Highland Potato Chips" printed on the sides above a picture of a girl wearing a plaid skirt and blowing on a bagpipe, one knee lifted high in the air. These held ancient newspapers and magazines, pages yellowed and warped and stuck together by mildew and the weight of time: a library of *Collier's* and *Life* and *The American* and *Reader's Digest*. Once, stuck between a March 1947 *Collier's* and a *Saturday Evening Post*, he found a small comic book with crude pictures of a naked Popeye eating spinach and doing obscene things to Olive Oyl and a series of other females, one of whom looked disconcertingly like the Highland Potato Chip girl. Lonnie pushed the volume deep into the box where no one would find it and think it his.

In front of the shed stood a new and enlarged rabbit hutch, and it was through the open door of this pen that he believed the neighbor's dog had dragged his brother's pet. But the rabbit wasn't dead; it had gone under the building, and when, still shaking with anger and frustration, Lonnie walked back from cursing Dolan and Dolan's dog, it hopped out into the yard.

Across the road from the house lay a large open field, thick with weeds and brambles. Here a pack of dogs, hair matted and ribs showing, Dolan's runt trailing along behind, harried whatever they could scare up. Sometimes they ran at night, howling and screeching, and Lonnie would lie on the sofa beside his younger brothers, imagining the darkness among those weeds, frightening himself with visions of attacking dogs.

One morning a month after he had cursed Dolan, the hutch door again stood open, its broken latch lying on the ground. Lonnie crawled alongside the shed, peering under, but it concealed no rabbit. He trampled the clover patch, kicked down the weeds along the drainage ditch, even wriggled between stagnant puddles to peer through the culvert. But the rabbit was gone. That night the dogs howled in the field across the road, and the next night and the night after that; each morning Lonnie looked for the bloody patches and white fur that would declare the rabbit's fate. They never appeared. Neither did the rabbit, though Lonnie daily searched the field from the apricot tree, watching for a show of white in the tangle of the distant field. But to no avail.

Lonnie's father had gotten work as a construction laborer on the new housing project going up just half a mile from their home. Streets had been staked out on an old truck farm, and the foundations for the rectangular buildings had already been poured, four deep in six unyielding rows. There were no trees, no grass, just mud and concrete strung along the flats of the upper flood plain.

During the summer the buildings grew two stories high, then were capped with identical gray roofs. Sometimes Lonnie watched from his tree, over the vacant lot to where the cement trucks and the paving equipment were in constant motion, watched as the work progressed. And, too, his eyes strayed from the dusty glare of the project to the field, as he looked for a flash of white among the weeds.

As the summer wore on, he went on Sunday afternoons to inspect the half-finished streets and the drab rectangular buildings. He could not imagine people here, but his father showed him the hallways to upstairs apartments, the mail slots, and the cement pads provided for each building's garbage cans. Eventually he showed Lonnie the one in which they were going to live. The boy protested with an uncharacteristic tantrum. He did not want to move, to leave the tree and all chance of finding the rabbit. His father said soon trees would be planted in the project, that there would be a playground, children, everything. He said that it was no use watching for the rabbit. Something that big and white, that defenseless, could not survive in the wild. "He's just no match for a pack of dogs. He can't hide and there's no place to escape. That's a killing field for any rabbit, let alone a white one."

Lonnie's family moved to the housing project just after school started in September. Only four buildings were ready for tenants by then, but the others opened one at a time over the following winter and spring, increasing the population of

Liberty Homes—as the project had been officially named—daily. By moving so early, Lonnie's family arrived ahead of the sidewalks and most of the streets and curbs, and in the absence of grass the September rains churned all the unpaved areas to a thick mire. Residents took sheets of plywood from the construction area at night and built makeshift walkways over the worst places, but, inevitably, workers came to reclaim the material, often apologetically, sometimes angrily. After school and on weekends, the children—every apartment came with children—watched the paving crews as they inched along with the streets and walks. And the paving crews watched the children, convinced that they might, at any moment, run across a fresh pour, or place their palms flat on a new sidewalk, ruining forever the concrete's perfection.

Lonnie missed the apricot tree and the shed filled with magazines, and began to feel increasingly claustrophobic. As construction progressed, Liberty Homes in its entirety was being enclosed with a four-foot-high chain-link fence, anchored by posts that had been, themselves, secured in concrete. On three sides this barrier separated the project from empty land, the L-shaped bean field of a surviving farm thick on one side and narrow toward the river, and—on the third side—the big weeded lot that ran to First Street. But to the west the fence stood between the rectangular buildings and real homes: houses with brick chimneys and white siding; houses with trees and grass. And eventually, one after another of these houses grew a "For Sale" sign in the front lawn.

Among the project children, gangs and alliances began to form, usually half a dozen or more boys who wandered off together looking for things to do. Lonnie belonged to none of these and was untroubled by most of them. But one group was different: four or five boys, thirteen- and fourteen-year-olds, who gathered in the fence corners or lounged against parked cars, there to smoke and threaten the younger children. The leader, in particular, frightened Lonnie, not because he was the largest, or even the roughest-looking, but rather because of his manner, the contempt he showed everyone—even adults—who came near, the arrogant way he laid claim to the projects. He was oddly built, thick-bodied with short, stout legs, and took up a great deal of room wherever he went, demanding the complete width of the sidewalk for himself. When he leaned against the fence or perched on one of the oil drums beside the maintenance shed, he would take out a knife, not the regular pocket variety but a switchblade, and clean under his fingernails with its point, do it all in a very showy way, compelling attention toward that stiletto blade. His name was Mike, and the boys in his gang acknowledged his command in everything, swelling with confidence around everyone else but cowering before him.

One Saturday near the end of September, as Lonnie walked alone, the tallest of this group, together with another gang member called Mouse, came from behind, each grabbing an arm. They kept walking at his pace, and he did not resist.

"We're starting a club," the tall one said. Lonnie said nothing.

"Yeah," Mouse added. "A real club."

"And we're looking for new members." The tall one spoke now with exaggerated sincerity. "We wondered if maybe you wouldn't want to join."

"I can't join stuff," Lonnie said, trying to keep fear out of his voice. "But thanks."

"This is special," the tall one continued. "Real special. We're going to have a clubhouse. Everything."

"And dues, too," Mouse said. "Real dues."

"I'll have to ask," the boy said. "My folks don't let me join things."

"This is special," the tall one repeated. In his eagerness to sound congenial, he became shrill and whiny. "You can't tell, anyway. This is a secret club."

"Yeah," said Mouse. "And now that you're in on the secret, you got to be initiated."

By this time the three had walked to where the paving

equipment stood. The workmen, putting in overtime on a weekend, had stopped for lunch, and except for one man who sat sleeping, cap pulled over his face, against the nearest building, no one was in sight. The paving crew had left a troweling machine on a fresh pour that glistened with water as the concrete hardened. The tall boy and Mouse pushed Lonnie to the very edge of the fresh cement, to the end of the long troweling bar that extended from one edge of the slab to the other.

"What you got to do to be initiated is walk across on this machine. Just cross it. That's not hard, and then you're one of us."

Lonnie knew this wasn't a difficult assignment. The bar was at least six inches wide, and he could easily sprint across it. On the other side, beside the fence, stood a portable toilet for the workers, and beyond that a gate. Once across he could get away before the tall boy and Mouse could run around to catch him. Still, he hesitated. Would crossing mean, even if he got away, that he belonged to their club? Could he cross and not be initiated?

Mouse squeezed his arm. "What are ya waiting for?"

The tall boy began to push. "Just cross to the other side. No big deal," he said.

Lonnie mounted the troweling bar, balancing quickly as it shifted beneath his weight.

"Just cross before anybody sees you, before someone comes back."

Lonnie began to walk, gaining confidence with every step that carried him away from the tall boy and Mouse. Halfway over, he stopped and turned to face them.

"I'm not joining your club," he shouted. "I don't join clubs. I won't be initiated."

When they did not move, he turned, triumphant, to complete his escape. But while he was yelling out his defiance, Mike had come from behind the toilet and now stood on the opposite side of the concrete, knife in hand, flicking the blade in and out as he smirked at Lonnie.

Something, perhaps Lonnie's defiant refusal of membership, roused the worker beside the building. "Stay the hell off that cement," he shouted, and at those words, Lonnie stepped from the bar and ran across the fresh paving, leaving the faintest trace of his shoes on the still tacky surface.

For the next two weeks, he walked back and forth to school by elaborately circuitous routes, expecting Mike to step from behind every tree and shrub. He practiced this subterfuge until word got around that Mike was in the hospital, and would be for a long time, both legs cut off when he'd fallen under the freight train he was trying to jump.

That winter was a hard one. Bad weather and an economic recession brought all area construction, not just the work on the project, to a halt, and since most of the men in Liberty Homes were construction workers, unemployment ran high. Lonnie's father was laid off the week before Christmas and began spending his mornings at the Union Hall. On days when it snowed, he went to the wealthy section of the city where big houses were strung along a high ridge, went to shovel long, winding driveways and walks that connected them to the rest of the town. But it did not snow much that winter, just got bitterly cold and stayed that way.

Other men, many of whom had been out of work since Thanksgiving and who had given up on finding anything before spring, escaped from their apartments to the corners of the project, where they leaned against the fence, their coat collars pulled up against the cold. They sucked on cigarettes and faced the long, drab buildings in which they lived. They rarely spoke to one another; sometimes they shared a bottle. But mostly they just stood looking in toward some mysterious center of Liberty Homes. Evenings, when their children trudged back from school, their own collars pulled up and their hats pulled down, the two groups were distinguishable only by the contrast in size.

Winter passed slowly. Even when it snowed, four inches in January, the project remained a gray place, the frozen ruts in its yards cutting fiercely no matter how soft the covering. Bill collectors in business suits walked warily on the sidewalks, watching the house numbers out of the corners of their eyes. The previous summer credit cards had arrived in the mail, and now representatives of gasoline companies came to the door to demand their return. Salvation Army captains brought food to the more desperate families, and housing authority officials watched to ensure that those with incomes were keeping up with the rent.

But eventually the March thaw brought a return to work, both for the men living in the project and for those building it. Curbs and sidewalks were completed, and a project maintenance man came around to replace tiles that had popped up from apartment floors over the winter. And with work came new cars and trucks to the parking areas. Television sets, still a rarity the year before, began to appear in front-room windows. Also with warmer weather came a feeble sodding effort, as well as a planting of scrubby trees between the sidewalks and the street. Many of the trees were dead on arrival, but some showed encouraging signs of life. Even Mike, hobbling around as he learned to walk on his stiff new legs, seemed—though no less cocky—almost congenial. By the time school let out in June, workers had finished a play area at one end of Liberty Homes.

That's where Lonnie met Terry. Lonnie often walked his baby brother Joe to the playground, and there, often as not, swaggered Terry. Terry delivered the Sunday paper, the Des Moines *Register and Tribune,* and always had a metal-covered collection book sticking out of the back pocket of his jeans. He came for the same reason as Lonnie, sent to watch over a younger sibling, but he came aggressively, ordering other kids around with confident authority. If he did not seem quite the bully that Mike had been, he possessed a self-assurance that was, itself, intimidating.

Lonnie avoided Terry, steering his little brother away from the larger boy's path, ashamed of the fear that motivated these

maneuvers and yet always yielding to it. Yielding until the day
that Terry, who had entered the gate ahead of them, abruptly
turned and, in the suddenness of his movement, knocked Joe
down. Lonnie, usually so careful to avoid confrontation, flung
himself on the offender, goaded by shame for all the insults he
had evaded in the past.

Terry stood nearly a head taller and weighed at least ten
pounds more, but his surprise and Lonnie's rage evened out the
advantage. Children and mothers shouted encouragement or
ridicule as the two thrashed around on the ground. Terry's
nose began to bleed, and Lonnie had a long scratch down one
cheek. The fight slowed as anger and energy played out, and
as it slowed, the onlookers lost interest and drifted away. Finally
the two lay on the ground virtually abandoned: Lonnie had
Terry in a headlock and was himself being squeezed around the
chest, but little pressure was applied in either hold.

"You ever deliver papers?" Terry asked suddenly.

Lonnie was surprised but did not release the headlock.
"No."

"I need a substitute. Want the job?"

"How much does it pay?" Lonnie let him go.

"Depends," Terry said. He pushed his hair back and rubbed
the blood from his nose. "Nickel a customer if you collect too.
Two and a half cents otherwise." He pulled the collection book
from his pants, where during the fight it had raised a big welt
on his back. "I got enough customers for the both of us, if you
want to help."

"What do I do?"

"Sundays, you do half the deliveries. That's two and a half
cents. Collect when I can't. That's a nickel."

"Sounds OK," Lonnie said.

"Only thing is you got to get up early on Sunday, 'cause
papers come at five. Can you get up that early?"

"Sure," Lonnie said, and left the ranks of the unemployed.

Being paper boy in a housing project is nearly an indoor job.
Every Sunday the two boys loaded the papers—made bulky by

feature sections, comics, and extra advertising—into a red wagon, which they pulled along the sidewalks between the buildings, Terry carrying papers to one side, Lonnie to the other. At the downstairs apartments they placed the papers inside the screens, but for the second floors they entered hallways and climbed to the upper level, where they laid the news in front of closed metal doors. Since the distance from the wagon to the buildings was little more than the distance up the stairs, most of the morning seemed to be spent in the stale air of the project halls, climbing up the littered steps. And during the week, when he collected, even more of Lonnie's time was spent in these same hallways, waiting at half-opened doors, peering in at the uniform beige walls and gray tile that denied the private deviations of each family.

Two carriers could make the deliveries quickly, and by July, now an equal partner, Lonnie saw an opportunity to move outside the project. He convinced Terry that they should expand their business, and the two of them got their official route enlarged to include the houses scattered beyond the weed field along First Street and on past the junkyard and the city dump to Seventh Street. For two weeks they went door to door until they had sufficient subscriptions to justify the canvas newsbags they had to buy for deliveries outside the project. Their area grew to three times its previous size, and while deliveries took twice as long and collecting from the new customers added endless complications, profits rose, and they were proud of their accomplishment.

Lonnie especially welcomed the larger route and nearly every week volunteered to do the collecting outside Liberty Homes. He liked getting away from the project, and even though the houses were shabby cast-offs at the edge of the river bottoms, houses like the one he had left on First Street, they were spread out along the potholed streets and separated by huge elms and sycamores. Along these streets, nothing seemed predictable, not the dogs, or the people, or the adventures he might encounter.

At first the new customers confused him—courteous one week, surly the next, sometimes leaving a tip, other times ignoring his knock even though he could hear them moving around inside—but after a while he learned the patterns of their moods, which days to call, when they were serious, when joking. At one place, Dolbeck's, he learned to bypass the house on Sunday morning and leave the paper on the rotting front seat of an ancient Plymouth that had been rusting away on tireless rims longer than he had been alive. Dolbeck never stirred in the back seat, even though the door scraped loudly when Lonnie opened it.

But the most exciting moments on the expanded route came at the end of every street. Seventh Street concluded at the city dump, and often Lonnie stopped to watch the scavengers, Dolbeck's wife nearly always visible among them, turning and re-turning the most recent deliveries, checking every item against some potential use or value, either throwing it aside with a disappointed shake of the head or cramming it into a shopping bag. Sometimes, too, amid the rot of soft garbage, high school boys shot rats with .22's, or followed the old man who, every Thursday evening, came with a ferret to stir up shrieks of anguish in the rubbish heaps.

Fourth Street ended in a junkyard. Like the project, it was enclosed, surrounded by an eight-foot fence topped with barbed wire. Inside, among the wrecked cars and mangled refrigerators, roamed a German shepherd, all hackles and teeth. Lonnie liked to look in, trying to identify the brands of as many of the ruined cars as possible, but whenever he approached the fence, the dog, with a maddened snarl, came hurtling toward him, crashing mindlessly into the wire only to fall back and charge again and again. No matter how quietly he walked, or when he came, the dog seemed always to find him out and rushed from among the piles of twisted chrome and rusted steel with an infallibility and a malice equally inscrutable.

Other streets ended with black-and-white wooden barricades and dead-end signs, and beyond these barriers rose low, sandy bluffs, cut away by ancient meanderings of the river and inhabited by thousands of cliff swallows. Here the project seemed far away. There were ravines to explore, gullies to slide down, small hidden ledges on which to await the river breezes. When time allowed, Lonnie came to this place, his first haven since the apricot tree.

In August the polio began. There had been a few cases around the city, and the usual warnings from the Health Department, but by the middle of the dog days it was everywhere. Most of all, it was in Liberty Homes. The public swimming pool closed, but few of the project children had ever gone there anyway. The Liberty Homes playground with its swings and sandbox was locked—locking things had become the rule. Through August the heat and drought worsened. Hydrants were opened and children splashed in the spray. Then mothers panicked for fear the water, like swimming pools, could somehow carry the contagion into their lives, and the streams ran, without interruption, to the storm sewers.

In the beginning only a few people got sick, and they were taken quietly to the hospital. Sometimes Lonnie heard that one or another had lost the use of his legs or had to be placed in an iron lung. But mostly they just went away. Then children began to die.

First there was Gloria, the little girl in the building across from where Lonnie's family lived. She had come every afternoon to play with his younger brother and to watch children's shows on the new television set. Then one morning she ran a fever and had a sore throat. They thought she had a cold but it got worse. After a week in the hospital, she died. A baby in one of the apartments where Lonnie delivered the paper, a baby he always saw standing in its crib, a diaper hanging heavily from its hips and a bewildered look upon its face, died four days later.

Ambulances became a familiar sight as they wailed into the project, pulling over curbs and driving between houses to the unlucky doors. Mothers tried to keep children isolated in their apartments, but the days grew even hotter and the dead air in the narrow rooms drove everyone out again. Rumors that the city would lock the entire project, quarantining all of Liberty Homes, passed from building to building. Plans were made for breaking out. Those who could promptly left for extended visits to relatives in other cities. But most had to stay. And to wait. Every morning and evening all the project children swallowed to see if their throats were sore, and eventually the repeated effort of swallowing made them so. They bent their heads to their chests to prove that their necks had not stiffened with the first onslaught of the disease, until the bending itself caused their necks to stiffen. And every morning they watched to see if any new apartment had been visited, listened for the ambulances, waited for word of who had been singled out.

Because of the paper route, Lonnie entered every building and looked into nearly every apartment. Together with Terry, he kept the official tally. During his weekly visits, anxious parents volunteered their fears in exchange for news of the other corners of the project. He knew within hours of each new victim. Sometimes even sooner. When Mrs. Lassiter, a woman who had never seemed quite right in the head, pointed to the center of the living room and her stricken three-year-old son, insisting he had the flu, Lonnie told her what it really was. Of course, Lonnie's own mother worried, tried to make him give up the paper route, but she gave in to his pleas and his father's reasoning that Lonnie had already been exposed to everything in Liberty Homes.

Lonnie never feared the apartments but hated the windowless hallways with their smells and their unmoved air. He tried to hold his breath when he entered and to rush up the stairs without breathing, thinking that if he did not breathe until the apartment door swung open, and the light and life of the lived-in place came out to him, he would be safe. Sometimes he thought of what the disease must be like, but for the most part, he was caught up in his role as emissary and considered himself a neutral party going from one frightened camp to the next, keeping accounts. Once, when two new cases had appeared in as many days, he went with Terry to the swallow bluffs. They watched the birds dart into the small, dark caves, and let the breeze from the river brush off the dead air of the hallways. When they talked he told Terry how he held his breath as he climbed the stairs. Terry laughed. The trick, he said, was never to get sick. He'd never been sick, and wasn't ever going to. He said most of those who had been taken to the hospital were little kids, babies, or people who were already sickly, and Lonnie believed him. But the following week it was Terry who went to the hospital.

Sunday, after they had finished the deliveries, they sat, one at either end of the wagon, and divided up the week's collection chores. In two weeks Terry was going to visit his grandparents in Ohio, so they agreed that this time he would do all the collecting in the project and Lonnie would go only to the houses on First Street and beyond. They talked about expanding the route in the opposite direction, and about how they would handle the business once school started. Then they sorted out the loose leaves from the collection book, Terry taking the bulk of them, and agreed to meet again on Wednesday to see which of the accounts were still unpaid. Terry looked all right when they said good-bye, but by evening he was in the hospital.

When Lonnie awoke the next morning, his father told him of Terry's death. He could not comprehend it. Terry had sat in the wagon the same way as on all the previous Sundays. How could he be dead? Babies and little girls might die so suddenly—maybe—but Terry was half grown and strong. A car or a gun or a train could kill him, but how could sickness work so quickly? But when Lonnie saw Terry on Thursday, in a gray suit, with his hair neatly combed, and lying in a coffin, he was dead. He did not look sick, despite the waxen skin that made his freckles seem like splotches of Mercurochrome, but he did look dead.

Lonnie was one of the pallbearers. He watched the open coffin during the funeral, didn't look away, even when Terry's mother fainted in the heat of the church or when Terry's little sister began to shriek near the end of the service. Mouse and the tall boy from Mike's gang were among the pallbearers, but Lonnie was the only one who was actually a friend to Terry. He felt that somehow his was a special trust. He sat straight, keeping all expression from his face, all tears suppressed. He had once heard of a man who had been pronounced dead prematurely, and who had awakened during his own funeral, and so he watched the coffin, somehow convinced that the Terry who had never been sick, who could not walk without a swagger, that Terry would sit up and laugh at all the ceremony, and complain about the warmth of his wool suit.

But when the priest finished, and the coffin lid was lowered for the last time, Terry remained inside. And together with Mouse and the others, Lonnie carried the coffin and Terry to the hearse, and, at the cemetery, from the hearse to the grave. The young pallbearers never faltered as they marched two abreast, carrying their heavy burden between the older graves to the new pit prepared for them, and after Terry had been lowered into the ground, each of them threw a handful of dirt onto his casket and went back to the project.

On the Sunday after Terry's funeral Lonnie rose at four-thirty and went to pick up the papers. He pulled the wagon through the dark, and then waited at the corner until the truck came. The driver helped him with the bundles, lifting them down from the truck and into the wagon.

"Where's your buddy this morning?" he asked.

"Gone," Lonnie said, the word catching in his throat, its sharp edges stabbing at him as it worked its way to his lips.

"Left it all to you, eh?" the driver said. He liked kids. "Can you manage this lot?"

"Yes."

"Good boy," he said. "That's the only way to be in this business. You can't count on anybody being there when you

need 'em. Gotta be able to go it alone." He thumped the boy
on the shoulder. "Good boy." And as he climbed onto the
truck, "Next week, then. Do it all again next week."

Lonnie pulled the loaded wagon back toward his apartment.
There he cut the wires on the bundles, carrying into the kitchen
the papers for later deliveries. The rest he pulled between the
long buildings of the project, entering the bleak hallways to
leave them in front of upstairs doors or opening the first-floor
screens and quietly leaning the thick bundles inside. It did not
take as long as he had thought. No dogs had been left on the
stairs to frustrate his progress. No one came to the door to
complain. There was only the warm morning dark, silent except for the crying of an occasional baby or the rustling movements of the insomniac Jenks in his foul-smelling rooms.

After Lonnie had traced all the sidewalks that ran between
the project apartments, he returned home and loaded the remaining papers into the bulky shoulder bag. Full, it hung nearly
to the ground, so that he had to lean awkwardly against the
canvas strap; but as he walked down Seventh Street, and then
Sixth Street, the bag lightened as the morning sun began its
climb above the river, flashing brightly from the chrome and
steel in the junkyard. The dog that stood guard over the
wrecked cars and the broken refrigerators snarled at him
through the fence, daring him to enter. Lonnie did not stop but
continued on toward Third Street.

By the time he had left the last paper at Dolan's, the sun
stood well above the horizon, and houses stirred with the first
activities of the day. The apricot tree beside his old home
looked parched, its leaves dry and curled, and he turned from
it, crossing the street to the empty lot with its confusion of
weeds. In the distance he saw the long, ugly buildings of the
project, each one like the one that preceded it, and like the one
that followed, as terribly alike as the plots in the cemetery
where Terry lay. He felt very tired, and about halfway through
the field, where someone had dumped an old drainage culvert
he climbed up out of the thicket to rest. At one end the corru-

gated tube had been squashed into an oval, and he slumped onto the flattened metal.

Lonnie stared into the weeds and thought about Terry. It was not so much thought as a tangle of images, twisted hopelessly, but each vivid and alive out of the dead week: Terry sitting across from him in the wagon, flipping through the collection book; Terry in the coffin, waxen and still; the cemetery hillside; himself, marching across the grass; the sobbing mother; the weeping sister; himself, sitting in the wagon flipping through the collection book; himself in the coffin, waxen and still; Terry marching across the grass; all the project buildings; all the graves, strung out in an endless sameness surrounded by chain link fences and patrolled by junkyard dogs. All the killing grounds.

He folded the canvas bag, using it to cushion his head as he lay back on the culvert. Above him the sky was a perfect blue, and he closed his eyes against its indifference.

Dolan must have kicked his ratty dog out the door, because there came a distant yelp and a slam and then, close beside Lonnie, a rustling in the dry weeds. The boy began to raise himself, then hesitated. He settled back, feeling the warmth rise from the hard metal. Eyes closed, he watched a rabbit lift above the brambles in a great leap, its white fur gleaming in sunlight.

Dolan's dog continued to mourn outside the closed door, but in the dead field all movement ceased.

Epilogue

Always at this place, at this time, in the dark fifteen minutes of alder and spruce between the river and the road, the doubt surfaces. Either the ruts of the abandoned logging spur and the old truck are just a few yards ahead, or I have left the trail which, even in light, is barely visible among the chaos of second growth. Just when I am convinced I have lost the way, despair rising bitter in my throat, the timber ends abruptly beside the road.

I stop to check the fly line and shake the snags from my net. Behind me, in a clearing somewhere across the river, a coyote begins to cry, at first a series of yips and then, as his echo rebounds, the calls lengthen to prolonged howls. A half-moon has just cleared the trees, revealing the dark pickup and the man leaning against it. I walk toward them, waders squawking and creel slapping against my side. The man straightens and opens the door. I put the fly rod in the back, then add the net and creel. He waits till I have crawled into the cab, then starts the engine and switches on the lights.

"Slow night," he says, but he does not ask if I've caught anything. "You spent a long time in that beaver pool." That is how he knows I've caught nothing: by my lateness. I overfished the final pool, in one last effort to avoid a shutout.

The truck lumbers stiffly through potholes and rocks, its headlight leaping up an embankment of yellowed ferns, catching withered birch, then plunging down again. This has been the second dry summer in succession, no rain at all in July and hot even at night. Now young white pines, their roots still too shallow for a second season of drought, show the rusty evidence of their dying. Blackberry bushes reach out to the road's faint track, but the fruit they bear is hard and dry. At last, two weeks into August, there has been a frost, reddening those maples whose leaves still live; and a shower—not enough to raise the river or cool the water, but a promise.

"Nothing moving tonight," I say, statement and question.

"No," he answers. "Too warm. Too dry."

"It doesn't help," I say, "when you have to fish in a crowd. Half a dozen mergansers stayed ahead of me for an hour. Kept everything along that cedar bank in froth and feathers before they finally flew away."

"They're bunching up early," he says, shaking his head. "They feel an early fall. Even the ducks will be headed south soon."

"A nice brookie rose below the big beaver dam," I say. "Fifteen, maybe sixteen inches. Came right up from the branches at the foot of the dam. Wouldn't take the fly. Just one lazy roll and sank back down."

"Waiting for rain," he says. "Nothing will move till we get a hard rain."

The truck slams into a deep hole, hesitates, then lurches forward. I brace myself against the dashboard, then turn to look at him. Thirty years older than I, he's fished this river nearly two of my lifetimes. The deference I show him is respect for the latter, not acknowledgment of the former. But today he looks sixty-five and more. It's been eight months since his surgery and still he winces as the pickup caroms along the cratered road.

He glances over and sees me watching. "It's so dry you could come in here with a damned Cadillac," he says. "Be full of flatlanders if we don't get rain soon."

I am leaving tomorrow. Tonight has been more ritual than sport, a leave-taking for ten months, an occasion to imprint the river so deeply in mind that it will not fade through all that time but will endure so that a winter's changes can be recognized within the sameness of this place. I think of the stand of cedars where the current sucks the fly under the bank and of the fish that lurk among those roots. And of the big trout below the dam, waiting for rain, for the water to rise above the beaver's blockade and allow her to swim upstream to the spawning beds.

Two woodcock run ahead of the truck just at the edge of the headlight's beam. As we gain on them they stop their clumsy run and take to equally clumsy flight but soon sit down again in the darkness up the road. Time and again we catch up with them. They run, then fly into the darkness only to land once more in the center of the trail.

"They like this road," he says.

"Persistent but stupid," I add.

"Coming from a man who's fished every night for a week without catching a legal trout, that's some compliment," he says.

In the lights the scrambling woodcock, dusty and bedraggled as they run along the ruts, at last tumble into a clump of ferns that rise like yellow flames on the embankment. The logging trail leads onto a real road, a gravel road. We race through the night; tall maples and popple shut off the sky, forming a tunnel that runs to the next hill or the next curve, but leading irresistibly away from the river.

"It will rain tomorrow," he says. "You'll be loading in the rain again. And in the cold." He pauses, downshifting for the hill. "Trout are going to start moving. The September rains will be early, and there will be a godalmighty rush upstream. If you could stay two more weeks, so much water will be piled up behind that beaver dam." He smiles. "It will start early this time. This is the earliest fall of your life," he says.

"Yes," I say, helplessly, "yes."

Somewhere behind me a brook trout heavy with roe lies hunkered at the foot of a beaver dam, waiting to continue on against the current, to let her eggs drift in the shallows where sperm can wash down over them. How many eggs does one trout carry, how many uncertain trips does she make upstream in her lifetime?

"Next year," I say as we start down the last long hill before the path to my cabin, "we'll fish the Meadows. And I'll find a way to stay through Labor Day."

"You'll need a float of some kind then," he says. "The Meadows will be deep next year, too deep to wade." But he sounds uncertain, as though after all those years the winter is too vast an interval to bridge, even in thought. At the bottom of the hill I get out and gather my tackle from the back. Then I walk to his window, awkward in the waders. "Next year," I say.

"Yes," he says and then, knocking the shapeless old hat—his old hat—from my head, "get a new hat. You look like a Finlander going to church. And a float. You'll need a float in the Meadows."

I retrieve the hat, dropping the creel and net in the process. At last I have everything gathered up again and stand for a moment beside the truck. The moon is barely visible above the trees. It has a ring around it.

"It's going to rain," he says. "You're going to pack in the rain, just when the trout start to move." He is silent for a moment. "I wish you could see it after Labor Day. Everybody gone. The whole river to myself. And the fish going crazy like the first spring hatch." He hesitates. "I wish," he says, and then stops.

I laugh softly at an old thought.

"What's that?" he asks.

"Then beggars would ride," I say. "Then beggars would ride.

"Next year," I say, and start into the dark.

ABOUT THE AUTHOR

WAYNE FIELDS was born in 1942 on his grandparents'
farm near Wyaconda, Missouri. He teaches American literature
at Washington University in St. Louis. His articles on subjects
ranging from contemporary politics to the American prairie
have appeared in leading periodicals, including *American Heri-
tage* and *Playboy*. He is the author of *What the River Knows: An
Angler in Midstream* and *A Union of Words: A History of Presidential
Rhetoric*.

Phoenix Fiction titles from Chicago

The Bridge on the Drina by Ivo Andrić
Concrete by Thomas Bernhard
Correction by Thomas Bernhard
Extinction by Thomas Bernhard
Gargoyles by Thomas Bernhard
The Lime Works by Thomas Bernhard
The Loser by Thomas Bernhard
Old Masters by Thomas Bernhard
Wittgenstein's Nephew by Thomas Bernhard
Woodcutters by Thomas Bernhard
Yes by Thomas Bernhard
Acts of Theft by Arthur A. Cohen
A Hero in His Time by Arthur A. Cohen
In the Days of Simon Stern by Arthur A. Cohen
Convergence by Jack Fuller
Fragments by Jack Fuller
Pictures from an Institution by Randall Jarrell
A Bird in the House by Margaret Laurence
The Diviners by Margaret Laurence
The Fire-Dwellers by Margaret Laurence
A Jest of God by Margaret Laurence
The Stone Angel by Margaret Laurence
Fiela's Child by Dalene Matthee
The Conquerors by Andre Malraux
The Walnut Trees of Altenberg by Andre Malraux
The Bachelor of Arts by R. K. Narayan
The Dark Room by R. K. Narayan
The English Teacher by R. K. Narayan
The Financial Expert by R. K. Narayan
Mr. Sampath—The Printer of Malgudi by R. K. Narayan
Swami and Friends by R. K. Narayan
Waiting for Mahatma by R. K. Narayan
A Dance to the Music of Time (in four *Movements*)
by Anthony Powell
A Father's Words by Richard Stern
Golk by Richard Stern
An Innocent Millionaire by Stephen Vizinczey
In Praise of Older Women by Stephen Vizinczey
Lord Byron's Doctor by Paul West
The Painted Canoe by Anthony Winkler
A Coin in Nine Hands by Marguerite Yourcenar
Fires by Marguerite Yourcenar
Two Lives and a Dream by Marguerite Yourcenar